THE MAN IN THE BARRETINA HAT

THE MAN IN THE BARRETINA HAT

NANCY O'HARE

For permission requests, email the author at bynancyohare@gmail.com

Published by Nancy O'Hare at IngramSpark

ISBN: 978-1-7774017-5-7

First published on January 11, 2023

Edited by Susan Fitzgerald

Proofread by Mirror Image Publishing

Cover design by BespokeBookCovers.com

www.bynancyohare.com

Dedication

Written for my dad, a man of many hats

Epigraph

Routine can calm the soul, but once torn open exposes a tempestuous fury, one we wrestle to control and long to succumb to under the wild hopes of a life full of what-ifs and lucky turns.

Contents

CARLOS

———————

Carlos Ignacio pulled his hat lower, narrowly preventing a tempestuous gust from hurling it against the stone wall of the marina. He had nearly lost his treasured barretina cap last spring in similar winds. It had blown straight across to the Kalkara Marina, where he had collected it after a rather embarrassing run-in with the manager of the Regatta Club's restaurant. His thoughts turned to his friend Peter, who just last week had reminded Carlos to stop at the tailor to have a hole in the hat stitched. Peter Bustillo, a fellow professor who typically arrived early for their morning walk—and who knew every cobblestoned street that wound around the harbours of Vittoriosa, Senglea and Cospicua—had oddly not appeared this morning.

Peter's never-ending quest to lose five kilos had inspired their daily regime. While Carlos epitomized the lanky scholar, emphasized by thinning hair and tortoiseshell glasses, Peter leaned towards a more eccentric style. Only yesterday, he had paired flashy orange cargo pants with a sea-blue linen shirt for their stroll. Even a teenager on a skateboard had done a double take as he flew past. His grin rolled respect, jest and scorn into a single sardonic expression that adolescents do so well.

Carlos had liked Peter from the day they met. Over a year earlier they had joined an archeology club looking into digs on the island and had grown even closer. Malta had a curious history. A history at the heart of some interesting questions their group had been raising.

When Peter wasn't at their normal meeting spot this morning, Carlos had initially assumed he had started his walk early and they would eventually run into each other. But the sun was now well above the horizon. Peter had not shown up.

A fragment of a memory niggled the edges of Carlos' mind, like he had missed something on his walk, a detail that was intended to appear natural but for some reason sat askew in his subconscious. Carlos checked his phone once more to see if he had any new texts. Only one green notification popped up. His wife had sent a reminder: *Car, would you swing by Sasha's for a loaf of fresh rye, por favor?* Only Myriam called him anything but Carlos. Not even Peter in their most heated debates crossed into that most personal single-syllable sphere.

He recalled his last conversation with Peter, only fourteen hours earlier. Peter mentioned that he had uncovered some worrying connections and wanted to talk with Carlos face to face. Peter's whispered words had prodded Carlos' growing concern: "Say nothing to anyone. I will explain tomorrow."

Perhaps it was nerves, but Carlos felt a gnawing impulse to backtrack. He wanted to observe the place where Peter typically performed his daily ritual. After almost stepping in a fresh dropping some dog owner had failed to bag Carlos slowed his pace; he knew the next steps could prove crucial. Or maybe he was overreacting. Peter might very well be at home relaxing, nursing a headache after staying up too late engrossed in his latest theory and most likely partaking in a few too many glasses of his neighbour's wine. Not that Carlos could blame him. On more than one occasion, he had lost count himself of how many glasses of the smooth beverage he'd consumed while lounging beside the very vines that produced such a spectacular vintage.

"Stop rambling," Carlos muttered. Every instinct was telling him he had to be sharp. Something was off. He might be a near-retired IT professor, but he still felt pretty spry. Besides, he wasn't only involved in dry academics. More often than not, that side of his life already felt like a past life.

No point in calling the police—he really had nothing concrete to go on, and they had made such a debacle of the missing woman's case from a few months ago. Evidence had been destroyed and key witnesses overlooked. The papers blamed stumbling ineptitude, but hushed voices speculated about a more sinister narrative. No, he definitely wanted to do his own research first.

Glancing at his watch, he calculated he had four hours to retrace his steps, check in at Peter's house, make a few calls and, of course, pick up the grainy rye Myriam had requested. That would give him enough time to make his Monday lecture. Thankfully, it was his only course of the semester. Far too many distractions were pulling him from his usual scholarly life. Peter was not the only concern prying into his thoughts.

While returning along his route, Carlos had to dodge two people staring so intently at their phones they forgot to watch in front of them. Shaking his head, he finally spotted the reddish capitoli inset where Peter left a single flower every morning. Such devotional niches dotted corners of buildings all over the city. Usually they held the statue of a saint. The Knights of Saint John had mandated these tiny sanctuaries back when Malta's capital city of Valletta and its surrounding villages were originally built. Without fail, Peter's donation would be gone by the next day.

Carlos gasped.

A fresh blossom balanced just as Peter would have left it; Peter had been here this morning. As Carlos stepped back to lean against the cool stone building, a hand, seemingly from nowhere, clenched his mouth. One question flew across his mind: *What is that smell?*

Then, total darkness.

2

SASHA

———————

*W*hat a disturbing day, Sasha thought. Her morning had started out as usual. She had risen to ignite the ovens by 3:00 a.m., ready to start baking a dozen loaves fifteen minutes later. It had been easier when she lived right above the bakery, but she loved having a proper house with more space for her and her daughter to live. Besides, the two-block walk gave her enough fresh air to wake up without being inconvenient.

Although her customers were friendly, she knew even a five-minute delay of their beloved rye or tender ftira—a

THE MAN IN THE BARRETINA HAT

bread foreigners routinely confused with sourdough—might send them over to the baker on Triq Hanover. More than likely they would return the next morning, but these days every euro counted. The smaller community of Birgu did not attract the crowds of neighbouring Valletta despite sitting just across the bay.

Her only daughter had one year left to complete her master of science, and intern jobs paid little. On top of it all, that blasted Emanuel had appeared again this morning and requested her most expensive loaf. Naturally, he left without paying anything beyond a contemptuous glint of superiority. Her shoulder still ached at the thought of last month's "payment."

When the noon crowd had faded and the early evening rush had not yet begun, Sasha tried to enjoy a few minutes of solitude. She pulled off her hairnet to let her scalp breathe. No matter how much styling cream she used to smooth her waves, the Mediterranean air never failed to turn her auburn tresses into a frizzy halo by midday. She absently tucked a loose strand back into her hair knot and took a sip of iced lemon tea.

The drink cooled her throat, but not the irk still rolling around her head from the frantic call that had come during her busiest period. The caller had asked what time a man wearing a barretina had picked up a loaf of ħobża rye. Such molly-coddling these days. Then Cristabel, her daughter, rang to say she would swing by to help at the shop since her professor had failed to turn up for their afternoon class. This news set off another wave of frustration with the local university's lack of professionalism. These classes weren't cheap.

Sasha's mind swiftly turned to more pressing concerns. She could now make the entire meeting with her new group. Not long ago, she'd joined an alliance of sorts among small-business owners. The myriad of unfair, unmonitored and intricate financing rules of this small island nation made it impossible for most people to earn a reasonable living. If the officials could not sort things out, it was time the people took things into their own hands. Of course, she dared not let anyone outside of the tight-knit club know of her involvement. Even she, a small-time baker, knew the consequences of getting on the wrong side of the so-called right people.

The afternoon crowd eventually arrived. Later by the time the rush had dissipated, Cristabel came flying into the shop. Ever since she was a baby, people had commented on the intensity of her green eyes. Those eyes never missed a beat. Before the door had closed behind her, Cristabel had straightened the business hours' sign and picked up a receipt the last customer must have dropped. Sasha reckoned it was why Cristabel stayed so slim; the girl moved in a frenzy of continual motion.

Cristabel tossed her worn backpack under the

payment counter. As usual, the bag was crammed full of textbooks and flimsy magazines, their ragged edges poking out of the half-open zipper. Cristabel grabbed a Red Bull from the cooler and rushed Sasha out the door, encouraging her mom to get some fresh air.

Although her daughter's antsy nature might be trying at times, Sasha didn't complain. Tonight, she was keen to get out and clear her head before meeting up with her group.

Tonight's meeting would be held in the next village over, Kalkara, near the old Fort Rinella. Its name, like many, did not quite match the truth. The fort was not a fort, but a battery constructed by the British for an extra-heavy cannon. Regardless, between the occasional roaming tourist and the miscellany of actors who popped in and out of the nearby film studios, the area offered the perfect place to meet unnoticed. At low tide, those who knew which narrow gap to squeeze through could clamber down between the stone port walls and get close to the surf. Down there, voices scattered into nothing more than soundless rustlings amid the waves.

Sasha ran over her plan one final time.

At the last meeting, she'd found out Raymond needed vehicles. Lots of vehicles. As it happened, Sasha's uncle worked for a car plant in Japan. While she imagined the very rich commission she would earn, a nearly imperceptible flash of unease poked her resolve. Just as swiftly, the thought of Emanuel's greedy grin urged her forward. She had twelve days.

A phone light flashed. Her head throbbed. Sasha hated all the selfies people were constantly taking these days. She glanced backwards and noticed someone in a tweed jacket dart behind a building. *That's odd,* she thought. Her mind was becoming overly active. It was not like her to play games or take risks. Yet much of what she had done in recent months wasn't in her character. *What the hell, I only live once.* She hadn't felt this exhilarated since she took over Loaves & Buns thirty-one years ago. Now most people simply referred to it as the L&B.

Turning back around and straightening her shoulders, Sasha dialled the number she had so rarely called until recently.

"Hello?" Her uncle's stilted voice sounded distant. It was the middle of the night for him.

Taking a deep breath, Sasha replayed their last conversation in her mind when she had agreed to do as he asked—with one condition. Not noticing the overhead camera on the corner, nor the person in the tweed coat standing nearby, she began, a little louder than she realized. "Uncle Noa, I am in some trouble."

3

CRISTABEL

Cristabel rushed into her mom's shop. She was intent to get the place to herself, which apparently would be easy, as her mom seemed uncharacteristically eager to leave her darling business. With a short text to a trusted friend to keep an eye on her mom, Cristabel's anxiety dropped slightly. She figured she had a good forty minutes to dig around before the evening clientele started to trickle in. Kicking aside the worn Iranian rug, Cristabel grabbed the rusted iron ring bolted to the floorboards. It took a few hard tugs, but the section it was attached to eventually slid open.

Before climbing down she typed a few strings of characters into her mother's computer. Her two years of IT classes and optional forensic security courses were paying off already. Last fall, Cristabel had shown her mom a standard encryption function built-in to their bakery's accounting software. She figured if her mom wanted to hide anything, she would have used this trick. The screen flickered, then revealed a list of about eighteen files. Encrypted and filed in hidden folders, they would remain invisible to all but a trained eye. Luckily, Cristabel made a point of being trained, very well trained. She had brought a USB drive with the decryption tool she needed. While it ran to decrypt and copy the files, she slipped through the narrow shaft into the underground cavern.

As she climbed down the ladder, her nose detected the change. Musty dampness stifled any aroma from the bread ovens above. At the bottom, in complete darkness, she shifted her feet around until she felt them grip the uneven bedrock. With a tap, her phone's light lit up the smallish room. Arches above adjoining tunnels looked like furrowed eyebrows sending warning messages to leave, sparking scant images from a distant memory. Early on, she had learned never to ask about the time her family had crept down here. Early on, she'd learned her mother's boundaries.

Pushing her uneasiness aside, she stepped deeper into the space, feeling along the wall with her hands as she went. *Was the old board in the wall a figment of my imagination or does it actually exist? There it is!* She grimaced as her hand slid along the slimy surface. She remembered a knob, recalled stretching with her entire arm to reach it. Instead, her fingers ran into a cardboard box. It couldn't have been here long. It was dry, not soggy, despite the damp environment. But why had it been placed here, in an inconvenient location where nobody normally came?

Cristabel gently lifted the lid and beamed her phone light inside.

Documents, a stack of foreign bills and the butt of what looked to be a revolver were tucked inside. Before she could dig through further, a faint ring from the bell that hung on the bakery door jolted her thoughts back upstairs.

The customer jumped slightly when Cristabel suddenly stood up from behind the cash register.

"Sorry to startle you. I was digging around this bottom shelf to tidy up a bit." She added a partial smile to complete her rushed cover story.

Perhaps it was the extra flush in her cheeks or the freckles she had given up trying to hide years ago, but the man on the other side of the counter seemed more amused than shocked. He ended up buying five items and promised to return the next day. She found him creepy and decided she would certainly *not* be coming back tomorrow to help her mom.

Her thoughts returned to the box. Why had her mother stashed it in the underground shelter? And why was she hiding documents and a gun? Something was up. But she would search for more pieces to this latest puzzle before leaping to conclusions.

Before closing the bakery for the night, Cristabel received a text from her trusted friend: *9 p.m. @ usual corner.* She glanced at her watch and decided to close the shop a few minutes early. With her navy hood pulled low over her head and the files from her mother's computer safely saved on a USB stick, she threw her pack over her shoulder, locked the door and rushed down the street. Eight minutes later, she leaned against a brick wall beside a man wearing a worn tweed coat.

She had first met him years earlier after an ordeal on a bus. This tall dark-haired stranger had leapt up and tackled a guy on the sidewalk right outside the bus. The jerk had snatched Cristabel's bag as he got off without her noticing. This handsome stranger had seen it happen and jumped to her rescue. Ever since, the two had stayed close. He taught Cristabel self-defence and other modes of protection. Their bond grew. Stronger than she'd ever expected.

Tonight, vague memories of a great-great-uncle clouded her head as her closest confidant relayed what he had seen and overheard earlier in the evening. Her mind swirled. Why was her mother calling the son of a man her family had disavowed decades earlier? And what was she doing with a group of strangers down at the waterfront?

4

TRAPPED

———

Carlos' forehead pounded. He felt disoriented, especially because the only thing his fingers could feel around him was dust—the floors, the walls, everything was covered in it. He seemed to be in some sort of industrial cavity. Beyond the soft scratching of something a few metres away, the space remained unbearably silent. Eventually, a memory came back to him of a rag being forced over his mouth and nose as he stood near Peter's favourite niche.

Between the lack of windows and the musty scent, he

figured he must be in a storeroom or cellar. Disappointed but unsurprised, Carlos noticed his pockets had been emptied. At least they didn't take his barretina. It hid a scar he preferred not to explain, and without the hat people's curiosity invariably led them to ask how he got it. Given the situation, he definitely did not want to go there.

Eventually, Carlos pushed himself up into a sitting position. Myriam must be crazy with panic by now, whenever *now* was.

He felt around his wrist until his fingertips located what appeared to be a raised freckle. The patchwork of age spots on his hands and arms offered the perfect camouflage. He quickly pressed it twice, and relief flooded across his shoulders. Decades earlier, Carlos and Myriam had had tiny GPS messenger devices embedded in their wrists. A bonus of backing Castro before they had left Cuba was that their military connections meant they'd had inside access to advanced security gadgets.

Work networks went beyond social camaraderie. A few trusted colleagues in Carlos' tech department had fiddled with the devices' relays and reconfigured them to only transmit messages between the two implants, a closed circuit, so to speak. They called them dos enlazados, which roughly translated meant "two linked" or "two united." Dos enlazados represented a secret pact between his wife and him, regardless of what they faced. Myriam and Carlos may have appeared to be semi-retired professors, but they knew how fragile a serene life could be. They'd learned how to stick together. Carlos trusted her with more than his life—he would hand her his soul.

Only after activating his locator signal did he start to fill in his mental storyboard. Blank frames with a few bits of colour tumbled around inside his head.

Almonds. That was the smell he had noticed before blacking out. Pieces started to fall into place. His headache, his loss of consciousness. Someone knew how much cyanide to apply—and, thankfully, didn't overestimate it. It was easy enough to obtain on Malta. All but a few organic vineyards used it to keep insects away.

With little insight beyond knowing what caused his blackout, Carlos looked around his chamber. The walls and the floor were made from a rough cement. He ran his fingertips over grit and ridges—familiar, yet something was missing.

No grout lines.

The material was not manufactured. Carlos realized he could be inside the island itself. When the city of Valletta was built back in the sixteenth century, the island's bedrock was used for its foundation. Years later, people dug tunnels and storerooms that extended deep underground. Some were used for sewage channels and others, later, as bomb shelters during the Second World War. Carlos had heard certain people whisper about hidden shafts that ran like a subterranean lattice beneath the entire city. Until now, he had assumed the chatter to be urban legend. That changed today. If the rumours were true, there should be either a connector shaft or an access point somewhere. He intended to find it.

With absolutely no light inside the tiny compartment, his eyes struggled to adjust. Sheer blackness. Forgotten feelings rose from his past. He could not allow himself to panic. Instinct kicked in. On all fours, Carlos followed the wall to a corner. From there, he would map his prison until he had an image so clear he would know it better than his captors. *Create an advantage. Focus on the task. Stay in control.*

His fingers hit a small opening where the rock wall had broken down and been chewed away. Chunks of limestone lay on the floor. That explained the soft rustling sound: rats. Besides a little airflow, he wasn't hopeful the hole offered much help.

The discovery of a wooden door framed with metal proved more interesting. To the touch it seemed relatively new, without any apparent rust. His unease grew when he realized it had no handle on his side. He was certain someone would eventually come through this door. The question was *who*.

The rat hole offered his best glimmer of hope.

While his and Myriam's wedding rings looked like platinum or silver, they were actually titanium, one of the hardest metals on earth. And the pyramidal design they'd chosen offered more than good looks. Its sharp edges had come in handy on more than one occasion.

He knew a few students who would have described him as having sharp edges. Some called it tough love, whereas he preferred "pointed redirection." In most cases these people eventually thanked him. But there were always those unwilling to step up. Sadly, they blamed him for what they lacked.

No use pondering lost souls now. It was time to scrape his way out of this latest mess.

Carlos could fit only a couple of fingers inside the hole. He grated the edges with the tip of his ring. After what felt like ages, a chunk of limestone fell away. In this hushed space, the soft clink of it hitting the ground sounded deafening. He held his breath. Silence. Gently, he flicked the piece of rock into his palm.

As he eased his hand out of the hole, something caught his attention. It sounded like "Hey," only distorted.

Did he imagine the voice?

Carlos flattened his face to the floor and stuck his ear against the enlarged hole. He whispered back, "Psst, who's there?"

5

MYRIAM

Myriam felt a ping on her wrist. She stared at the faded freckle, not believing the little device still worked. At first, feeling self-conscious, she had applied self-tanning lotion to try to hide the obvious spot on her otherwise unblemished skin. Over the years, she dropped the habit. Looking down now, the raised dot seemed to scream out once again as artificial.

When the contraption was inserted she had wondered if it was excessive, but now she considered its song a lifeline. Six minutes longer and she would have resorted to calling the police—a dreaded action. The five o'clock gongs from their grandfather clock had been her self-imposed deadline. Thankfully, she could hold off for now. Carlos was alive.

The past eight hours had felt like eighty. During that time she had called the baker, who seemed unusually gruff on the phone. Myriam was a long-time customer but realized afterwards that she had probably called at peak time.

Carlos' dear friend Peter was nowhere to be found either. She had tried ringing him multiple times with no luck. For the rest of the afternoon, Myriam had walked the wharf. She retraced every twisting street and dead-end road across the entire Three Cities bay area. The trio of interconnected towns, Vittoriosa, Senglea and Cospicua, was Carlos' favourite walking route. By the end, she was exhausted.

Standing less than five feet tall, she had once kept fit merely by keeping pace with Carlos' long strides. Nowadays, she swam four times a week and practiced Pilates almost daily to stay healthy.

Finally, the buzzing mole had given a starting point for her futile hunt. Still, she desperately wanted more clues, more signs about where her husband had disappeared to. Kneeling down beside their antique wooden desk, she rolled back the burgundy rug. The handle was still intact, tucked below the floor surface in a small divot. Without intentionally doing so, she held her breath as she tugged the narrow wire ring. The panel slid upwards. Loose straw remained where she had scattered it the last time she and Carlos had accessed the spot. Beneath this innocuous cover lay their old laptop. Carlos pulled it out once a year to update its software and ensure the machine still functioned, but typically she gave it little thought. Until now.

She drew the curtains. Normally just being in this room comforted her. The gentle ticking of the grandfather clock she had listened to since she was a child mixed with the faint scent of aged furniture would reassure her that all would be right in the world. Now, she did not feel so certain.

Carlos was the IT guru. Myriam, on the other hand, had worked in pharmaceuticals for the government before they left Cuba. Malta had seemed an ideal destination, with a familiar island lifestyle and tight Latin American community where she could continue her work part-time. Through her doctoral studies, she had delved into how medicinal plants used by Indigenous peoples could help supplement modern medical treatments. As Cuba had been under trade sanctions by much of the world, its medical community turned inwards. Medicine flourished, but often at a different pace and along alternative branches to those in North America or Europe. Her favourite subject, Ocimum gratissimum, a type of basil, treated a wide array of diseases from anemia to typhoid. Indigenous peoples across the Americas had used it for centuries without the harsh side effects of many of today's advanced drugs.

Through her long days of research, she'd become pretty adept at using a computer. And the contacts she made training biotechnology interns from all over the world had proven invaluable over the years. Her experience defined her—as did the striking bolt of grey that ran through her bangs. The tracking system buzzed on her screen and she turned back to the task at hand. Time to sync.

While the tracking software tried to pinpoint Carlos' location, Myriam left the room to turn on the kettle. She hadn't slept well the previous night, and her adrenalin was fading. A boost would have to come in bean form. She still preferred Cuban coffee, grown a few kilometres from her family's home. Its brew had a richness she had not been able to match with anything from Malta's markets.

The news played on the radio, talking about another discovery of ancient grooves and basins carved into the rock on the northeastern side of the island. Myriam lowered the volume just as a local archeologist was being interviewed. He spoke of the unusual style of this latest find.

By the time she returned to the desk in the upstairs

office, the laptop displayed a list of links on the right side of the screen. The left panel—the GPS section—showed a dismal grey.

"Coño!" she cursed under her breath. How was it possible that Carlos' device pinged her yet remained invisible on the GPS tracking system? She stared at the screen disbelievingly before clicking a few keys in the hopes of re-engaging the system. Nothing. Nada. Blank as her intern students' faces on the day she introduced therapeutic biological compounds and EGF deprivation by active immunotherapy. Completely vacant.

The tech team had supposedly outsmarted typical jammers and metallic diffusing capabilities to allow their GPS signals to get through almost anything. Maybe newer technology had surpassed their tricks.

Was Carlos even still on Malta? She started feeling frantic as she realized nearly a dozen flights had already taken off since this ordeal began. Time to dig deeper. She started with online inquiries into what might be interfering with Malta's remote communications.

Over the past twenty-four hours, the island's main satellites had undergone a scheduled round of maintenance shut-offs. *Isn't that convenient?* she thought. *Coincidence? I think not.* She kept reading. The notice advised that the outages should not have disrupted general activities. Essential services had been notified in advance to put backup measures in place.

With this development, Myriam thought immediately of her old friend James. They had worked on a few projects together during her master's program. James now oversaw the R&D arm of a small agtech firm out of Vancouver. Last time she'd talked to him, he was tracking carabid beetles to correlate their movements with disease spread. If anyone knew the ins and outs of tracking, it was James. Although they hadn't spoken in ages, she knew she could count on him.

The landline rang, breaking her focus. She glanced at the number, relieved it wasn't the university calling again to ask about the whereabouts of her husband. Myriam wasn't ready to disclose anything to anybody. Not yet.

She picked up the receiver. "Hello?"

"Is this Professor Ignacio's wife?" a muffled voice asked.

Myriam hesitated, considering whether to be truthful. "Who is this?"

"I want to help," the voice said. "The professor once gave me a second chance, and I owe it to him. Something weird is going on."

The unnamed person directed Myriam to check her mailbox the next day at precisely 3:33 p.m., long after the regular post would be delivered.

Myriam stared at the phone after the person had hung up. Was this unknown person to be trusted? She knew her husband had taken an interest in helping the occasional student who struggled to find their way, but only if they showed promise. Was this a student he had helped? Or was someone using that as an excuse to get close to her? Maybe they were ticked off by what some perceived to be a reckless approach to nudge floundering undergrads? In any event, not knowing put her at a disadvantage. She needed a plan.

James, on the other side of the globe, would likely be cycling to the office or squeezing in a breakfast meeting as he often did. It would be best to send a text. She dared not contact Carlos' old colleagues in Cuba. Surveillance was heavy on anyone associated with the government.

Carlos' files. She needed to see what project he was working on, which students he had turned around and who had failed despite his good intentions. And there was that new archeology group he had joined. Surely that was incidental and not worth her time?

With a slow gulp of coffee, she turned her attention to his file cabinet. Before she could insert the key, a thundering bang filled the room. The entire house shook. Myriam darted to the door frame, holding tightly to it for support. Particles of debris and drywall dust filled the room. In a moment of apparent calm, she dashed away from her protective cover to grab the computer and her phone.

Just as Myriam grasped the items, she felt something sharp pierce her leg. A frenzy of wind, water from a broken pipe and shards of wood exploded around her. The roof collapsed inwards. A moment later, searing pain shot through her head. Stunned, she froze.

Everything blurred.

And then turned black.

6

DEAD ENDS

Yesterday Cristabel had questioned her choice of supervisor. Professor Ignacio's vibrant teaching style normally challenged her thinking, yet it irked her that he hadn't bothered to tell his students class was cancelled. Instead he just didn't show up. Her annoyance turned to concern when he neglected to meet her as planned to review her dissertation project. She had spent most of the weekend reworking it based on his previous advice. Even though its ultimate submission was not due until next year, she needed all of that time to do what she wanted—to pass with Distinction, Summa Cum Laude. Without a reliable supervisor, her goal would be practically impossible to achieve.

When her dear friend then texted an unexpected question asking about the same professor's whereabouts, her concern shifted to alarm.

After walking up the driveway, Cristabel stared at the house where her professor lived. *Former house*, she noted. The local news had reported a low-intensity tremor yesterday, but she had ignored it as inconsequential. The size of the resulting sinkhole said otherwise.

She stared at the cardboard tube in her hands. Its bright pink bow seemed a useless diversion now. The ribbon reminded her of a photo hung in Professor Ignacio's office. His wife's huge grin was half-obscured behind the rosy blooms of a fuchsia plant. Using the professor's reputation for helping lost students, Cristabel had certainly succeeded in getting his wife's attention. But she wasn't sure if the woman was even alive now. The rolled-up maps and transcripts Cristabel had so carefully secured in plastic wrap would have to wait.

It still amazed her how these sinkholes could be so precise. Buildings on either side of the professor's home were hardly damaged. From the yellow tape that surrounded the sinkhole, she knew the ambulance and police had been and gone.

Taking a moment to gather her thoughts, she sat on

the curb. Observe. That is what Professor Ignacio would have advised. In a world where the physical and abstract intersected, the greatest lessons were often triggered by tiny anomalies often missed. She recognized that those same rules would apply here. Breathe. Look. Absorb. Shattered glass. Buckled wood. The entire top floor had caved inwards, smashing most windowpanes. Only one window on the upper level remained partially intact. Large shards around the edges implied that it had broken from the centre outwards. The window frame itself looked relatively untouched. Anomaly noted.

Slowly, Cristabel stood up from the curb, took a few photos on her phone and tried to casually carry on towards the campus. Everything had turned so complex. Nothing made sense. Recapping what she had figured out created four piles of information with no obvious overlap. Her favourite computer science professor had disappeared. His wife may or may not have been hurt from a random tremor resulting in a sinkhole beneath their home. Her mother was meeting strange people and acting weird. And it was all happening as an amazing discovery of ancient markings that raised more questions than answers in the archeological community hit the papers.

If it wasn't for everything else going on, the new site would have offered the perfect subject matter for her final project for her anthropological technology class. She had hoped to discuss it with Professor Ignacio at last night's archeology club. Not only had he failed to show up, but so had another member. *What was his name? Steve? Paul? No, Peter.* The group required at least eighty percent quorum to go ahead. Without it, the group's secretary had cancelled the meeting.

Although Cristabel had hoped to simply drop the package for her professor's wife in the mailbox and head straight back home to sort through the files she had downloaded from her mother's computer, she now needed to adjust that plan. For one, she was not convinced the sinkhole was entirely random. Ill intentions at an opportune moment seemed more plausible at this stage. Tremors were frequent on the island, but they rarely caused major damage.

Too many red flags to ignore. She really needed to find and speak with the professor's wife. The hospital was the obvious place to look. Time to make an impromptu blood donation at the hospital's clinic—they were always calling on citizens to do their part. From there, she could do a little reconnaissance of her own.

She checked her bag to be sure she had thrown her extra scarf and old jacket inside. Once she was incognito, just maybe luck would turn her way.

On her walk to the clinic, Cristabel grabbed a chilled ruġġata at her favourite stall, where they still added shaved cloves to the traditional spiced drink. It was far better than any frappé sold by the chain cafes, especially since she had more pressing concerns than hanging out in air-conditioned comfort.

After all that had happened this morning, she was finally able to settle down once surrounded by strangers in the hospital's blood donor lineup. While everyone else filled out forms or stared blankly at their phones, she eyed exits and checked which doorways were least used. Her thoughts trailed to the maps she had planned to leave in Myriam's mailbox. The pattern on them was obvious. Tourists thought they got the lowdown on Valletta's so-called secret underground tunnels, but the mystery lay in what they weren't shown.

For a class project she was working on, Cristabel had used the tunnels' angles to test a pattern-finding program she designed. In theory it should have spit out commonalities between corresponding angles and alternative exterior angles. It didn't. No matter how many times she checked the code, its result threw her off. Still, she was convinced her approach was right. When she dug into older maps—unapproved versions from the city archives—she found something surprising.

Certain tunnels in the early drafts were left out of the final, city-approved blueprints. In every case, the missing sections fell precisely forty degrees from the tunnel angles she was testing and, in turn, shifted the angle of her expected offset in the final blueprints. For every single tunnel with a disparity, an undocumented sister crawlway existed. According to the draft drawings, these extra legs were dead ends. What she couldn't get straight was whether the ghost sections had actually been built and for some reason omitted from the final blueprints or simply never constructed. When she tested her program on earlier draft maps, it ran perfectly.

Why would the old city planners try to hide some of the channels? She tried overlaying the location of historic buildings on the old drafts in case they revealed a pattern. About a third of the oldest buildings sat directly above the mystery tunnels. Her stomach tightened when she figured out that these same historic structures had all been sold over the past eighteen months. Public records didn't disclose who was buying them up. Or why.

Between her professor vanishing, the unexplained tunnels and the recent property purchases, Cristabel reckoned the maps were somehow connected. At the very least, they offered a starting point. She needed to get them to his wife. Maybe Myriam could spot a link.

7

DUALITY

———

Following the dim beam of an old flashlight, Sasha stepped deeper into the cellar. There it was, the rough shelf and the shadow of the box she had placed there days earlier. But the lid was lopsided. She stared at it unbelievingly. A bolt of numbness hit her chest as if the shelf itself had jumped out and clobbered her. *How can this be? Hell, barely anyone knows this place exists, let alone has access to it.* This was her safe space. It allowed her to survive when all else failed.

Barely breathing, she nudged the lid aside. Everything

looked to be as she'd left it. Maybe she had bumped the box without realizing it the last time she was here. Although unconvinced, she desperately hoped this was a careless error on her part, but alarm bells warned her that her vigilance might be waning. She should never have left it on the vault's access panel. No slip-ups, not now. Feeling around the stone wall, Sasha located her faux rock. She had chiselled it into a knob herself. She moved the box inside the separate vault where she should have put it in the first place.

She couldn't believe anyone else would have come down here. Cristabel had surely forgotten the incident from so many years ago. Sasha, on the other hand, would never forget the echo of bricks smashing above them while she covered Cristabel's ears in their subterranean hiding spot.

Looters had turned her precious ovens into piles of rubble and had ransacked every last display case. Her family hid in this cellar while the chaos took place overhead. How do you explain to a four-year-old about rogue overlords trying to blackmail businesses? After that, her grandfather insisted she take his old revolver from the war. It was their last conversation before he passed. She remembered his words so clearly: "If it can stop Mussolini's hawks, it can stop whoever wants your loaves."

For months back then, she placed the Closed sign on

the door when the flow of customers slowed in the early afternoon. It gave her time to rebuild her shop. It also gave her space to refurbish another part of the building.

No one noticed the extra supplies for wood shelving or iron reinforcements. No one cared that some of her construction expenses were for materials diverted down below. By the end, she was quite pleased with the secured vault hidden in her cellar. Originally, the space had been intended only to keep her family safe. Back then, she would have never guessed how things would actually play out.

It started out as an innocent game. Actually, it was her grandmother who inadvertently came up with the idea. During the Second World War, her grandmother nearly achieved the status of a saint in the hearts of her customers for it. She was a baker too, but worked out of her home. Regular sieges by the Italians destroyed fishing boats. German forces attacked on land: homes, businesses, everything. Despair hit every family. Sasha's grandmother felt helpless to the pain she witnessed on her friends' faces day in and day out. That is when she started her scheme.

Originally, she crocheted tiny dolls or socks as gifts and then wrapped them inside waxed baking paper before hiding them in a loaf of fruit bread. Friends and loyal customers were delighted, and surprised at first, to find these handmade gifts tucked inside their loaves when a daughter or son had a birthday. Life for a time turned bearable.

But these were times of war. Even virtuous secrets did not stay secret for long.

Hidden gifts turned into covert communiqués.

Sasha's mama dropped the practice as it was no longer needed when she took over the family bakery. Yet years later, many of Sasha's own most loyal patrons were connections passed along from the days of her grandmother's message-filled loaves. Business had improved since Malta joined the European Union in 2004, but even so, inflation stung. Prices for everyday items skyrocketed, and underground demand for cheaper goods flourished. With it, the need for confidential messaging resurfaced. Sasha, finding her savings account short on substance, happily helped to fill the gap. Her grandmother's special bread became a hot commodity once more.

The special bread evolved. Nations were competitive and communications tight. Cryptic memos rolled inside silicon tubes and parchment paper kept the L&B alive. Sometimes she slid the notes inside ħobża rye, and at other times her courier was a Gozo grain. Sasha named all her buns Gozo, after the small sister island to Malta, and she saw them as mini versions of her regular loaves. Although Sasha offered this special service to only a handful of customers, each paid well and showed their appreciation generously. They had an unwritten arrangement. Sasha never read the notes. Nor would she reveal who received such loaves to anyone but her client. In return, wealthy politicians and long-standing executives made lucrative deals or relayed intel undetected. Her commissions meant Cristabel could attend university. They meant Sasha could serve more than bread and garden vegetables at her dinner table.

Feeling calmer, Sasha gently shut the cellar latch behind her. Rays of sun bounced off the loaves and her little bakery felt safe once again.

She glanced at her calendar. *Tuesday.* Another week had flown by and she knew Emanuel would soon come calling again. He relished pestering her, a not-so-subtle gesture to remind her he was following her movements. Sasha had eleven days to deliver. Her uncle had promised samples by the end of last week and they still hadn't arrived.

A familiar tightness spread across her chest. Its burning grip seemed to be creeping up on her more and more frequently. Thankfully, a hazy plan was beginning to gain traction. When she'd spoken with her uncle the night before—nearly midnight in Japan—he'd confirmed the shipment of vehicles had left Nagoya's port fifteen days earlier. He had double-checked every detail himself and assured her the product was carefully concealed.

Sasha knew bringing the product to Malta was a savvy

business move. Perhaps not entirely legal, but the logo would be legit. She silently thanked Raymond, her new acquaintance from her underground entrepreneurs' group. He had unknowingly filled the final hole in her game plan.

While Raymond wanted access to new trade routes, she wanted an undetectable sliver of commerce. And her uncle's position in a foreign vehicle manufacturer was the foundation for her way forward. Black markets thrived on the streets of Malta. Everyone wanted the latest smartphone. Few had enough euros to pay for new models sold at traditional stores. This discontent sang opportunity for those willing to take a risk. And she was in the fortunate position of having discreet connections with those in powerful positions.

8

RAT HOLE

Carlos' mind raced at the gravelly voice he heard steal through the rat hole. Could this be possible? Was his friend its true source, or was someone trying to fool him? He needed to think fast.

"Friend, tell me your vice."

Peter and Carlos had used this phrase since the first day they met at a performance of Shakespeare's *King Lear* in the San Anton Gardens. Maybe it was their Cuban background, but they had both memorized the same quote, which fell shortly before the second intermission:

Through tattered clothes great vices do appear;
Robes and furred gowns hide all. Plate sin with gold,
And the strong lance of justice hurtless breaks.
Arm it in rags, a pigmy's straw does pierce it.

Seconds passed. They felt like minutes. The heat pressed down as he waited to hear a few faint words back from his nameless neighbour.

At least he still had his favourite hat with him. It was a little more crumpled than normal, but its wool fibres fuelled his strength. Men all around the Mediterranean had traditionally worn them. Ironically, their floppy style implied a nationalistic, stoic nature. Carlos had learned the barretina's backstory within a week of arriving on Malta and had immediately bought his own.

Malta attracted a fair number of Cubans like Peter and Carlos to its shores. It may have been the warm island breezes or the general hardworking attitude, but for one reason or the other, Cuban professionals gravitated here. Carlos and Peter's friendship had grown out of more than a shared heritage and profession. They both loved the arts and, in particular, cultural antiquities. Their conversations generally leapt from the latest technological white papers to the uncanny acoustics of Greek amphitheatres. Carlos' wife tended to dodge their conversations for fear of igniting a heated debate, like the time she had asked about the usefulness of solar versus lunar trajectories. The two men had debated their applications for hours.

Carlos' thoughts were quickly yanked back to his dank hovel. The whispered response burned his ears. "A Cisk and a cigarette would taste mighty nice."

Cisk was Malta's pride in the brewery business. It was first produced in the 1920s and embodied Maltese grit and perseverance. But it bore no relation to Shakespeare's drama.

Peter would have spoken about being dressed in rags or some other disguise in order to stay true to their Shakespearean verse. So the voice came from no one Carlos knew—or at least nobody he could readily trust. He also picked up the stranger's implication that he had been stuck here for a very long time.

It had been far too optimistic to think his old friend sat in the adjacent cell. Still, Carlos felt disheartened as the reality settled in.

Carlos' tiny cube of a cell smothered even the smallest glimmer of hope. His only connection was a stranger, contactable only through the airway of a rodent's lair. The lack of street noise, blaring cruise ships and whirring fans, which normally irritated him, turned oppressive. It was time to gain an ally, or at the very least, to gather information.

"I'll take you up on that cool Cisk, on me if we ever get out of here. Hey, do they bring any food into this hole?"

"Mate, got me a tray of scraps and jug o' water days ago. Hard to say how many. I woke up as the grub was shoved through a rusted slot in the wall."

The bedrock absorbed every third word or so, but Carlos made out the gist of his neighbour's message. Someone wanted to keep them alive, if only barely. For how long and why remained murky.

He couldn't help wonder how this guy had gotten caught up in whatever plot had snagged him and Peter. Time to share a little in the hopes he would learn more in return.

"Buddy, I'd take scraps at this point. How'd you get here? I was standing on a street corner thinking about the Hibernians' next game when some jerk threw a cloth over my face." Carlos chose not to give away too many personal details. The national football team offered a safer topic.

While waiting for a response, Carlos decided to check his own holding cell for a food slot. He had been pretty careful in his first inspection and, except for the door, had felt nothing remotely resembling an access point. Water seeped through one corner, not enough to drink but enough to dampen his pants when he knelt in it. Its mildly septic tang stung his nostrils as he edged back towards it.

Ignoring the unpleasantness he rolled his heel over the area, rubbing gently in order to detect any intrusion or variation in substance. Nothing. When he ran his shoe higher across the damp wall, it slipped on one section. That certainly didn't feel like stone. By now, his eyes could discern where the walls met the floor and a slightly darker patch for the door.

Just then his neighbour's voice trickled from the rat hole. Distracted, he caught only the last part of the sentence: "... slick job to pull a bag from some guy's car ... never found nothing."

Whoever this petty thief was, Carlos was stumped how his foiled larceny could be tied to Peter's disappearance or his own. It did not fit into his limited set of theories.

Before he had the chance to respond, the high-pitched squeal of rusted metal grating against itself sent him back into his clammy corner. The section of the wall he'd been examining opened. Something came flying through the chute and crashed to the ground.

Neither man spoke, sensing that their captors could be listening.

Carlos moved closer to inspect what had landed in his cell. A bottle of water rolled against a plate of something. He carefully unclipped the cover on a small tray. No concerning sounds. No curious smells. Instead, four strips of dried meat, a lump of ħobża and a couple of stale pastizzi, or Maltese pastries, stared back dishearteningly. Although he could have inhaled the entire unappetizing plate, he figured rationing was the wiser approach. Yet he was not keen on attracting rats by holding on to food either. He would take a few sips of water and eat a quarter of the food before replacing its cover.

Carlos decided to use the corner opposite from his food chute and furthest from the rat hole as his toilet. It wasn't pleasant, but he had little choice. Sometimes humanity sucked.

Returning to the driest corner, Carlos shut his eyes. He always thought better with his eyes closed. Turning inwards let him see more clearly outwards.

Carlos was convinced he must still be on the island of Malta. For one, he had only gone to the bathroom once since waking up. But how long he was unconscious remained a mystery. Second, the bedrock surface of his cell matched the underground infrastructure used by Valletta and other towns on the island. Third, since pinging his wrist, he had received no response from Myriam. That further confirmed his suspicion that he was holed up somewhere beneath the city. He knew it was not uncommon for owners of older buildings to update their bunkers to withstand modern warfare—such as blocking cyber signals.

He only had to think back to late last year, to October. The wettest month of the year had left his favourite loafers a soggy mess. He had cursed as he walked the two blocks between the bus stop and conference centre, the rain pooling on the rutted cobblestones. Valletta's prestigious Mediterranean Conference Centre sat on an impressive site overlooking the old fort and the incoming ships, but parking on the area's fortified streets terrorized even the most steadfast of drivers. Carlos had suffered from cold toes and soppy socks during his entire speech to members of the Malta Chamber of Commerce.

The chamber of commerce had asked Carlos to speak about how its members could protect themselves from cybercrime. Safety measures were much the same whether you had millions or not, but having a larger sum to safeguard often motivated people to act. As he scanned the faces in the audience, puckered brows and the perma-frowns of middle-aged executives stared back. Sadly, they would likely continue down that path and become gloomy grandparents with double the estate value. They were a captivated audience, though, especially those involved in the more common than not case of lawful enterprises covering up for less scrupulous operations.

Perhaps the very people Carlos had been trying to help had turned his advice against him. The firewalls and physical barriers he recommended to withstand hackers could have been twisted into a sinister lair rather than a safe haven. A secure backup site could double as an impenetrable holding cell. He grimaced wryly as he realized he might be trapped inside his own web of protective advice—sage words given to the wrong character. He'd recognized more than a few connected dealers and "creative" entrepreneurs in the audience.

His speech had followed a standard pattern: background context, shifting international forces, examples of what could go wrong and, finally, best practices to avoid the worst outcomes. Then the discussion was opened to questions from the audience. Most queries seemed benign: How often should I back up? Can I still trust a safety deposit box?

Yet he recalled one attendee who approached him after most people had left. Carlos would have escaped this interception if his assistant had not been sick that night. Instead, he was still packing up when a wiry man in his sixties burst into the conference room. The man apologized for missing the lecture and then insisted on a private talk over a drink. Their "short" talk ended up seizing the rest of Carlos' evening.

Based on the man's penchant for twenty-one-year-old Scotch and his glistening Bontoni shoes, Carlos sent Myriam a text saying that he might have found a new benefactor for the university and would be home later than expected. His department was on a continual hunt for funding to support their high-tech research projects. Unfortunately, this retiree's true interest lay in digitizing archeological maps and ancient scripts related to Malta's megalithic temples. Carlos endured a semi-interesting chat, but ultimately failed to unlock any funding. The man wanted to protect his beloved collection of maps and physical drawings, whereas Carlos' forte was safeguarding electronic images and encrypting data.

The man passionately explained how Malta's seven free-standing temples represented an elite cluster of buildings rarely found elsewhere in the world, certainly not this old. In his mind, these septem structurae also held a powerful spiritual significance. He talked about how the megaliths represented the dawn of a new consciousness. Not only were they built before Egypt's famed pyramids, he told Carlos, but their elaborately designed domes, chambers and multi-level burial rooms indicated a worldwide connectedness that bordered on omnipresent.

Thinking the talkative elder was solely interested in protecting his treasures, Carlos explained key safeguards and imaging tools that could be used to make backup copies. He wouldn't forget the sting in the gentleman's response: "Copies won't secure the percipience hidden within the temples."

It sounded innocent enough, but Carlos felt unsettled long after their conversation had ended.

9

GAUZE AND HAZE

———

A recurring beep plucked at Myriam's thoughts. Abrasive, initially. She thought she was back in Zambia. She was crunched in the back seat of a car. A tsetse fly dove at her legs repeatedly. She swatted at it, over and over again as it tried to bite the back of her knees and nibble her ankles, which were protected by only a pair of thin socks.

Sluggishly, Myriam's mind grabbed on to the only tangible sensation it could find. *Beep … beep … beep.* Her consciousness gradually thrust her to the surface.

Myriam tried to open her eyes. Heavy. Something pressed down on them, holding her lashes closed. The beeping became regular. It pierced her ears and she realized it must be her own heartbeat being monitored by a machine nearby. Then she heard a whirring sound. It seemed to be moving. Maybe a fan? Although she felt no breeze.

She wanted to feel her face, to figure out what was covering her eyes, but her hands did not respond. Where were they? Why couldn't she lift her arms? It felt like her brain was switched on, but her body had fallen into first gear.

Oh, where is that throbbing pain coming from? It's filling my entire head. My leg aches. Myriam heard her breath heave without realizing it was her making the sound. Her body felt disconnected. It exhaled groans before she could stop them.

Distant clatter. Shoes. Someone was approaching. *Inhale. Slow down. Control.*

Images of falling ceiling beams burst into her consciousness. Shattered glass. A stinging dampened by a warmth that spread and calmed her. *Breathe out.*

The laptop. She couldn't remember if she had grabbed it. Then the memories stopped. Cut off.

What had happened? Where was she? Carlos, where was her dear Carlos? *Breathe in.*

A door clicked open and rubber soles approached. Myriam exhaled very slowly, very deliberately.

"Now, look, your gauze is loose. What have you been up to, Miss Jane Doe?" The voice had a subtle shake, divulging the nurse's rough age—an indication she knew what she was doing. Myriam thought it came from a woman, but the hoarseness could also suggest a man. "Nod your head if you can hear me."

Myriam held still.

"They will crack you wide open before you leave this place, dear." The sharp words ensured the tepid breath seeping through Myriam's facial gauze was not the only cause of her racing heart. Although the garlic funk that settled across her nose caused sufficient distress in its own right.

At the next whispered words, a numbing sensation compressed Myriam's chest. "I have seen what they can do."

Ever so slightly, Myriam tipped her chin to the left. She felt a chill as a bony hand cupped her shoulder.

"Your USB stick is safe with me. But they took your laptop." The hushed voice leapt back into caregiver mode. "Silly lady, let me tighten your dressing. Your wounds will never heal in this state."

Seconds later, Myriam heard heavier steps enter the room. "Eva, how is our patient doing?"

"Doctor, she remains unconscious with occasional

bouts of semi-lucidness. Normal twitching and rustling after such a trauma, but no signs of alertness. I gave her another dose of morphine and expect we can switch to paracetamol with codeine by the morning." The nurse sighed almost imperceptibly. "Doctor, I will remain at the station overnight if you need anything." Eva left the door ajar before returning to the front desk.

Myriam wondered if that last statement was more for her own ears than for the doctor's.

The practiced warmth in the doctor's voice began to fade. "Myriam, I am going to ask a few simple questions to test your cognition. Tell me your maiden name."

What an odd question, thought Myriam. And she distinctly recalled the nurse calling her Jane Doe.

The doctor silently waited for a response. The sound of distant shuffling drifted through the doorway.

"Come now, let's try something easier. Can you recall your first pet? Perhaps a wee pup." Light keystrokes interspersed his words.

Myriam focussed on her breathing. *Inhale. Exhale. Steady. Think.* Maiden names and childhood pets. These were typical password questions. She was not that naive.

A click echoed through the room as the door snapped shut.

In the quiet room, the fluorescent lights hummed. The soft tapping of typing ceased. A chair rolled closer to

Myriam, its wheels squealing mildly under the weight of a sizeable individual.

"Eva is always playing games. She'll retire soon, but for now I have to put up with her antics. I know she never gave you more morphine. Your diagnostics would read totally differently. I also know you can hear me."

Without a chance to respond, Myriam felt an almost imperceptible prick.

Burning tendrils spread across her limbs. She felt like a tree with its branches alight, turning from solid matter into feeble ash. Myriam focussed on memories elsewhere, using a technique she had learned in the military. Control your mind and you control your body.

Blue waters lapped the shore. A gull echoed overhead. Then hot lava oozed once more across her body, bringing her back to the present. *Depart again. Escape.* Soft jazz played as she stirred lumpy cookie dough. It must be a Saturday afternoon because Carlos sat reading the paper at the kitchen table. She relaxed as the wind gently rattled the range hood. She heard the buzz of an oven timer. It tried to penetrate her concentration. *No, no, it's not time to open the door yet.*

The doctor's clipped accent became more pronounced the longer he spoke. "I can only get you out of whatever mess you have gotten into if you cooperate. Gunshot wounds and imploded homes do not tend to follow the innocent. So don't play virtuous with me. I am paid to heal only those who provide answers. Play my way and you may walk out of here alive. Play your way and that needle sticking into your arm will be the nicest thing you feel for a long, long time. Consider what I can do to make you wish you had been left buried beneath the rubble, alone in that house. Now, tell me your maiden name."

Myriam agreed there were games underfoot. She didn't trust the nurse's subversive offer of help either. There was no USB—everything was saved on the laptop. Myriam heard its familiar jingle as the computer powered up.

"Ardelean," she murmured. It was the furthest name from her Cuban-Polish background she could think of. She also knew it would give her a few precious moments while the doctor tried to hack into her laptop.

Slow, deliberate clicks of a keypad scratched at Myriam's ears.

She felt the bands tighten around her wrists and ankles. Everything else felt numb, any sense of pain lost. A haze began to cloud her thoughts. Images shifted to moments from her past. She was sitting on a tan leather seat. Her father sat in front of her, steering his old Buick. His shoulder moved up and down as he changed gears on the sticky gear shift that stuck out from the steering wheel. Then she tasted something sweet. The fog reformed.

She was back in her lab. Her eyes hurt from the

microscope lenses, which dug into her skin when she stared into them for too many hours. No time for a break. The officers would arrive any minute. They had no patience for research or study, only answers. She knew the medicinal herbs better than anyone else. She understood their uses after countless years working with Indigenous healers and visiting abandoned sites. This field was her specialty. Now she needed to recreate an ancient medicine that could fight a modern disease.

But the black cloud started its unavoidable descent towards her consciousness. Time had run out.

10

BLOOD DROP

A cheery nurse called Cristabel's name. "Good morning, sweetie. We'll get you signed up and into the lab in no time. Just sit yourself down here. I have a few questions the government requires me to ask every blood donor."

The nurse had already filled in the upper section of her clipboard. Standard questions. It often surprised Cristabel how trusting the medical system could be. No one verified her statement that she had not travelled in the past five years. Even though the same government charged with protecting its citizens' health also monitored their comings and goings, its bureaucracy was too thick to integrate the two departments. Today, Cristabel used this weakness to her advantage.

The nurse remained unaware that she'd travelled to Guatemala and Honduras three years earlier, during a renewed Zika virus outbreak. Nor would the health system have any trace of her trip four summers ago to the Ivory Coast to volunteer at a local college. Cristabel was confident she had not contracted anything—her blood was clean—and figured her succinct version of her whereabouts played to everybody's best interest. *White lies were virtuous, right?*

The nurse sent her to another waiting room further inside the Mater Dei Hospital. Access into this hospital would hopefully give her a chance to find Myriam. Under normal circumstances, the Mater Dei Hospital was where ambulances rushed victims from car crashes, violent crimes or severe accidents. Cristabel feared this was not a normal situation. She needed to be sure.

Slowing her steps, Cristabel took note of every label on every door she passed, building a rough mental model of the corridor's layout. It helped that, a month earlier, an investigative journalism documentary had exposed the hospital's inner workings, with video coverage of the Emergency Department and several surgical wards. The police had been searching for a missing woman and had failed to follow the basic protocol of checking at the island's main hospital.

Considering Cristabel had spoken to Myriam on the phone yesterday afternoon, she knew Myriam was likely at home when the tremor occurred. She had seen for herself that damage to the house was extensive. And where was Myriam now? Cristabel was certain she was seriously injured and in need of hospital attention. If she had been brought here, to the Mater Dei Hospital, there might still be a chance that the whole situation was a huge misunderstanding. Although Cristabel's gut told her otherwise.

Cristabel followed the nurse's instructions to go down the hallway and turn left. She passed a bold red arrow pointing towards the Emergency Department. Door signs confirmed a similar pattern to the last hallway she had walked down, suggesting a consistency in the hospital's design. The next intersection of hallways showed the Pathology Department to her left and a secured door, barring public access, to her right. Before Cristabel ducked into the Laboratory Services waiting room, she noticed the sign posted above the restricted door: "Acute Care: Authorized Medical Staff Only." That hurdle would pose more of a challenge.

Twenty minutes later, she had given three vials of blood. A male nurse led her to the donors' waiting room to rest. Besides a mild ache in her left arm, she felt completely fine. Slipping into the bathroom, Cristabel went into the far toilet stall and tied on her headscarf and threw on her jacket. The narrow backpack hung flat against her back, making it easier to haul herself up and out of the stall. The ceiling air vent had a simple mesh cover, which she quietly replaced after she had climbed through it.

Two access panels further down led into the maintenance room. She had noticed its sign on a door during her walk from the lab. Bingo. Its cover slid aside easily and she dropped down into a small space, trying not to knock over anything as she landed. Buckets, mops, cleaning solution and the grand prize, coveralls, were all neatly stacked. Snug but tidy. Plan A was falling nicely into place. Too nicely.

The door handle swivelled when she had two buttons left to do up on her borrowed uniform. A lady wearing a torn hairnet and smeared pair of coveralls jumped back at the sight of Cristabel. "What're you doin' in here, missy?"

"Oh, ma'am. Sorry to scare you. First week on the job and I spilled bleach all over my coveralls! I thought I had this room to myself to swap into a new pair. Give me a minute and you can have whatever you want in here." Cristabel took a chance on her believability. She had long ago decided that people who talk assertively were listened to, and she desperately wanted this lady to listen right now. Maybe she should have studied sociology instead of technology.

The woman, however, wasn't falling for her story. "I never hired you. What are you up to?"

Great, just her luck to run into the floor supervisor. Cristabel's mind raced and she blurted out the first thing she thought of. "Sorry, ma'am. I am working over in the obstetrics department on backfill. That floor is way too cramped." Cristabel grabbed a pair of disposable gloves from an open box and cruised past the lady before she had a chance to ask any more questions.

After getting through the next swinging door, Cristabel snagged a cleaning trolley sitting outside a public washroom. Glancing around, she silently thanked whoever had decided to take an unofficial break and leave their half-full cart of disinfectant wipes, antibacterial spray, garbage bags and other cleaning supplies out in the open. She then spotted an arrow pointing towards the Emergency Department. Two nurses sat behind the station desk. One stared intently at her computer screen while the other looked blankly at some invisible spot above her as she spoke into the phone—likely a distraught patient was taking all of the nurse's attention.

Cristabel embodied her role as cleaner and decided to play it up. She glanced at the nurse's name tag while slowly sanitizing the adjacent wall. When the nurse hung up the phone, Cristabel acted as if they knew one another. "Akira, can you believe that earthquake on the western shore?" She bought some time by carefully knotting the station's full waste bag before replacing it with an empty liner.

"Oh, I never heard about any tremors recently. Thankfully no one was hurt, at least no one admitted here." The nurse barely looked at Cristabel and quickly went back to the phone as another line beeped and lit up bright red.

Finally, she had confirmed one fact. If Myriam had been taken away by an ambulance, it had not rushed her here. Time to check another potential ward.

Acute Care was not so easy to get into. Its main door was locked and needed an access pass to swipe a sensor located next to the handle. Cristabel hung around the area. She slowly wiped down the baseboard then gingerly disinfected the wall. In time, she moved on to sanitize each light switch. Eventually a medic rushed out, but the door slammed shut before Cristabel could duck inside.

She decided to move closer. Over and over, she scrubbed the door handle. It would be the cleanest knob in the hospital. A pair of interns finally came out and held the door open for her to reach its inside edges. Thankfully, neither checked her badge. She continued inside the ward. The knot in her stomach eased slightly.

Cristabel had always imagined Acute Care to be full of doctors running around, nurses rushing from room to room and alarms blaring constantly—basically hallways running amuck with organized mayhem. In reality, the quiet stillness of the ward gave off a sense of serenity, a controlled crisis instead of barely contained chaos.

Perhaps her fears were unfounded. Breathing in confidence from the air, she pulled her shoulders back and made her own rounds. In room after room, she wiped, dusted and observed patients. No one looked anything like the photo she had seen of Myriam. Besides one woman in her twenties, all of the patients were elderly.

Cristabel decided Myriam had not been brought to this hospital. This only raised further questions. Who had authority to divert ambulances from Malta's main hospital? Or did they move Myriam without officials even knowing someone had been injured from the sinkhole? The more she probed, the more questions arose.

II

JAMES

––––––––––

Carlos buckled over on all fours in the far corner of his cell. It felt like a dagger had been slammed into his stomach and ravaged his insides. Whatever had been in that food, he wouldn't touch it again. So much for his overseer trying to keep him alive. The last thing he remembered was the advice from his so-called friend next door to eat all he could. He retched once more. Nothing came out.

Over the past hour he had heard nothing but his own wheezing. Then loud grating noises and what sounded like a scuffle shook his nerves. He figured his neighbour was being dragged out, or maybe released for keeping his part of the deal. After that, Carlos blacked out.

When he woke, he didn't know how long he had been unconscious. The darkness of the cell started to change colours. His eyes were playing tricks. Between the lack of food and insufficient water, the chemicals in his body had been thrown out of whack. Carlos had to remind himself that this was normal, that he could fight it and hold on to reality. He had suffered worse.

Pressing the mole on his wrist, he tried one more time to contact Myriam and relay his location.

A soft click came from the far wall, prompting him to edge out of the way. The movement set his stomach into revolt. He pushed down another surge of nausea. Backed into the corner, he squatted and hugged his abdomen.

A narrow beam of light shone through a crack into his cell.

"Shhh, I'll get you outta there."

The door without a handle was roughly nudged open until it hit a ridge on the floor. Clearly, the door was not used often. Not knowing who was on the other side made him wary. But getting out offered options. And at this point, he needed options.

"C'mon Carlos. Can you fit through this gap?" The voice sounded familiar.

All he needed was a few inches to slide his body

through sideways—and a bag to hold over his mouth. The ceiling lowered near the door, making it impossible to stand. Carlos lay on one shoulder and pushed with the toes of one foot to shove himself through the gap. He grimaced. Rough rock grated against his shoulder and hip. Now he knew what it felt like for the lemon he zested on his favourite tagliatelle.

He was blinded by a bright light inside a dark space. Now lying on his back Carlos felt walls push against both shoulders. He presumed he had entered some sort of hallway.

"Oh, sorry." The penlight flicked in the opposite direction so Carlos could see the face of who had rescued him. Bony cheekbones and hollow eyes. The hair was a curly mess of dark blond, shorter than the last time Carlos had seen his friend. James had gone to school with him and Myriam and the three of them had become close.

Before Carlos could ask James what he was doing in Malta or how he'd known Carlos was in this place, he heard the word for a second time.

"Sorry."

Carlos jerked his head to the side. It was faint, but he felt the sting, and then warmth spread across his left arm. *What the—?* His thoughts blurred, and the penlight dimmed. He imagined a heavy jacket being pulled over his arms and wrapped snugly around him. Oh so tightly.

***

James looked down at his friend, more gaunt than he remembered. The beard was new, and likely scruffier than usual. At one time they had been inseparable.

JMC, that's what they had called themselves: James, Myriam and Carlos. They earned master's degrees at the same university in Kingston, Canada. After graduate school Myriam had moved on with some aid organization. Carlos had turned theoretical and started teaching. James preferred to leap. He wanted action.

Money drives everything in the world and businesses make money. James teamed up with some entrepreneurial buddies who believed the west coast of Canada was the place to be. Vancouver offered a technology hub with access to investors. It also brought him closer to Canada's unpopulated spaces. For an unconventional idea, the location fit almost too perfectly.

James and his partners dove into research and testing. A handful of foreign private investors funded their work. Results were kept quiet. Even his cohorts did not realize that the research tactics James had devised were actually probing a bigger issue. He worked feverishly. The line between work and his personal life disintegrated.

Even so, James never quite left the JMC triad.

One evening, back when the three of them were hanging out and drinking minty caipirinhas or hoppy cervezas negras almost every night of the week, their relationship changed dramatically. They had returned to James' apartment late one evening. James started ranting about his advanced IT class. He felt his final project about bringing GPS tracing methods into agriculture's biopesticide industry was genius. The professor disagreed. James—being the least affected by the quantity of alcohol coursing through their veins—proceeded along an increasingly charged warpath about how he would prove the professor wrong.

Carlos and Myriam started to fidget when James threatened to dig up dirt on his hated professor and smear her reputation before her morning coffee. He pulled out his laptop, seething at the chance to ruin the professor's career.

Myriam interrupted him and challenged James to track her and Carlos' matching moles. He knew it was intended to be nothing more than a diversion, to distract him. James figured they were beyond drunk.

Myriam was the first to give it away. She grinned and held out her wrist, showing him the tiny raised brown mole that coloured her skin. "Try to track us." She promptly passed out and collapsed on Carlos' shoulder. Before long, Carlos started snoring.

James' thoughts about his hated professor evaporated. Who gets GPS trackers embedded in their skin? Five minutes earlier he had been certain his friends were just innocent classmates, but now he was not so sure.

James tried all of his standard search techniques. The clock read well after three in the morning by the time he had finished. The two GPS devices simply did not exist. Invisible. *Shit.* Were they messing with his head? Were the supposed trackers nothing more than growths of skin?

The next morning, neither Carlos nor Myriam mentioned the bet. James, on the other hand, could not get it out of his head.

A week later, between rereading his thesis and studying for an operations management exam, James tried once more to trace Carlos' and Myriam's GPS trackers. He bounced around across thirteen different servers before getting blocked by some sort of national security-level firewall. He couldn't believe it.

James kept at it. Every six months or so, he would try to find them. Every time, he came up empty. Six years into his personal project, his luck changed.

Under his current role, James headed up a team that tracked pest infestations in crops. The crew specialized in sub-Arctic, prairie and arid lands. By last quarter, they had signed three memorandums of understanding with northern communities trying to grow produce locally using specially constructed greenhouses. The data fed into an innovative forecasting tool the company had developed. Ongoing prevention and treatment support came with the service. In tandem with devising a new type of insect management system, his company was quickly selling their patent-pending brainchild to farmers around the world.

His latest technology progressed more than one goal. When he loaded Myriam's and Carlos' GPS tracking data from university into his company's system, their location stood out like a shark's fin in placid waters. *Gotcha!* By then, additional questions rumbled around his consciousness, set there by people he knew and trusted.

His opinion of Myriam and Carlos took time to shift. James had other friends, boyhood friends. When most teenagers studied calculus and Tolstoy, James was introduced to psychoanalysis and back-channel cybersecurity. During his adolescence, Komsomol, Russia's Communist youth league, recruited James. While he finessed his crisp North American west-coast accent, those boyhood friends called him Yakov. It was not coincidental that two of these friends also attended the same university as him and later invested heavily in his start-up. Although undocumented in the company's private placement papers used to attract investors, the friends' interests spread beyond insect detection and control.

For James' first international mission, he was sent to the same university where Carlos and Myriam studied.

Trying to make a name for himself, he forged a seemingly casual yet tight relationship with them. Although secretly associated with the Cuban government, Myriam and Carlos remained oblivious to James' tie to Russia's intelligence service. Even trusted allies had to keep an eye on friends.

During those university years, James met his old friends over coffee and played one-on-one basketball. Their conversations quickly branched into shadowy connections and thwarted plots. They traded folders stuffed full of photocopied pages, often barely legible. Thick black lines struck out certain names and locations. Still, the underlying message rang clear to James.

Elsewhere, patterns of subterfuge within Cuba's national intelligence began to emerge in joint procedures with Russia. Routine communications increasingly contained anomalies. Undisclosed operations were not looked upon kindly within Russian hierarchies, allies or otherwise. Reports filtered through to James suggested a possible link to Myriam and Carlos. Yet James was convinced they were uninvolved and harmless.

That view changed when Myriam challenged him to track their moles.

After graduation, James moved to Canada and Carlos and Myriam returned to Cuba. Years later, as their Christmas card informed their friends, the couple relocated to Malta. Move for move, James monitored their whereabouts. Myriam left Cuba first, and James watched from afar. Carlos followed soon after, once the deans at the universities that hired him co-approved his transfer. James watched. Their transmitters emitted a low-level signal, strong enough for James to follow.

From then on, a separate team was tagged with on-the-ground surveillance. James focussed on his Canadian project. On the surface, the business developed pest control in remote locations. Underneath, James had a more explicit mission. His investors cared solely about gathering geospatial data and information about military outpost movements—or lack thereof—in Canada's Arctic.

So when Myriam had sent an obscure text about Carlos mixing caipirinhas and blacking out, James knew something was up. His mind carried him straight back to that night in his dingy flat. It was as if he could still touch his threadbare corduroy couch. He also knew the pair hadn't worked out his true identity.

When Carlos' GPS did not respond, James hopped on the next flight to Malta.

12

REUNITED

———

Cristabel had left the hospital the day before feeling dejected. She felt she had missed something. Throughout the night, memories of other failures came reeling back into her head. Her hand on the shop doorknob. Breathless, after running back to the bakery. The yellow school bus whizzing past just as her mother dropped a tray of hot loaves. Cristabel had forgotten to move the cooling racks closer to the oven on her way out.

Then, years later, sitting at the back of a muggy room. It was her final literature class. Everyone else nodded eagerly, but she couldn't grasp the concept of the duality of character hidden within *The Great Gatsby*. The teacher deconstructed layers from the story and droned on about societal inequities that simply made no sense to Cristabel.

Now, once again, she found herself falling one step behind, struggling to bring all the pieces into focus.

In any case, she knew where Myriam was *not* located. What troubled her was having no idea where Myriam *was* being held.

It felt like the world was running out of control. Unseen affairs moved faster than Cristabel could keep up with. Her gut sunk even lower while showering. It was already Wednesday and she still had to write a paper and read about a hundred pages in the next two days for her classes. Normally, she would have run to her favourite professor and supervisor for advice. Normally, that professor would be sitting in his office marking papers or highlighting journals for the next classroom discussion, not missing and out of contact.

Groaning inwardly, she sulked and finished drying her hair. Once back in her bedroom, she pulled on a clean T-shirt and called her most trusted friend and mentor. "Gerardo, I've come up dry. We need to regroup, and I think we need help from the others."

***

Gerardo had been waiting for this call. He grabbed the tweed jacket splayed on the bed, where he had flung it last night in frustration. Initially he had worn it as a joke, telling himself it would help him fit in on campus. It had pilled over the years and the elbows had worn thin. But season after season, it suited his needs. A little extra warmth. A touch of wise old man for his ego. Eventually, he convinced himself that the texture helped him think more clearly.

His fingers ran over the threads, instinctively moving back and forth over their ridges as he tried to sort through the latest quandary. He needed its calming clarity once again. Cristabel might have answered certain questions, but he needed a plan to unravel the rest.

***

Thirty minutes later, Cristabel turned on her laptop. A stale pot of coffee sizzled on a burner that should have been turned off hours earlier. She had planned to wake up soon after her mother left for the bakery. Unfortunately, Cristabel tossed all night and had overslept.

She sank onto her arms, nodding off without meaning to. It was nine in the morning. Two minutes later, Cristabel jerked awake when mail came flying through the slot in the front door. The postman was certainly precise. Four envelopes and the daily newspaper skidded across the floor. She glanced up from the kitchen table and saw a third of the front page blazoned with an ad for some fanatic's roundup for a new spiritual awakening. The advertisement coaxed readers, claiming that Malta was at the crux of every ancient religion and that the upcoming grand ceremony on May 14 would reveal new evidence to prove it. So much for the stereotype of slow island life. Not on Malta. Moments later, Cristabel fell into a deep slumber and dreamt she was lost in the ruins of Great Zimbabwe, searching for a message from the Queen of Sheba.

Cristabel woke to her phone buzzing. She had been asleep for another hour. Three voicemails and a meeting notification flashed red, all from Gerardo. She had twenty minutes to get over to the outdoor gallery on campus, a favourite gathering place thanks to its lush palms and discreet nooks. With her mind feeling fresher after her nap, she splashed cold water on her face and swiped mascara across her lashes.

During the drive, the Top 40 station won out after thirty seconds of listening to a religious enthusiast spouting about some grand discovery at the latest archeological find. He was probably trying to drum up interest for the same convention that the morning's paper advertised. Normally she loved the talk show's nouveau themes, but this interview proved too far-out even for her ears.

By the time Cristabel reached the park cafe, the others had already gathered around Gerardo. He wore his usual tweed jacket, which suited his ruffled brown hair and prominent jawline. The group hadn't met together in public for nearly two years due to the COVID-19 pandemic restrictions. Instead, they had communicated mainly through darknet chatrooms and hidden video channels. Little had changed except that Saul had grown a beard and now wore torn jeans instead of a tailored suit.

Celia was explaining her findings. With an eyebrow nod in Cristabel's direction, she proceeded to detail what she had figured out since their last video briefing.

They already knew that, since 2015, five executives had bought over ninety percent of Valletta's historic buildings, excluding municipal property. It turned out that the same five individuals had all graduated within two years of one another from the University of Tartu in Estonia.

If any member of the group gathered in the shade hadn't been paying attention before, this point yanked them back.

Estonia had a reputation in tech circles. Since its independence, Estonia had become one of the world's most technologically advanced countries. Ninety-nine percent of government services were offered digitally.

Skype's key strategist and its earliest employee, Taavet Hinrikus, and its co-founder Jaan Tallinn, both came from Estonia. Hinrikus later upended the global cross-currency exchange industry when he launched TransferWise, which offered lower fees than traditional banks and was available to anybody who wanted to send money abroad. The company proved hugely successful. Another Estonian, Markus Villig, became the youngest founder of a billion-dollar company in Europe that he launched back in 2013. He, too, had studied at the University of Tartu. Undoubtably, the school had proved itself to be an impressive institution.

Cristabel glanced around the tight-knit circle, noting everyone's eyes were fixated on Celia. The small team listening knew that if the five executives of interest went to school together at the University of Tartu, they were capable of something very big. Perhaps not as successful as their more well-known alumni—Hinrikus, Tallinn and Villig—but worth paying attention to nonetheless.

Celia absently twirled a piece of grass between her fingers as she spoke. She paused, looking up to check if anyone had a question or point to add before continuing to explain her findings. Although obscure, a further anomaly linked the businessmen. Whereas the parents of all five men held active memberships with the Russian Orthodox Church, the men themselves all claimed non-denominational status in their municipal filings. Beyond this, Celia had found no other connections. No common memberships or clubs or other apparent associations. In a centre as small as Malta, it almost looked as if these compatriots were actively trying to avoid one another.

Next, Ana updated the group. She traced outgoing communications off the island in search of particular keywords of interest. On more than one occasion, she had been reminded to ignore critical topics such as uranium supply, assassination plots and subversive political groups. A separate, more senior intelligence agency handled these activities on a global scale. This left Ana to seek less obvious regional undercurrents for their small field team's assignments.

Chatter about black markets spiked after Parliament had announced a new retail levy a few months back. Two of the five executives of interest had been tagged as participants on separate recordings. But these indirect links had no apparent crossover between their reactions or underlying industries of concern. Although unregulated dealings were likely to gain traction, Ana dismissed the trend as not critical to their current mission.

Ana had uncovered another bizarre theme. It related to a handful of recent donations made to archeological excavations across Malta—all paid anonymously. They stood out because the payments were made through shell companies and hidden behind a web of transactions and multiple foreign entities. Red flags shot up because what normally would be a straightforward donation was instead a hide-and-seek mess.

Ana would continue to dig, but she expected the source of funds would eventually lead back to the men in question. It seemed an odd scheme. After all, the actual fieldwork was run by two non-profit organizations. However, these entities tended to follow the bare minimum of disclosure requirements, making the money difficult to track.

Cristabel's internal alarm bells clanged. She was certain a fragment of information she had picked up related to Ana's update, but that bit of intel remained hidden in the shadows of her mind. What was she missing? She decided not to say anything. After all, she didn't know what she could say. Not yet at least.

13

SEVEN WORDS

———

Seven simple words. Words that would start a new level of business: *Port of Marsaxlokk—08 19 midnight—TM359TYR8P-XT*. Sasha wrapped her message first in parchment paper and then in tinfoil before burying it inside the cranberry and walnut dough. She smiled at her hideaway while singing an old nursery rhyme: "*Iddendilt mal-kannizzata / Qisni kelb tal-kaċċatur.*" She barely thought about the murmured words' meaning: "I climbed up the vine trellis / Like a hunter's dog." Yet they kept rolling around in her thoughts like a toy train looping around its tracks, unending and never needing to stop for passengers. Let the pursuit begin.

Sasha marked her special loaf with a slash of her knife. Its identity glared obvious to her, but once the loaf was baked, her customers would not notice it.

As she slid the batch into the fiery ovens, her mouth felt parched and her head ached. The bakery was unusually stifling. She reached for the glass she kept beside the sink. The clear liquid soothed the dryness. Her tension eased and her brows relaxed. Better than water. Normally she never touched vermouth. It was her secret ingredient for tomato and olive pastries, but today it proved far more useful in her drinking glass than stuck inside the cupboard. No one would know any better. Sasha returned to her singing, only this time a little louder.

A noise from below shocked her from her daydreaming. She stood stock-still, staring down at the floorboards. Silence.

Forgetting to draw the window blinds, she dashed to the cellar's access panel. It looked as it always did—hidden under an old rug, dusty and undisturbed. Every time Sasha closed its lid, she sprinkled a handful of flour around the rug to achieve this look. Glancing around, she convinced herself the noise had been a figment of her imagination. Her nerves must be ramped up. *How could anybody be down there?*

Then a shadow crossed the window. Someone walking past turned their head away as soon as she looked up. She was used to window-shoppers, but they weren't normally embarrassed about peeking. *People are certainly fickle today.*

She decided to fight her urge to go down to the cellar and instead grabbed a ball of dough and started kneading—perhaps a little too strenuously.

Another person crossed in front of her store. She was sure they had eyed her up through the window before wandering off. Trust ranked low on her radar this Wednesday morning. *Forget them!*

For the next forty minutes, Sasha dashed around her shop. She refilled a basket of ricotta rolls and topped up the display of fig and Gorgonzola loaves. When she could put it off no longer, she pulled out the mobile phone that was stuffed deep in the pocket of her apron. Only one number had ever been dialled from it. Before losing her nerve, she hit redial.

The familiar voice answered with a grunt. They had agreed on this nondescript communication earlier to keep their discussions brief in case anyone overheard. Sasha spoke aloud the message she had rehearsed about fifteen times to herself. "Six fish in the nets at the harbour, descaled in one day's time."

Even though the Port of Marsaxlokk now received over seventy percent of Malta's total imports, locals still called it the fishing harbour. That meant using the code word *fish* for the delivery point wasn't much of a mystery. To help build her cover, Sasha had been intermittently ordering snapper and dorado from various fishmongers over the past three months. Luckily Cristabel figured her mother was on a health kick to raise her omegas.

Months earlier, Sasha and Raymond had agreed on a few communication "rules." They would say *descaled* to mean customs clearance. *Fish* represented the vehicles. The incoming cars were clean, straight from a factory outside of Nagoya. Her Uncle Noa assured her the shipment's paperwork was in order. This was the part of the transaction she felt confident about.

It was the murkier items hidden inside the "fish" that concerned her. She had one day to sneak into the port, access the sealed container with the vehicles, remove the contraband and then get herself out of there without getting caught by the surveillance cameras, dogs or guards that swept the port. Unconsciously, her right hand began to twitch uncontrollably until she gently rubbed it still.

The prospect of breaking free felt so close. Raymond knew nothing of the black-market phones tucked inside the vehicles imported for his dealership. If all went to plan, he never would. He needed a reliable supplier and she delivered—for a small fee, of course. Other dealerships across Malta had to use one of three importers, all heavily taxed. Raymond had vocalized his frustration at their group's first meeting, explaining he'd heard the levies were often diverted into corrupt pockets before hitting federal coffers. Sasha offered an alternative.

Her scheme generally followed the rules, in part by playing with import classifications to ensure shipments stayed within the lowest emissions' category. Then, through one of her connections, she managed to reduce the registration fee normally charged. Its far lower rate meant her friend's retail prices could better match mainland Europe versus the typically inflated island prices. Powerful connections were proving lucrative for her.

Rumblings beneath the floorboards interrupted her thoughts again. *What is going on down there? The building can't be shifting.*

Sasha pounded her foot on the floor. Cristabel had not been to the shop since Monday and no other customers had entered for at least an hour. Satisfied after a few minutes of silence, she went to the cupboard and pulled out the vermouth. The olive and tomato pastries would have to take a break tomorrow—she needed their key ingredient today. With a slightly clearer head, she tried to run through her plan. She hardly noticed the twitch in her fingers or the strain in her neck muscles.

Two days earlier, Sasha's uncle had described where

he hid the phones. He was sure his employer did not suspect anything. He explained everything clearly. First, a clear envelope would be stuck to the windshield of each hatchback, containing a copy of the waybill and an authenticated purchase agreement along with all the required stamps. This was standard protocol for vehicle imports so officials could spot-check any auto at random. The second, more plump envelope hidden under one particular passenger seat was not standard protocol. For this first shipment, the concealed envelope contained a dozen imitation mobile phones and a signed document to pass along to Raymond, Sasha's vehicle dealer.

If Emanuel's boss was satisfied, Sasha's uncle would send hundreds more each month. She calculated her commission. It was worth the risk.

She had intended to retrieve the concealed phones herself, but then another idea started to form. But her thoughts were cut short when the little bell on the door jingled.

Well, wasn't it fitting that *he* happened to walk in at this very moment?

As if on cue she smiled wryly. "Oh dear, your favourite pastries just came out of the oven. You'll have to wait a minute. They'll be too hot to wrap just yet." She felt in control and savoured making this scoundrel wait.

Emanuel glared back. "No more delays, my dear. Boss

wants his sample." He grabbed the right hand she was leaning on and twisted sharply.

Something popped. Sasha cried out, in part from the jolt of pain and in part because she hadn't expected him to come at her so fast. She relied on that wrist. Now it would be almost useless for weeks.

She stared him squarely in the eyes. "Stop. They are at the port. Come with me tonight. Now that you've bashed up my hand, you'll have to retrieve them yourself."

"You're on your own, lady. Have them for me at this same time on Friday or more than your wrist will hurt." Emanuel grinned and popped an entire pecan tart into his mouth. Turning swiftly, he left the door swinging, its bell jingling uncontrollably.

Sasha hoped he burned his tongue on the tart. She knew he enjoyed mocking her. Well, he wouldn't control her forever. That she could change.

Cristabel sailed through the door. Sasha grimaced inwardly at the timing, but forced a wide grin. "Darling, how good of you to stop by. Don't you have classes today?"

While Cristabel launched into a long story of a missing teacher and impending dissertation project, Sasha wrapped a tea towel ever so tightly around her right wrist. She barely heard the words flowing from Cristabel's mouth, but kept smiling and nodding to deflect her true thoughts.

"Is everything okay, Mom?" Cristabel gripped her mom's shoulder.

Sasha hoped Cristabel didn't catch any whiff of liquor. For her daughter's sake, she normally cursed the stuff.

"Yes, yes. My arthritis is acting up, so my mind is a little scattered at the moment." Sasha fell back on an old ailment that hadn't actually bothered her for years. But she noticed Cristabel's brow relax. She then threw back a couple of extra-strength paracetamols and rubbed a thick layer of her arthritis cream on her wrist for good measure. For once the law played in her favour. It required all retail businesses to keep a medical kit on their premises. Ages ago, she had also stashed a spare tube of joint-pain cream inside the container.

Clunk.

Cristabel did not even blink. It was as if she hadn't even heard the noise beneath their feet. Well, better she didn't notice.

Then, with perfect timing, Raymond strode into the shop. Cristabel, oblivious that this person wasn't a random customer, headed out the front door to deal with some other matter.

"Good to see you this afternoon." Sasha slid the marked cranberry and walnut loaf into a paper bag. "I do hope you enjoy this loaf and all the goodness it entails."

Her friend handed her three euros and change. "I do

look forward to trying this new flavour." The man winked and left as quickly as he had arrived.

Sasha started to sing the familiar tune once more: "*Iddendilt mal-kannizzata / Qisni kelb tal-kaċċatur.*" A squeal like rusted hinges pierced the floorboards and put an abrupt stop to her song. *What is going on in the cellar?* She kicked the floorboards to be certain there was not a rogue rat scurrying around before shoving the mat out of the way. Without bothering to flip the shop's Open sign to Closed, she bent down and lifted the vault's access panel.

14

ALLY AND FOE

Someone was shaking her shoulders. A voice screamed, and incoherent words plummeted from some unknown source. Myriam could not make out what they meant. Her eyes were taped shut. The shaking rattled her concentration. With each touch, volts of pain slashed through her shoulders and arms. Then everything turned cold. Cool liquid seeped through her bandages, and within seconds, every part of her body felt saturated. Heavy, sopping cotton pulled her deep, like she was being dragged to the bottom of a well where no light reached and wisps of silence wrapped her in their cocoon.

Time passed quickly or slowly; she had no idea. One moment she thought she heard voices. Sharp words in a language that reminded Myriam of the staccato notes on her grandmother's piano. Distant utterances. Fading into a low drawl. Gone.

Later, or maybe earlier, she heard clicks from random directions. Something slid beneath her. Her feet burned. Then her attention faded.

At one point, a female's voice brought her back. "Myriam! Myriam, do you know where you are?"

Myriam was not sure why or how, but her body nearly felt normal. How much she had merely dreamt versus what they had actually done to her, she had no idea. It did not matter. For now, her thoughts were clear.

She cracked open her eyes.

A woman, her face framed by long black hair, gazed down at her. Strain around her eyes and furrowed brows hinted at her concern. Then Myriam saw the cold stare of her pupils and the white knuckles gripped around a clipboard. A fair attempt, but not true compassion.

Myriam's defensive wall rose like an invisible cloak. *Gather information.*

She was lying down in a small room with beige walls. Without moving, she could see a window partially shaded by blue curtains. Outside a pigeon balanced on an electrical wire. The bird cocked its head, probably seeing its own reflection in the glass. She figured she must be on the second floor, or maybe the third.

"Myriam, tell me where your husband is." The unfamiliar woman moved her mouth but the words did not fit. Strange how disconnected she seemed.

Then Myriam realized the lady was chewing gum. She was not speaking at all. Myriam blinked her eyes, trying to grasp what was going on.

A second woman rolled her chair into Myriam's view. "We know you know more than you have said. Your house was destroyed. Your husband disappeared. You have nowhere to go and no means to run. Now, I don't want to put you through anything worse than you have already endured. So let's work together. Tell me where your husband is hiding."

This woman looked to be in her late fifties, with blond hair and matte red lipstick. Her accent was subtle, but Myriam recognized the mild Russian influence immediately. They should be allies. Although not formally, since Myriam had long given up her work with the Cuban military. She sighed inwardly. One never really leaves the service.

"Comrade, you know my husband is a smart man. Even if you find him, what do you think he will tell you?" Myriam sparred, trying not to reveal too much but also looking for inroads as to why she was being held in the first place. Considering she was lying here—and still alive—she needed them to keep thinking she did know where Carlos was located. It was her only card to play.

"Darling." The woman stretched out the word, as if searching for how much detail she should share. "Professor Ignacio, as he likes to call himself nowadays, has been running a lot of unsanctioned searches over the past few months. Ally relationships are based on trust. We don't like to be kept in the dark when friends get nervous."

"I suppose you thought by abducting me and then torturing me, I would warm to your cause?" Myriam had no clue what searches this lady was talking about. Sure, the progression of technology and ancient science were passions of Carlos. But the nexus of Russian–Cuban covert operations was a topic she was certain he steered clear of—no matter how enticing.

"Dear, you know, since we let you live, that you must be a favoured friend. You also know we have little patience for people who refuse to work with us. So, what special project was your sweet husband hunting down that kept him working late for three straight months?" Although the woman's words might have sounded kind, their cunning intent was clear.

Myriam felt her face pale. Carlos had been dabbling in some new club lately, but she had paid little attention to it. Now this lack of information put her at a disadvantage.

The Russians didn't often give second chances, certainly not a third. She had already used up her first opportunity when the doctor had asked for the password to her laptop.

Discreetly she pressed her mole. The hidden GPS was a long shot, but it was all she had.

Her mind raced. If she explained Carlos' interest in archeology and his newfound club, the lady would think she was either lying or diverting, or both. Regardless, it would diminish Myriam's value and might even drop her into the useless bucket—a fatal move. On the other hand, she could plead ignorance—although she feared that route would certainly lead the Russians to deem her worthless. And being worthless meant they had no reason to keep her alive.

She decided to go out on a limb and use the two pieces of information she had learned during her short span of consciousness. "He was cross referencing data from archeological sites with old military projects to see if there were any correlations."

The woman stared at her. After a long pause, she spoke the one word Myriam dreaded: "Why?"

Myriam had to think fast. "His interest was piqued after he gave a few talks about cybersecurity. An odd pattern of questions started to pop up, all from different people at different conferences. So he wanted to figure out where they were getting their ideas." In truth,

Myriam had no idea what Carlos was doing with his archeological club. But, as this lady had told her he was tracking something and insinuated it was related to the military, her story practically wrote itself.

"Thank you, and sweet dreams." That simple phrase confirmed that her comrade believed her tale was a valuable lead. The lady then turned a dial. A clear liquid began to flow from an equally clear sack that hung above Myriam's shoulder.

Myriam watched the trickle travel down the IV line. The woman's behaviour echoed a typical modus operandi: disappear, validate the newly acquired data and reconvene. It meant Myriam had bought herself time. Unfortunately she would be asleep for most of it.

Moments later, her thoughts vaporized and the lights dimmed.

15

FISHERMAN'S HUT

Carlos' right hand reached around and felt where James had inserted a needle into his arm before everything had gone black. Still dazed, he surveyed the wooden slats on the floor, blinking a few times before raising his head. He saw James sitting a few metres away, watching him. Carlos' eyes locked with James', both seemingly asking questions the other could not or would not dare to answer.

Carlos knew not to challenge his friend—although nothing made sense. How did James manage to find him, and what was he doing on Malta in the first place? The questions rolled around in his mind, but he was determined to keep the conversation light. "Ahh, buddy, I feel awful. I didn't appreciate that jab, but you got me out of that hellhole, so thanks."

Carlos looked around the dingy room, trying to get a sense of where they were. Reels of fishing nets, once coiled with care, lay forgotten along one wall. A mess of twine twitched when a Mediterranean shore crab scurried across its mildewy fibres before dodging behind the baseboard. Carlos noticed dried blood splattered down the cracked front of a cooler that was tipped over not far from where he was lying. A shrivelled fish tail was stuck to the corner alongside a blob of congealed guts. Carlos imagined what this ragged hut looked like from the outside—abandoned. It would surely be covered in peeling paint with streaks of turquoise or strips of yellow that matched its weather-worn wooden panels.

Wind whistled through cracks around the windows. The air felt damp and, by the overlapping calls of seagulls, he presumed they must be in one of about a hundred harbours dotted around the island. Practically every inlet across Malta housed a handful of old fishing huts.

Inside the hut, formerly-white-now-yellow bits of paint curled around the edges of the window frames. Crystallized salt water was smeared across the panes, dried from too many storms to imagine. A thin black scar revealed that the window had recently been cut away and inconspicuously replaced. Glancing towards the door, Carlos noticed a uniform layer of damp dust covering the warped floorboards. It looked like, other than for their recent entrance, the door had not swung open to disturb the hut's filth in a very long time. The perfect hideaway—or the ideal prison—in an abandoned fishing inlet. Invisible in its normalcy.

He paused, feeling more confused than ever, before turning back to James. "What are you doing here, wherever here is?"

"Myriam contacted me. She was worried about you. I guess she remembered I tracked insects and figured you were a more worthy target."

***

James decided Carlos didn't need to know that all he had received from Myriam was a text to call her when it was convenient. Unfortunately for Myriam, a small tremor got in the way of convenience.

Fortunately for James, he knew more of what was going on than anyone suspected. He tried not to think about it and risk giving something away in his expression.

James was sure Carlos had no idea about his true identity. In Carlos' mind, James was simply his buddy from college. Yakov did not exist in Carlos' world. James had landed the perfect scenario in which to extract information without the other party knowing whom they were dealing with—the ultimate trio of disorientation, surprise and deception.

Carlos would likely assume James had met with Myriam. The two of them could have tracked him down using his GPS marker.

Carlos appeared satisfied, moving on to the broader question, "So, where do we go next?"

James intended to keep Carlos isolated. He needed time and space to draw out information, even if it meant ruining their supposed friendship in the process. It was hard to completely ignore the good times the three of them had had together. James reminded himself of an important lesson he had learned early in his training: cause and effect. Carlos and Myriam would not be where they were today without some sort of cause. Their actions were out of his control. He merely added the effect. "I think it's best you hide here for a while. Whoever you ticked off is going to come looking for you once they realize you escaped their little dungeon."

James paused. "I've secured the door, so this hut will look like every other fisherman's hut around this island—locked up and unloved." He then looked intently at his friend. "So, whose craw did you stick, anyways?"

***

Something seemed off to Carlos.

Why wasn't Myriam here? She would have wanted to be the first person he saw after the rescue. And how did James, a techie insect tracker, get inside the bowels of Valletta's underground cisterns and access its impenetrable channels? Carlos reminded himself that on top of his own predicament, Peter was still lost and likely stuck in those same tunnels. Would his own freedom further endanger his friend's safety? Carlos needed to figure out which wildcard he could control, and fast.

"I don't know who took me. It must be related to a friend who disappeared the same morning they grabbed me. We walk together almost every day. Does Myriam know you found me? Where is she?"

"Whoever kidnapped you and your friend can't touch her. She's in a very safe place." James had slowed down his speech, not realizing how ominous his accompanying smile looked to Carlos.

"Can I at least talk to her? Maybe through a clean set of mobile phones that can't be traced back to us." Carlos did not like being separated from his wife. It felt like another round of imprisonment, which was the very reason he and Myriam had had the GPS moles embedded in the first place.

"Until we learn more about your abductors, I don't

think that's a wise move." James reached into his duffle bag and pulled out a rolled-up Therm-a-Rest mattress, some blankets and a laptop. He pulled on a nozzle at one end of the the plastic air mattress. "I've used this to sleep on during field trips up north. It's more comfortable than you might expect."

Carlos pulled himself up onto a rickety-looking chair. He was not keen on staying in this dank fisherman's hut without contacting his wife, but decided he needed to play along placidly. For now. And James was right—he didn't have a clue what his captors were planning or might do next. Refocussing, he tried to fill in the missing pieces to a rapidly expanding puzzle. "So, what day is it?"

"Wednesday. I took the red-eye flight after Myriam got in touch." James looked like he was still jet-lagged.

Two days had passed since his ordeal. "Did you see anyone else where you found me?"

James paused to reach into the bag and pull out a bottle of water along with a ham and cheese wrap. He handed them to Carlos. "I jumped down a manhole. A couple of guys in maintenance overalls had come out and left its cover partly off. They had their backs to me and were heaving something into the back of their truck when I ducked below. After that, any voices from the streets above disappeared pretty quickly."

Carlos cracked the seal on the water bottle's lid and

looked quizzically at James. *What is he holding back?* "Did you see what they were putting in their truck?"

"No." The laptop chimed on. "Let's start with the names of everyone you and your missing friend both knew and their relationship to each of you."

Carlos was more interested in gaining insight than in data points. Whatever connections Peter had stumbled across the night before he disappeared must have scared someone—somebody with far-reaching power who was accustomed to being in control. Unease gnawed at the back of his mind. Just then, a seagull's piercing call rang like twanging steel. He took it as a reminder to trust his instincts.

16

INTRUDER

———————

Sasha tried to think straight as she stared at the open hatch in the floor. Reconsidering, she ran to the front door and flipped over the sign and also closed the blinds. *Okay, calm down. Take a breath.* It had already been a long day and she was tired. Her wrist had started to swell. Once back near the till, she opened her medical kit and took an ibuprofen, hoping it would be strong enough. In one hand she then grabbed her best Wüsthof carbon-steel paring knife, and in the other her solid marble rolling pin. Whatever or whoever was making noise in the cellar would soon stop. Light from the bakery illuminated a small patch on the floor. *Wait. Listen.*

Satisfied, Sasha secured the knife and rolling pin between her apron's waist ties before cautiously stepping down the ladder. She leaned back instinctively to keep her balance against the decline. Once her feet touched the floor, she shuffled back against the wall and scanned the small space around her. The rock walls absorbed all sounds from the street, making the darkness feel like a separate world. With her right hand, Sasha untucked her familiar blade and clutched it in a very unfamiliar and menacing manner, while the rolling pin became an extension of her left arm. Anyone seeing her might have mistaken it for a stubby baseball bat. Thankfully, the pain reliever had kicked in and her wrist ached a little less. Balancing her penlight between her lips, she panned its beam across the room.

A light tap coming from the inner vault caught her attention. All of her notes and documents for the car imports and phone deal were stashed there inside her old shoebox. *Damn.* This was her private space.

Whoever was behind the door had surely found it. She crept closer. Slowly, as if detached from her own actions, she reached across the outer ledge until her fingers found the knob. It had already been unlatched. The sound of rustling papers and glow of light filtered through a narrow gap where the vault door had been left ajar.

She flattened her back against the cool stone. She focussed on the noise.

Someone was approaching from behind the vault's metal door. It swung open to reveal the dark outline of a bulky person slightly taller than Sasha. The shape emerged, backlit by the dim bulb she had replaced only weeks earlier.

Instinct took over. Sasha slammed her right fist into the person's gut, followed by a harsh left swing with the rolling pin. The person let out a high-pitched gasp before falling to the ground. A separate clunk hit the floor nearby.

Sasha shoved the vault door wide open for more light. The sneakers on the intruder looked familiar. A shrill scream escaped her lips and she fell to the floor. Shock radiated through her limbs as if a slow-motion freeze had taken over her body.

Sasha reached over and tugged the person's hoodie. Dark hair tumbled down. She knew that hair. Cristabel stared up at her mother, bewildered. Blood pooled around her waist.

Sasha screamed. "No, no, no, no. Cristabel!" Tears streamed down Sasha's cheeks as she rolled her daughter onto her back and pressed down on the wound. "What are you doing down here?"

Cristabel groaned. Cursing softly, she rolled her head over to look at her mother. "I ... I was worried about you."

Cristabel tried to move her arms. Pain coursed through her body. Her phone had skidded somewhere close. She managed to grab it and slip it into her pants pocket without her mother seeing. Cristabel had taken photos of what she'd found in the vault, and they were now safely tucked away.

Her mom propped Cristabel's back up against the wall. Cristabel thought she might black out.

Then her mother laid the heavy rolling pin on top of the gash and draped Cristabel's arm over it to hold it in place. Cristabel fought to stay lucid.

"You need a doctor," her mother pleaded.

Cristabel knew she was hurt badly. Yet every cell in her body screamed no at the prospect of visiting the hospital. She worried someone might recognize her from when she had tried to find Myriam. Nor did she intend to explain the true circumstances of her injury to anyone. Gerardo had a medical background and could help—later. She had to dissuade her mom.

"Mom, I feel all right. Remember when you stitched up Paws? I just need a couple of stitches to close the cut."

"Okay, I can try. I'll get the first-aid kit." Her mother ran to the ladder.

Cristabel hissed into the darkness. "You've got a few seconds. Get out of here."

A low scraping sound from the far end of the cellar confirmed that Gerardo had closed the old side panel behind him. Cristabel hoped he hadn't left any trace.

***

As Sasha looked for her medical kit upstairs, she remembered stitching their pet cat's paw years ago when Paws had gotten into a tangle with a neighbour's tomcat. She grabbed a handful of clean towels and rushed back to the cellar.

One, two, three rungs. In her hurry, she released her weight an instant too soon before the final step.

For a second nothing caught her foot. The ground evaporated. In an instant it returned, though lower than expected. Sasha plunged to her knees. The towels scattered around her. Her palms skid on the rough ground but hardly enough to buffer her fall. The wrist Emanuel had wrenched twisted awkwardly inwards.

"Mom, what happened? Is that you? Mom!"

Sasha pulled herself up and cupped her wrist. "'I'm alright. I just missed a step. Are you okay?" She wiped grit from her palm. It was already turning purple. Light-headed from the pain, she ran over to where Cristabel slouched against the wall.

At least Cristabel was conscious.

Gently, using her one good hand, Sasha unzipped Cristabel's hoodie and lifted her T-shirt. Blood stuck to the cotton, making Cristabel wince when her mother peeled the cloth away. Sasha gasped when she saw the gash. The bleeding had slowed but the wound looked nasty. She did not want to touch it. An urge to run away washed over her.

Pull yourself together. Sasha took a deep breath and started to swab the area clean. She daubed a big glob of lidocaine around the wound's edges. Since she'd have to stitch with her less-dexterous left hand, she smeared on a little extra and waited for the skin to become numb. In the meantime, she wiped lidocaine around her right wrist and taped it.

Twenty minutes and eight stitches later, Sasha covered the area with a sterile dressing. Rubbing her own shin, which had started to throb, she asked, "What were you doing down here?"

"Lately, I've had weird dreams about this place. I know we hid down here when I was little, but I hardly remember it. You never wanted to talk about it, so I didn't push it." Cristabel spoke quickly.

She's not telling me the whole truth. Still, Sasha realized all the sounds she had been hearing down here were just Cristabel poking around. Although it explained a lot, she wasn't sure how much of the past—or the present—she wanted to reveal. "That was a long time ago," she said. "Rough gangs went on a rampage, trying to control the streets. The L&B got in their way. The cellar saved us.

Eventually the police got a new commissioner and things changed."

Sasha started packing the first-aid supplies back into the kit. "And now you know there's nothing down here but a forgotten cavern. I want to keep it that way."

Sasha paused, her fear that she had killed her daughter now turning to anger. "Your rattling about down here made me panic and now my wrist is busted." Even if it was actually only a bad sprain, she needed to put a stop to Cristabel's nosiness.

17

GERARDO

Gerardo pushed the heavy door closed behind him. Moments later, he heard Cristabel's mother return on the other side. Sweat dripped into his eyes. He dabbed his hood against his forehead. *What the hell had just happened?*

Since Cristabel's mother had returned to the world of the sane and decided to help her daughter, Gerardo could get back to the reason he had been scrunched in this underground hovel in the first place. He slipped the razor blade encrusted with two tiny ball bearings back into its sheath. The concept had worked better than expected when he slid it under the old door to ease its weight and roll it open. Next, he needed to get back to his computer and analyze the photos they had captured. He hoped Cristabel had connectivity. He really needed her images of what was stashed inside that shoebox abandoned in her mother's otherwise empty cellar.

The subterranean maze was rotting and ill maintained. Gerardo retraced his initial steps exactly. Normally he would have liked to spend a little more time exploring alternative access points, but now walking hunched over for even the short distance back to his entry point set off his back. After wiping the grit from his fingertips onto his shirt, he rubbed his sore right shoulder.

In his twenties, he wouldn't have thought twice about creeping around potential informants' basements or crawling into dissidents' hideouts. Nowadays he sat in an ergonomic desk chair most of the time and scheduled an hour of physiotherapy fortnightly. Getting back out in the field was proving a shock to his body. It had become more doughy than he liked to admit.

Sunlight jarred his eyes when he finally reached the low entryway. Similar doors dotted the streets for maintenance workers or building owners to access the underground network. Most of the doors were originals despite rotting bases and weather-worn surfaces. Their squatter shape compared to conventional doors made them expensive to replace.

A dark-haired man leaned against a lamppost. Before Gerardo's eyes could adjust to the sunlight, the man stepped backwards into a recess in the adjacent building and disappeared. Observe or be observed.

Otherwise to Gerardo the block looked empty. Assuming he was alone, he turned to discreetly shut the tunnel's entrance panel and then walked away.

Gerardo unlocked his car and sank into the front seat. His secondary phone vibrated. An overseas call was displayed, yet the caller ID was blocked. It could be one of two people who had this number. He did not want to talk with either of them. But he also remembered the last time he'd ignored one of their calls. Seven months of remedial training back in Camagüey had reminded him of the tenacity of the agramontinos, his people. Respect seniority—without question.

Eleven years had passed and the lesson burned as intensely as ever.

Gerardo tapped the green phone icon. "Yes?"

Six minutes later the call ended. It felt more like sixty. Gerardo looked up at a gallarija that had been freshly painted blue and longed to sit behind its clear windowpanes. The space reminded him of his childhood refuge under the stairs where he would listen in on the adults without them knowing. Gallarijas—Malta's quintessential enclosed balconies—swept across almost every building as if the indoor space were stretching outwards in an attempt to reach the afternoon sun. More and more gallarijas were being restored, leaving apartment blocks looking less like Gothic stone behemoths and more like a parade of pastel checkerboards. Looking at the cool tones and carved columns had a surprisingly grounding effect. Gerardo needed it.

Nothing Gerardo learned from the call could be shared with his team. Yet the urgency of their operation cranked up.

Gerardo's main phone vibrated. The sender's ID read "Cr". Relieved to know Cristabel was well enough to send the pictures, he watched as the JPEG files funnelled into his inbox.

By the time he entered his home office, Ana, Saul and Celia were already online. He divvied up the images. Celia investigated names. Saul studied the deal documents. Ana tried to verify the agreements' validity.

Six cars, with potential for hundreds more, would be imported from a vehicle factory in Japan to sell at a local dealership. The first order had arrived this morning. Ana confirmed the paperwork was registered and filed correctly. Saul confirmed there was nothing of concern besides Cristabel's mother taking a commission on the deal with impressively favourable import duties. The car dealer was clean.

Among themselves, they decided Cristabel's mom probably didn't want to admit she needed more money than her little bakery could earn. Gerardo was annoyed by the distraction. He was also relieved his team came to this conclusion themselves. It made it easier to shift priorities without raising questions. He'd wasted too much time over somebody being either overly embarrassed or excessively proud to admit they had more bills than income, an all-too-familiar story and not his problem.

Gerardo replayed his boss's words in his mind. More than one high-ranking veteran was missing. The police acted oblivious. Sparse details left the group grappling for even remote theories, let alone for a most likely scenario.

Their immediate focus turned to the Tartu Five. "Trail and bug these guys and track down everything that exists on them," Gerardo told the team. "Find out what they are up to. I want to know anything else pertinent in their public image, but more importantly, their private affairs. What are their interests? Where does their money go? Tell me everything from what gets stuck under their fingernails to which church their mothers go to in order to pray. Leave Cristabel to me."

With the team charged with their latest mission,

Gerardo debated what to do about Cristabel. She was a competent field agent but easily distracted by anything to do with her mother. He got it. She thought her mom was all the family she had. In reality, Cristabel had been recruited specifically because of her family connections. He was one of three individuals who knew of the relationship. Even Cristabel had no idea of the arrangement.

And now, under his watch, she was out of commission. He intended to bring her back.

Gerardo had had time to think since her accident. And she would have had time to rest by now. Plus, he loved driving at night. The quiet roads calmed his nerves.

The streetlights flickered and clouds hid the moon's glow. It always surprised Gerardo how dark the residential streets of Birgu could get despite being directly across the water from the bustling hub of Valletta. Tonight he thanked the local women who had fought against bringing fluorescent lights into their timeless alleyways. The darkness gave him a chance to visit Cristabel unnoticed.

Cristabel had texted him earlier. She'd managed to climb out of the cellar and upstairs to her old bedroom. Later in the afternoon, she sent another message. Her mother had told her that she was going to a friend's book reading that night and given Cristabel two tablets of paracetamol with codeine before leaving for the evening.

Gerardo had his own plan for Cristabel.

Thankful for the uneven stonework, he managed to scale the wall of the bakery to Cristabel's second-floor window. She had left the shutter unlatched. Once inside, he drew the curtains and turned to see Cristabel lying on a makeshift bed.

Cristabel must have seen his surprise because she explained how her mother had turned the space into a storeroom when they moved from living here to their current place. Grinning, Cristabel admitted the sacks of flour made a decent enough bed to lie down on. Then she held out her hand, showing him the second pill her mom had asked her to take. It seemed stubbornness ran in her family.

Gerardo wasn't sure what he had expected. "As long as you are comfortable, I will see what I can do." He unrolled his medic bag. The wound looked worse than he'd hoped. Its stitches were a mess—they looked more like a haphazard SOS message of dashes and dots than a row of sutures. A child could have sewn a straighter line. Whitish-yellow goo oozed from one edge.

Gerardo sighed and went to work.

Half an hour later, clean gauze protected a line of equidistant stitches. Cristabel could not sit up, but she could form a coherent sentence. It was encouraging, considering her state when Gerardo first arrived.

"You rest for a few days," he told her. "Don't worry

about your mom. She's simply earning a bit of side cash. It's nothing to get bothered about. We did our due diligence."

Cristabel's shoulders relaxed marginally at this news.

Gerardo continued. "The team is pressing forward. If you think of anything relevant, text me using my safe line." He handed her a small jar. "Rub this salve on your wound twice a day. And relax. You'll be back on duty in no time."

He tried to sound confident, but could not erase the image of the abstract collage of goo and torn tissue inside her.

Cristabel had fallen into a restless slumber by the time Gerardo pulled the shutters closed behind him.

18

SWITCH

Sasha's hands were shaking when she returned to the ground floor. She could hardly believe the incident with Cristabel had just happened. Thankfully she had had the foresight to lock the front entrance and close the blinds. In a partial daze, she circled the shop to shut the store properly. She kept envisioning the pained look on Cristabel's face, her limp body and the blood radiating across her shirt.

Shadows crept into Sasha's thoughts—memories repeating and morphing into different slivers of the same awful deed. The sensation of the knife, resistant at first and then sliding in so easily. Her breath mixing with her daughter's. Sasha couldn't accept that she hadn't recognized her own flesh and blood, even backlit in the cellar doorway. The reel tortured her mind, replaying the horror again and again. Each time, the image of the knife in her hand looked bloodier and the exact sequence of events was more vague. What had happened to her? She felt her sanity slowly slipping through her fingertips and disappearing, like a single grain of sand falling onto a vast beach. Blending. Consumed. Gone.

It shouldn't be like this. She wasn't supposed to raise their daughter alone. Flashes of dark hair, a kind smile and comforting shoulder crept to the edges of her mind. Push away. *No. No regrets.* Decisions had had to be made. Actions taken. *Think of Cristabel.*

The heat of the ovens jolted her back to the present. As Sasha switched them off, a switch clicked in her head. *You can fix this mess. Pull yourself together. Tonight, extract the mobile phones. Let Cristabel rest. Tomorrow, mend your daughter.*

The medical bag lay open where Sasha had tossed it on the counter. The ache in her right wrist clouded her thoughts, but adrenalin pressed her forward. She grabbed a wooden spoon with her good hand and snapped the handle in half to make it shorter. It would function as a splint. Once she got the first few coils of medical tape awkwardly wound around her wrist and the spoon, the tape became easier to unroll. She continued to secure the makeshift brace up her forearm and along her palm using her free hand.

Sasha's confidence shot up. *You can do this.*

Before heading out, she crept up to the top floor. Sasha pressed her ear close to the storeroom door where Cristabel had stretched out on sacks of flour. Only the soft sound of a car passing spoiled the silence.

Time to act. Opening the Bolt rideshare app, Sasha ordered a car. Step one: build a cover. Gain an alibi.

That night an old classmate, Fiona Winslow, happened to be speaking as part of the Malta Book Festival to promote her new release. Sasha planned to go early and get her copy of the book signed. She slid the thin paperback into her bag. The event was being held at the Birzebbuga Sailing Club, conveniently located across the street from the port where the cars had been unloaded. She knew her friend would assume she stayed for the entire event. That gave Sasha sixty minutes of leeway before she needed to return for the end of the reading to solidify her cover story.

They had spoken a few days earlier. Fiona was angling for a heated debate. The excerpt she planned to present touched on controversial themes, begging for good press coverage. Controversy liked attention, and Sasha decided to play into that desire. She planned to congratulate Fiona afterwards on such a provocative discussion, giving the impression she had listened to it all.

Her plan for obtaining the phones was more complicated. She needed to bypass port security to access the shipping container that held the recently imported cars. Her friend from the underground entrepreneurs' group had already given her the access code to open the container and check the vehicles. Because her contact needed to stay at the dealership every afternoon to approve special deals for his salespeople, they had planned that she would view the cars herself after the units cleared customs—tomorrow. He didn't need to know that she would pay a separate visit before their agreed-upon inspection.

He also gave her the container's grid coordinates so she could locate it in the myriad of containers stored at the port. Over fourteen thousand ground slots made up Marsaxlokk's commercial container section.

As people settled into their chairs for the reading and discussion, Sasha slipped out the emergency exit door near the washrooms. She tapped her stopwatch to start a sixty-minute countdown.

Within five minutes, the sound of lapping water eased her nerves—marginally. Soon a steady hum of security lights played alongside, interrupted only by the occasional clanking of chains. She made her way around to the Wied Ix-Xaqqa, a neglected inlet adjacent to the port depot. Few of the locals used it anymore. Fewer still knew that the end of the tunnel opened directly into the port's fenced enclosure. When she was growing up, kids would try to crawl through the eroded tunnel at low tide. Whoever built the fence likely assumed the hole was an abandoned rabbit lair and ignored it.

Sasha had been practicing yoga for years to help with her arthritis. She considered herself pretty agile, even with a damaged wrist. This next step would test her. Taking only a minute, she slipped into a pair of black tights and a dark long-sleeved shirt. The dressier jumpsuit she took off folded into an equally small bundle as her athletic wear and slid flat into her narrow tote. She slung the bag across her back like a tiny backpack tucked between her shoulder blades. Despite grazing her forehead on a chunk of limestone and getting damp knees, she crawled through the narrow channel without any major dramas. Eight minutes later she stood a metre inside the port's perimeter fence.

The moon reflected over the water, drawing a jagged line for her to follow back to the book festival—and safety.

Security cameras panned the fence line but did not monitor an inner loop closest to the containers. Using this to her advantage, she walked parallel to the fence and tried to spot location reference numbers on the containers: 175C, 176C, 177C.... Her target of 357F must be further inside and in a different quadrant. She got down on her hands and knees, not wanting to trigger any sensors, and slunk close to the ground. Pebbles poked her skin through her pants. The company who operated the port never bothered to lay asphalt. Presumably to save costs they simply levelled the rocky earth. She wished they had at least swept the main corridors; her knees were screaming after only a few minutes. Three steps, four steps, two more and she would be behind the first row.

A soft jingle rang through the breeze.

Sasha froze. The wind whipped her hair and howled around metal corners. One more step.

There it was again. The jingle sounded closer.

Damn. Guard dogs.

Sasha lunged to the nearest container and scrambled up the metal rungs that ran up its exterior. Once on top, she flattened her body flush against the top of the crate. The ocean wind roared up here, obliterating all other sounds. She peeked over the side and spotted a guard with his dog sauntering between the first and second rows of containers.

His flashlight swung between the crates and across their sides. Diligent, except he only aimed its beam at eye level and below. The dog practically pranced, apparently happy to be out walking and clearly uninterested in anything other than his evening stroll.

Sasha held still and barely breathed.

The man stopped right below her. "Gus, what's that in the dirt? Dang rabbits. They are always tearing up the ground."

The dog was more interested in sniffing the air than any scuffs in the earth.

The guard's walkie-talkie beeped and crackled. "Hey, Martin, get back here. Halftime is almost over. I told you to wait to do your evening rounds."

The wind blew vertically, swirling upwards off the crate's roof. The man jerked the leash without noticing his dog briefly shake its tail. It pointed its nose up, trying to catch the breeze before the guard yanked his leash a second time and they headed back towards the office. "Gus, I put fifty euros on this match. The Reds better win or the missus will send me to the couch—second time this season."

A thin layer of blown sand covered everything. Sasha edged forward. Her foot slipped and sprayed grit down the side of the container.

The dog paused, now about sixty metres away.

"What's up, Gus?" the guard said.

Sasha's heart thudded in her chest. She dipped her head lower, hoping her eyes didn't reflect in his light.

The flashlight's beam scoured the aisle where the guard and the dog had stopped. The dog and man stood unmoving while it scanned the containers and traced the earth.

The wind howled and seagulls squawked. A paper label that had peeled off a neighbouring container fluttered in the breeze.

"Hey!" Giving up, the man turned around and continued to the office.

Sasha checked her watch. She had eighteen minutes before she needed to rejoin the reception. *Please, no more delays.*

After practically sliding down the side of the container, Sasha regained her footing on firm ground. She sprinted along a narrow passage and then cut right, nearly crashing straight into a massive metal box. Large letters were scrawled across its face in white chalk: 357F.

With shaky fingers, Sasha pressed the code she had been given into the keypad. Seconds passed. A green light blinked.

Tears of relief flooded her eyes. Then her uncle's words replayed in her head: "Make sure you oil the hinges. They rust from the salt water at sea." The last thing she wanted was to alert the guard dog with a metallic screech. She pulled out the tiny can of WD-40 she had brought from the bakery to spray the metal rollers. *Okay, you've got this.*

At first, all Sasha saw was complete darkness. She stepped in tentatively. Needing to keep moving, she pulled out her phone and tapped on its flashlight. Going directly to the third car—in a distinctive sea-glass pearl shade—she opened its unlocked passenger door. Careful not to disturb the protective covers, she knelt down and reached under the seat. At first, her fingers grasped only empty air. Then stretching deeper, they touched a lumpy envelope. *Oh thank you, Uncle Noa!*

With a few minutes to spare, Sasha scrambled through the tunnel and ran back to the sidewalk leading towards the Birzebbuga Sailing Club. Mission nearly accomplished. She walked past an ATCO trailer at the entrance to the port. A TV screen flickered through its window. She smiled at the vague echo of someone frantically yelling, "Pass. Pass the filthy ball!"

Before returning to the intrusive street lights, Sasha stripped off her dirt-stained clothes and stuffed them into her tote. She had never before used its convertible backpack straps until tonight, but now she silently thanked their ingenious designer.

She slipped back into her navy jumpsuit and sprinted one last time for the evening. Sasha could see a stream of light coming from the sailing club's emergency exit door, which had been propped open for airflow. She hurried. In no more than three steps she would be back inside and heading to congratulate her friend.

Just then, a tall form stepped onto the path in front of her. She nearly collided with the man. His features were obscured, backlit by the streetlight.

Then she recognized the glint. Emanuel's beady eyes locked onto hers.

19

FIND AND SEEK

Carlos resisted the urge to spill everything to James. To be honest, he missed the camaraderie of working side by side on covert operations. For the past fifteen years, he had suppressed his craving. In Malta, he worked alone. Not even Myriam knew that the only way they had been able to escape Cuba was because of his current assignment—on a different island but with the same tethers.

Sure, teaching one class a semester kept him grounded in semi-normality, but it was his side pursuits that challenged his spirit. Peter understood this—at least in part. Peter tended to skirt due process, allowing his mind to dive into the world of conspiracy and shadowy connections.

Peter had left Cuba decades earlier. The tight grip of the upper echelons of government grated on him. His true passion lay in patterns, trends meant to stay hidden but inescapable if you knew how to read the data. Peter wrote the programs that read the data. He then layered on flexible perspective capabilities so his programs spit out reports that sliced and diced the information in umpteen different ways.

Carlos had been sent to Malta to monitor potential incendiary activity churning in the Mediterranean. His role as professor gave him not only cover, but also access to advanced technologies without raising suspicion. Early on, close friends advised him to get to know Peter. It turned out the two men had a lot in common. Both questioned why things happened as they did in the world.

Even their offices at the university shared a common wall. This meant they often ran into one another in the department's archive room, usually trying to track down some forgotten journal article from some unsung author. They joked about how many nuggets of knowledge were lost on most of the scientific community even though they were laid bare in these less-than-famous but nonetheless peer-reviewed articles.

Carlos developed a true affection for the man.

One afternoon Carlos sat rummaging through a box of geospatial weather studies on the archive room's old mustard-yellow sofa. Peter slouched over his own box next to him. The couch spanned the entire width of their little archive room. On more than one occasion they had debated whether to move it to free up space. Yet the piece remained, too convenient and decidedly too integral to their operation of finding and seeking.

Peter, visibly fed up by his own search for interarcheological studies on the mysterious cart lines of Malta, shifted his gaze to the periodical Carlos was holding. The cover showed lines radiating in various directions. Three lines pointed towards cartoon personifications of climate phenomena: the Pacific Ocean's El Niño and La Niña and their cousin, the Indian Ocean's Dipole. Peter wondered out loud if there could be a connection between the parallel cart lines on Malta and overarching climate patterns.

Carlos looked up. He had been lost in thought trying to distinguish the weakest points susceptible to human intervention when mapping ocean patterns geospatially. Once he'd cleared his head and thought about Peter's comment, he carried the concept further. "Do you think we could delineate where natural and manmade trends intersect?

"Imagine if we pulled apart those differences created over time—like erosion, decay, abandoned disrepair and such—versus manmade technological advances to mitigate nature's forces. From there, we could see layers of trajectories, each representing a unique breakthrough in human technology in comparison to underlying weather patterns."

First, they needed to figure out if anyone else had already tried.

Since that initial discussion on the couch, their little project had gained momentum. Innocent at first, before it morphed. Troubling inconsistencies began to emerge. Then there was Peter's last call. He had mentioned worrying connections.

Now, Carlos took a bite of his ham and cheese wrap and looked up at James, uncertain of how much to reveal. He wanted to trust his old friend. But Carlos wasn't the naive university student he used to be. Right now, James had become a worrying connection in his own right.

Still, James did not seem to know who had kidnapped Carlos.

The Cuban authorities did not know either, or Carlos would be speaking with them and not his buddy James right now. Myriam, his most direct point of contact, was highly skilled with the technology to find him, yet even she had failed to reach him on her own.

"James, you need to be frank with me. How did you know to drop metres underground and crawl around Valletta's subterranean tunnel system to find me?" Carlos needed to get past this before disclosing anything that might help find Peter.

James paused before looking Carlos in the eye. "Do you remember that night, way back in our university days, when I was angry over a mark on one of my projects? The professor didn't agree with the concept that I later ended up building my entire business model on—which has been successful, I might add."

"Vaguely. I think I was pretty drunk that night." Carlos remembered more than he cared to admit.

"Well, you two convinced me that you had some new-age GPS implants. You caught me at a weak moment, and I believed you both. Anyways, your little game motivated me to keep working on my project—beyond class."

Carlos tried to act casual. But the slap to his ego burned. He liked to think he and Myriam were better than most agents, but slipping this intel to James so many years ago showed poor judgement. "I wasn't sure if I dreamt the conversation or if Myriam actually challenged you to track us." He was careful not to specifically admit they had GPS devices embedded in their bodies. Rather, he wanted to observe James' reaction.

"Yeah, well, you know me. Never say no to a dare. It took me ages, and to be honest, I only found you by using the technology my company later developed. By that point we had graduated and lived in different countries. I didn't mean to be intrusive, so I never said anything." James grinned sheepishly and hung his head.

When he looked up, he appeared genuinely curious. "So, how did you manage to get such advanced tracking technology as students?"

Carlos weighed the risks. His so-called friend had secretly trailed him and his wife. Then this same friend had rescued him from some brute's hidden dungeon that served spoiled food. Carlos believed in alliances. You can do more together than alone. Peter had proved that theory. Nevertheless, Carlos did not trust James.

"We signed on for some clinical trial that needed young, healthy adults and paid us five hundred dollars each. We needed the money, so we answered a few questions and let them test a new device touted to be the next generation of ultimate physical health monitoring. It reminded us of *Star Trek*. And we thought it would be cool. That was long before anyone worried about privacy and protecting personal information. Now, would you show me where Myriam is located? I'll feel better knowing where she is."

James turned his laptop to face Carlos and adjusted the screen to reduce the glint from the window. "It's surprising that any glare can make it through all that salt on the glass," he said.

Carlos stared at the blinking red dot on the screen. The map was zoomed out too far to read street names, but he could see that the dot marked the Xewkija Industrial Estate. He had been there once. It was situated near Victoria, over on the island of Gozo. He was pretty sure the industrial area was near the island's main hospital. That knowledge alone gave him hope.

Carlos let it slide, but noticed James remained silent on whether the conditions where he was keeping Myriam were any nicer than where he had brought Carlos.

He crafted his next words carefully, sharing only those details James probably already knew. "Peter and I both worked in the university's IT department. Peter retired from teaching years back but kept an office to continue pursuing certain pet projects. I guess you could say our curiosity brought us together. We were both captivated by ancient archeology and how people managed to reason such complicated concepts with such basic instruments. I would be lost without my computer and can't imagine calculating astrology patterns or forecasting weather from stones and conjecture."

James nodded. "Sure, none of us could do much without modern technology. But that doesn't get us kidnapped. What did you guys get into?"

"We started looking into the latest discoveries on

Malta. My distrustful side couldn't believe that three brand new sites could suddenly appear. It's not like Guatemala, where the jungle devours forty-metre-high Maya structures or completely grows over vast water reservoirs in a matter of decades. Malta is a rock island. Period. Trees don't grow here. Grass forges on in its own ridiculous struggle. The occasional vineyard you see is propped up by a forced irrigation system rigged to a desalination plant." Carlos was used to lecturing and he knew an audience needed a simple premise to compare to a challenging concept.

He carried on, but kept to himself the knowledge that Peter loved to disprove theories, especially by folks trying to gain influence or power where it wasn't due. "Peter, being an IT-minded person like me, loved to play around with data. Sorting. Comparing. Mining for more intricate details and unthought-of models." Carlos stopped there. He did not want James to know that in their quest, Peter had actually devised a way to feed archeological data points into a program that basically cross-referenced any other dataset. Nor the fact that finding the right points of reference had become their greatest challenge in recent months. They had spent weeks, months, gathering information and updating files.

Carlos shivered. Just a week before Peter disappeared, they had actually stumbled across a correlation. Shocks of disbelief prickled his arms just thinking about what they had detected.

"It was early days. We were searching for a theory—even if a barely working one."

James leaned in, encouraging Carlos to open up more. "So you think you found a link between the Malta ruts and another unrelated design?"

Carlos felt a surge of exhilaration roll across his chest at hearing the idea verbalized by someone else. It was as if the possibility became real once spoken aloud.

And James had hit the nail exactly on what he and Peter had uncovered—but without doing any of the background work. It wasn't a normal conclusion to jump to, from the vague description Carlos had just disclosed. Not unless James knew things he was not sharing with Carlos. Things that gave credence to the theory.

The conversation carried Carlos back to the afternoon when he and Peter had put the pieces together. He vividly recalled how each set of the recently detected parallel grooves pointed exactly to the site of a fallen civilization. The Giza Pyramids in Egypt. The Maya city of Tikal. Persia's royal ruins of Persepolis. Either the history of humanity was linked beyond anything science had ever been able to prove or someone had spent a lot of time and energy in the hopes of making every person around the world question what they believed.

Regardless, the sheer magnitude of James' words hung in the air.

Neither man spoke. Although not admitting it out loud, they both understood that the money required to create such a mirage would be immense. The power required to pull it off was even greater.

20

NECESSARY MEANS

Nausea ruptured from her stomach. Her hands tingled. Turning onto her side, Myriam curled her legs up towards her waist. She tried to wipe her mouth, but her hand hit something hard and plastic before it reached her lips. She opened her eyes a crack and saw the low ridges of something resting on her cheeks.

The fog in her head edged away. Fear took over, the type that starts as a mild concern and slowly blooms into outright terror. Bigger. Stronger. Out of control.

Myriam breathed normally; however, the oxygen mask

felt abnormal. Its chemical scent disguised the clean air it was meant to circulate. Manufacturers never thought of this part. They never stuck the unnatural bulb to their own faces while they tried to sleep or felt its suction tug on their cheeks after it had fused with their own drool. Drugging her into unconsciousness was one thing, but controlling what she inhaled scared her more.

Myriam had previously worked with Russian intelligence. When the United States closed the door on Cuba, Russia stepped in. Aiding. Devising experiment upon experiment. She knew their methods, remembered cringing from the other side as she observed pain and suffering. Payback and the so-called necessary means that operation teams loved to dish out. Tactics were their game.

Her role was that of an associate, basically an observer on ally operatives. She monitored behavioural changes and pain thresholds and then reported back to the Cuban authorities.

Myriam recognized the electrical wires outside the window. So her Russian captors hadn't moved her. For now, she lay alone in her single cell. Cold and isolated. Rubber ribbing ran around the door, sealing her inside. Even the air vent appeared ominous, blowing whatever they decided to spray into her space.

The Russians were known for their love of thallium, a key ingredient in unregulated rat poisoning. Since Soviet times, *rat* usually referred to something other than the four-legged rodent. Vomiting, headaches and tingly limbs were telltale signs a rat had been stung.

A flash of movement through the door's window caught her eye. Dark hair across a white collar slipped out of view. Seconds later, a whirring noise kicked in.

Myriam's eye itched, but her arms had become too heavy to lift. All she could do was imagine what toxins were spewing into the mask stuck on her face. She strained as hard as she could to lift her hands. Her skin stung where she had earlier tried to tear off the wrist straps they had initially used. As she lost energy, her thoughts clouded. She was hardly aware of it when her eyelids drooped. Before everything disappeared completely, she caught a blur of platinum hair and blob of red lipstick staring at her through the window.

***

Nadya turned away. She could not bare to watch her patient lose consciousness yet again. Even though she had dedicated her life to her country, the medical oath she had also sworn—to refrain from causing her patients any harm or injustice—haunted her subconscious. This mission in particular required her to ignore what she had studied for years to uphold. Pushing aside petty grievances, she nodded to the dark-haired nurse to switch off the vapours. Something held her back from pressing Myriam for more. Thankfully, they were making progress as a result of the information she and her team had garnered elsewhere.

Nadya's team included an eclectic group of specialists she had recruited herself. Since her supervisor liked to shave her budget—preferring to siphon funds to his long-time navy buddies' operations—her team had learned to work lean. She had become accustomed to the lack of recognition and underhanded maneuvers that limited her career progression.

It didn't matter. Certain eyes knew exactly what was happening and who accomplished it. In time she would rise. For now she pressed forward with surprising insight from her small group of four. Her two field agents, a seasoned nurse—who also covered administration for the team—and her own hands-on involvement made for a strong team. A smile crossed her lips as she thought about the tracks being laid, so blatantly obvious yet completely unnoticed. Those who could not see would become irrelevant.

Nadya's team brought together concepts of archeology and psychology to construct a possibility no one else in the intelligence agency had considered. In a world of extremism and teetering world superpowers, such a level of conniving made Nadya cringe. The potential of where it could lead helped her forget her neglected Hippocratic oath and focus on the task at hand.

Four pieces of information stood out.

First, new archeological sites were being discovered on the archipelago of Malta at an unprecedented rate. Second, for reasons unknown, a team of technologists had formed to study the ancient markings. Third, Myriam's husband was one of its members, and he, along with another member, had disappeared—both on the same day. And finally, any record of the ad hoc group's existence had also vanished. The university claimed ignorance and social media posts about the club had been wiped clean.

If it hadn't been for Myriam's bizarre reference to her husband's archeological group, Nadya would never have latched on to this strange sequence of events. Although her boss did not say so directly, she knew he figured she was wasting her time. Her team, on the other hand, knew not to assume anything. Experience had shown them never to discount events that lacked logic. A reason always existed, no matter how obscure it was or how deep you had to dig to find it.

Over the past two years, two new sites had been discovered on Malta plus one on Gozo, Malta's smaller neighbouring island. This was a significant number, considering how barren the islands stood, with virtually no trees or natural features to disguise ancient relics. All three contained parallel grooves etched into the limestone, similar to a handful of older sites already known to archeologists. On the surface, they looked like the ruts from carts.

Except that all of these so-called cart ruts were plagued by inconsistencies, not only the newly discovered sites but others found years ago all across Malta. Some were narrow and others wide. Certain grooves ran deep, while several merely grazed the surface. One set would require an axle over two metres above the ground to roll along its tracks. In a few locations the tracks headed straight off cliff faces, while elsewhere they extended from the shore into the ocean for great distances. Because of these discrepancies, the simplistic-looking ruts had mystified scientists for decades.

The archeological group Myriam had spoken of took a fair bit of hunting to track down. Its members came together informally. The university did not recognize the association. In fact, Nadya doubted anyone of authority even knew it existed.

The group's schedule also appeared fluid. Only a handful of meetings had actually taken place, with varying numbers of days or even weeks in between. Presumably they only met when everyone was free, and likely in random locations like members' homes or around a table at a cafe or jazz club. One investigator in Nadya's team said he imagined it resembled his mother's knitting group, with members negotiating dates around grandkids' visits and medical appointments.

Overall, their initial intel seemed about as promising as the knitting group's doilies were contentious. Still, she could not believe the archeology bunch were entirely benign. The fact that two of the five members were missing *was* significant. Why this group? Why these two members? Next steps would focus on the remaining three members. Who were they and where were they now?

Alternative sources of information were needed. Since they'd had no luck decrypting Myriam's laptop, a glimmer of hope remained with Peter. Little had been known about him until they hacked into Carlos' phone records. Nadya's most computer-savvy technician knew his way around standard firewalls and blockers.

As usual, the phone provider stored the most recent twenty minutes of each SIM card's activity in an isolated and encrypted database. Companies got around privacy laws with the justification that they required certain records to ensure billing integrity, even though they were not technically allowed to record private calls. Typically, only internal audit departments had access to these records and only referenced them on a test basis to cross-reference with billing records. In any case, that was the procedure established by most service providers because it had received the courts' blessing.

Billing records showed numbers and durations, but the recordings stored on secured data drives contained more elaborate evidence. While the public remained oblivious of this, many senior officials were aware. Unofficially, some government operatives possessed various means to tap into these files, all under the guise of national security. Usually they were valid probes to prevent illegal transactions and eavesdrop on terrorist communications. Nadya presumed it went further, into a deep chasm where government oversight and military protectiveness blurred. However, that was not her current concern.

Nadya's team accessed every facet within reach. Twenty-two minutes of conversation on Carlos' mobile phone still existed, floating in the virtual world, waiting to be snagged. Hackers called this task fishing. This particular fishing expedition came back empty handed. Besides a number of messages for Peter and four calls to students with borderline grades, it had yielded nothing useful. No calls had been made since the morning he disappeared.

No one had filed a missing person report for Peter. He was single and worked alone. His tenure kept him associated with the university, but he maintained that relationship at a distance. Nadya's team confirmed he had not taught any classes for the past three years. Nor did he mentor or involve himself in anything related to students or staff. Instead, he immersed himself in research.

He kept a small office close to the department's archives. Although most journals were digitized, some of the more obscure and less popular publications sat on shelves or lay stacked inside boxes. Time to get to work and find out what Peter was so interested in.

21

SPIRAL

———

Instinctively Sasha slipped her injured wrist behind the protection of her other forearm. Before she could step backwards out of Emanuel's reach, he moved closer. His stale breath jabbed her eyes. She jerked away.

Emanuel grabbed her shoulder. "Not so quick."

"I've got your damn samples here. Let me get them out of my bag." At this point, Sasha was more relieved that she had actually been successful at the port than that she was making a sale to this thug.

"Don't move. I don't trust you. Turn around. I'll get

them out myself." Emanuel looked like he was more used to dealing with twitchy crooks who would be happy to bump him off. Sasha presumed many of them preferred to shoot first and negotiate later, which was probably why he liked to catch them—and now her—off guard.

Sasha shrugged her bag off and held it open for him, wanting to get this over with and get back inside.

Emanuel impatiently combed through the top layer in her bag. "You've only got dirty clothes in here!"

"Dig down. The envelope's at the bottom." Sasha couldn't believe such an inept guy was the right hand to one of the most powerful businessmen in the country.

Emanuel bored deeper, looking disgusted by this scavenger hunt. Then he must have felt the bubble-wrap envelope containing his smartphones because his expression lightened. He pulled the package out.

"Just wait," Sasha grabbed the lumpy package. "I need to get some paperwork." She tore the envelope open. Inside, an extra copy of the critical sales agreement for the vehicles had been carefully stamped and sealed to pass along to her friend, Raymond. It was the only way to finalize the deal using her uncle's back channels. Sasha had told Raymond that in order to fast-track the new agreement, her uncle had bypassed the plant's normally cumbersome internal mail system and couriered the final documents directly to her. Thankfully, he hadn't questioned her story.

***

Emanuel grabbed the envelope back and disappeared into the manicured hedge. Once hidden in the shadows he slumped against a cement wall and closed his eyes. Eighteen years ago he had arrived on this horrible island. At the time, it had looked like paradise compared to the megacity he came from.

Corrupt officials, inept councillors and a poorly educated populace had made life difficult at home. Electricity cut out more frequently than it ran. Most months his landlord "forgot" to schedule fumigators, preferring to save the money and let tenants deal with the rodents and insects themselves. Water from the faucets—when it ran at all—carried a yellowy tinge. Empty water bottles littered the streets and jammed the drains. After having his first child and struggling to find a reliable job, Emanuel felt desperate.

The idea of his son going through the same undignified life depressed him. Naively, Emanuel believed a man dressed in a smart suit who quoted the bible and promised work for decent pay. Of course, he would have to travel abroad. To save his family, he needed to leave his family. Emanuel filled out the paperwork and handed over his passport, along with most of his life's savings.

He arrived in Malta two months later, keen to earn a

fair wage. His plan to send money home to his family so they could move into a home with its own water tank and backup generator fuelled his drive. He imagined lights for his son to study by long into the evening. He imagined a future better than his past. Back then he still had hope.

Then he learned about the spiral. His boss held his passport for one reason after another. Excuses became a regular occurrence. More immigration fees. Higher employment taxes. One more job commitment. His wages turned out to be paltry compared to what he had been promised. However, because he had no paperwork to support his case, no one listened. No one cared. Last month, he sent thirty euros home to his wife.

He knew if this deal didn't come through, his boss would hold his passport for another five years. That was not going to happen again.

It had been nearly twenty years since Emanuel left to give them a better life. Both his son and wife now had to work at multiple jobs just to pay for their rent and food. Nine years ago his son had had to leave school to get a job. He was only ten years old and he sold shampoo packets to drivers on a busy intersection near their home.

With this latest black-market phone deal, Emanuel convinced his boss to share fifteen percent of the profits. Emanuel would be responsible for supplying the product. His boss had connections to get it out onto the street. Emanuel saw a path forward. In order to have his passport released, he had to reimburse five hundred euros of fictitious expenses to clear his supposed debt. But this understanding was only the latest in a series of revolving-door promises.

***

Sasha stood outside the door for a few seconds after Emanuel disappeared into the brush. More than anything, she wanted to run inside to the bright lights and protective crowd. But she didn't trust herself to look natural. Her friend would see her fear, feel the tremor in her grip.

Breathe. She blinked rapidly and let the ocean breeze drift across her face for a moment. Her eyes cooled and she began to feel normal again. She popped a lozenge into her mouth, dissolving the catch that had latched firmly inside her throat. Humming softly, she felt her voice return.

Once she was inside, Sasha's shoulders relaxed. Checking herself in the bathroom mirror, she casually flicked strands of hair forward to cover the scrape on her forehead. From there, the bathroom hallway led her straight into the reception area, where she nearly bumped into Fiona.

"You did wonderful!" Sasha gushed. "The discussion was more thrilling than I expected."

Her friend looked vibrant, still hyped from her talk.

"Do you think? Was I alright? It all feels like a blur. I hardly remember what I said. Knowing you were sitting in the audience gave me confidence. I imagined I was talking directly to you, even though everything looked black beyond the second row because of the lights. Thank you so much for coming, Sasha." Fiona grabbed Sasha's right hand and squeezed it affectionately.

Sasha winced. Fiona looked puzzled. "I know you love to bake, but did you have to bring your wooden spoon with you?"

Trying to laugh it off, Sasha said the first story that came to mind. "Oh, you know me! I tripped at the shop and didn't have time to go to the hospital for a proper brace. I wouldn't miss your talk for the world, and this old spoon works surprisingly well."

"Listen, you work too hard. And I need a break after this book launch. Close your store next month and let's take off. A friend of mine has a B&B on the Amalfi Coast and she said I can stay there any time. Think of it, we can have a proper Napoli pizza and visit Pompei, like we always talked about!"

Sasha couldn't leave now. Not with Cristabel recovering and this phone scheme just about to take off. She scrambled to find an excuse. "I'd love to do that, but maybe next year. Cristabel gets so busy with university. I need to be here to be sure she eats at least one decent meal a day. And the new bakeries are so competitive, my customers might leave for good if I shutter the doors for long."

"Are you sure you're not just scared of leaving your comfortable routine?"

"No, really, we'll go next year." In truth, Sasha almost wished she could dive back into her dull treadmill of a life. But something inside tugged her forward. Hope. Hope for more financial security. Hope that someday she could take that trip abroad and say goodbye to everyday stresses. The thought energized her. She would make it happen. Besides, she just might need to disappear if Emanuel didn't stop his harassment when she wanted out.

Then there was her other dream of running away with a certain someone, a vision she would never lose sight of. It played out in an idyllic world and ran deep in her core. Sasha gave her girlfriend a more confident smile, easing the mood.

Sasha then opened the Bolt App on her phone and ordered a ride to take her home. She hugged her friend with her left arm. "I enjoyed your talk so much!"

Sasha's little lies spiralled outwards.

When her car pulled away from the Birzebbuga Sailing Club, flashing red and blue lights caught her attention. "What's going on over there?" she asked the driver.

"Over by the port? Who knows? Probably someone smoking weed by the beach got too close to the cameras."

The driver turned left and headed back towards the Three Cities.

22

CONE OF SILENCE

───────────

It looked like something hovering two hundred metres under the ocean. A solid mass pulsed, its tentacle-like arms projecting upwards, reaching to grasp invisible particles that hung in the night air. The beat pumped. Plumes of smoke streamed out from machines and glided around the centre of the dance floor. Most of the clubbers came here for a release—a Thursday-night therapy session to escape the stress of classes. The DJ worked his dials, shifting from deep house electronica to the occasional Daft Punk or Depeche Mode classic.

Gerardo sat with his team in one of the second-floor alcoves of The Current nightclub. Few noticed their tight group within the tangled crowd of students.

At the moment, Celia was speaking. Her words evaporated half a metre from where they were spoken, drifting into a tide of white noise and throbbing bass.

Saul motioned for the four to lean closer into a cone of silence where the mayhem surrounding them fell away. Gerardo liked it like this. Compact. Innocuous.

The team had dug up quite a bit of information on the mysterious men of Tartu. Personas had begun to take shape. To keep discussions untraceable the Tartu Five were given code names: Man A, B, C, D and E. The team framed the assignment like a student would compose a drama production, building a grid-like repository of potential characters.

Ana started the update. "Man A was born in Kuressaare, Estonia. It's the largest town on the island of Saaremaa, where most residents farm for a living. The agricultural island became a military restricted zone in 1946, with plenty of Russian overlords keeping order until the people of Estonia regained independence in 1991. The islanders had a reputation in the union for being a nationalistic, strong-willed bunch and, although not generally admitted publicly, they were excessively repressed during Soviet times."

Ana took a quick sip of her drink of choice, tonic water

with lemon and mint. "Man A's parents were both killed when the island was under military restriction. Little explanation was recorded, although it was rumoured they were part of an underground resistance. Apparently some local heroes used to hide inside haystacks and travel through hand-dug tunnels to take their communist regents by surprise."

"I think those two should find their own haystack." Celia nodded semi-discreetly towards a pair grinding their hips a short distance away. Her lip curled when the man's hands began to prowl below his partner's beltline. "Eww. I don't want to see that!"

"Focus team, we want to get out of here before last call." These distractions were exactly the reason Gerardo picked this venue to meet. No one would notice his boring team because nobody came here for deep discussions.

Tucking a stray piece of hair behind her ear, Ana continued. "After graduating with a bachelor's in business administration, Man A worked his way up to the executive level of one of the fastest growing banks in Estonia. His wife stays at their house in Kuressaare, where he usually returns on weekends. During the week he lives in a penthouse in Kadriog, Tallinn's most exclusive neighbourhood. He recently bought a vacation property in Malta, in the town of Sliema, north of

Valletta. He comes and goes intermittently, usually taking a run on his yacht. Clearly, Man A has money."

"Must be nice." Saul glanced around the group, seemingly avoiding eye contact with Gerardo.

"Hey, I remember when they didn't give any raises for over five years. We're lucky we get our rent supplemented. Ana, good job. Please carry on." Gerardo had heard Saul's grievances many times. He wasn't about to get distracted and bring them up with the entire group. Besides, head office made all the salary-related decisions.

Ana hesitated and then regained her train of thought. "Okay. Man B drifted around Latvia for much of his life. His parents were devout Christians. They donated the majority of their estate to the Sigulda Evangelic Lutheran Church, minus taxes and a small payout to their only living son. Not long after, their beloved son—our Man B—spent a few years at the Central Prison in Riga for defrauding that same church. He's stayed under the radar since getting released. An officer meets him quarterly and submits a report. However, it seems more like a formality than any in-depth scrutiny. The last four years' reports have read verbatim for every filing.

"When he was thirty-eight Man B attended Tartu University; presumably an attempt to start over. Recent photos captured him driving an Aston Martin on the streets of Riga and, a month later, handing the keys for his Audi A8 to a concierge on Saint Elmo Place here in Valletta."

Celia made the connection first. "So, we have two men with money—two potential leaders."

Ana carried on. "Man C came from Mestia, a mountain village in Georgia, where he trained as a bricklayer to maintain the famed Svaneti towers.

"Man D grew up in an Armenian border town with little notoriety. Semi-trucks going to and from Iran kept most family-run businesses in his village alive, including the guesthouse that Man D's folks ran. They refilled soda bottles with homemade wine and sold it to the drivers. It was a common trick that allowed the drivers to take their favourite drink across the Iranian border, where it was illegal. After school, Man D was in charge of the family's wine cart. He must have liked dealing with the drivers because he moved into the auto business when he grew up. He now sells fleet vehicles around the Mediterranean, including in Malta.

"Man E was born in Ulaanbaatar, in Mongolia, where he took over his family's business. He's a big-time property developer there and has more recently expanded into Malta and Gozo. One of his projects is that large resort along the north coast. Its foundation was laid over a year ago, but now it sits dormant without any walls."

Saul spoke up, perhaps trying to recover after Gerardo

shot down his last comment. "So, there isn't much overlap between the five men. They don't seem to have any common interests or links from childhood. What are we missing?"

A couple who were more focussed on their roaming hands staggered into the team's space. Gerardo was fed up. "Get yourselves another room!"

The two side-eyed Gerardo and his circle of friends, laughing disinterestedly. "Chill, buddy." The girl dragged her partner back out into the hallway.

In Gerardo's attempt to shoo the pair away, his elbow bumped something through the curtain that ran behind the bench he was sitting on. Curtains had been strung together to make the upper floor appear to be a series of private rooms, but they were not solid enclaves.

Whoever Gerardo had brushed against was no longer standing so close. Considering the music drowned out voices more than half a metre away and how Gerardo's team had been huddling around the table, he was confident no one could hear or lipread anything they said. His team continued their discussion, uninterrupted by the distraction.

For reasons yet unknown, all five men attended the University of Tartu between 2011 and 2015. Besides being born in ex-Soviet nations and owning property on Malta, there were no obvious connections between them. However, as the group shared their various findings,

160

similarities started to emerge. Hints of nationalistic fervour, free-spirited sentiment and money-driven ambition motivated each man. Perhaps it was those same beliefs that brought them together.

Just then, a ripple appeared in the drapes. Gerardo saw polished black leather shoes walk away briskly. He pulled back the curtain, cringing when his fingers touched something wet. He noticed the corner of a long leather coat disappear into a crush of people moving in sync with the music. *Weirdos. There's always someone hanging around too close and too drunk to keep their drink in their glass*, he thought.

Their next angle would centre around private-interest groups, chatrooms, memberships and anything else that might define these men's personal bents. Each team member took on a task. The group separated and filtered outside into the heart of Paceville, a popular nightclub district.

Music from other clubs bled into the street. Food trucks lined the sidewalks, feeding cravings with falafel, souvlaki wraps and pizza sold by the slice. A police car edged through the throng of pedestrians staggering about. Violence was rare—most people came simply to unwind and chill with friends.

Suddenly, someone grabbed Gerardo's arm, twisting it behind him, and shoved something into his back. Gerardo was pushed through the crowd and onto Triq

Sqaq Lourdes. At this time of night, few others retreated to this alley behind the Bay Street Shopping Complex.

Normally Gerardo preferred quiet streets. Not tonight.

23

ARCHIVES

———

Dim bands of light radiated across the second-floor hallway. The emergency exit lights glowed from the stairwell doorways on either end. A brighter light seeped under the edges of a blind covering the window of one office door, likely a professor trying to get through a stack of papers before tomorrow's class.

The few students still studying in the common area on the main floor had been too caught up in their laptop screens to notice the two men passing by. Dmitri guessed most students would more likely be out at the club than here on a Thursday night. Regardless, both he and his partner, Dominik, wore rubber-soled loafers and dark colours to keep quiet and blend in. It worked—they had made it upstairs unnoticed.

Nadya had not been clear on where exactly the archive room was located. Such duties fell to her team. Before coming to the University of Malta's Department of Information Technology, Dmitri had downloaded the building's layout from an orientation package available online for new students. Assuming the outdated materials stored in the archives were of little interest to most students, he and Dominik figured the room would be vacant for the evening.

They hoped to locate what Peter had been researching before he vanished. Had he tapped into something controversial? This was a department archive, not part of the university's library, so they hoped that it used a more casual sign-out system.

Dominik switched on his headlamp and focussed it on the door handle. He crouched down to work on the lock. Dmitri knelt at his back, keeping his eyes peeled for any movement.

"Okay, we're in."

Just then, the click of a door handle caused them both to freeze. The blind on the window of the sole room with its light on swayed.

"Move."

In one smooth motion, Dominik swung open the door and whipped into the archive room, while Dmitri swivelled from his crouched position outside to a similar crouched position inside, albeit facing the opposite direction. They squatted directly adjacent to one another and softly shut the door.

Dmitri whispered, "Dom, pull that blind shut so we can stand up. My knees are killing me."

Dominik's shoulder almost knocked Dmitri off balance when he reached up to pull the blind's string.

Seconds later, they heard a hinge creak, then a door being shut. Footsteps approached the archive room, slowing outside the door.

The two men held their position, huddled low with headlamps switched off.

Finally a set of keys jangled. A man's voice muttered something unintelligible and the footsteps resumed down the corridor.

Dmitri and Dominik relaxed slightly, stood up and started their search. Sure enough, a logbook sat on a table by the entrance. On the first two pages, Peter's and Carlos' were the only names. Apparently, not even other professors found this room of interest. Scanning the list of journals and books gave no obvious leads. The men decided to pull the publications themselves to see what they contained.

An hour later, a pattern started to emerge.

One article about the renowned Kensington Runestone explained how the nineteenth-century engraving had been mistakenly passed off as a fourteenth-century Viking inscription. Before it was debunked as a hoax, historians had recast the entire theory of Norse migration. Another paper detailed the once-esteemed but now-disgraced archeologist James Mellaart, who fabricated a long line of finds discovered as fakes after his death. A number of the texts that Carlos and Peter had consulted dove into carbon-dating inscriptions and methods to validate stone carvings. The men lost their trail when they came to the last document signed out by Peter. It was missing.

While the room screamed order, with its neatly stacked shelves and reading lamps aimed at a precise forty-five-degree angle, the corner of a well-thumbed magazine protruding from under a couch cushion whispered of disorder. In addition to its placement, its title did not match anything noted in the sign-out registry.

Had someone brought this into the library for light reading? If so, why would they have left it here? The magazine included an in-depth write-up about how scientists could cross-reference one archeological dataset with multiple discoveries to better understand commonalities and, perhaps more importantly, to flag inconsistencies. It seemed the study of interrelationships across cultures was gaining interest among a niche group of specialists. Several lines in the magazine had been underlined in pen. Just as intriguing, on the last page someone had circled the name of the person who had funded a research study referenced in the article: Juris Stokmane. Neither Dmitri nor Dominik recognized the name.

Unsure as to what it all meant, Dmitri took photos of everything they uncovered. They left everything exactly as they had found it. It was five in the morning by the time they slipped through the campus gates.

***

Nadya looked through the images her team had taken. Considering the two missing professors had dedicated their entire careers to information technology, she knew her light inspection wouldn't grasp the full extent of what they had learned. Regardless, the crossover between archeology and technology fascinated her medically inclined mind. She needed to get inside the heads of Peter and Carlos. What had they discovered that made someone want them out of the picture?

Nadya called an old colleague. "Yakov, tell me, what have you gathered so far?"

Five minutes later, she pulled her team together.

"You've got to go back to the IT department tonight. I know it's almost the weekend, but we can't slow down now. Dmitri, you focus on Peter's office. Find out whatever you can on the programs he was running. Check for any that cross-referenced data from the latest discoveries on Malta, and any findings he might have debunked. Dominik, cover Carlos' space. Look for handwritten notes, computer files, phone records—anything that might help explain what they were thinking or might have suspected. We have intel that they didn't trust what was being reported. Go home, get some sleep and be ready for another full night."

After the room cleared out, Nadya closed her eyes and tilted her chair back. She was still surprised her team had been allocated any resources at all to find out about a potential scientific hoax. Despite her supervisor's apparent disinterest, someone in her government must have been worried about the far-fetched theory. Motivations affected outcomes, and she wanted to get in front of whatever grandstand show had the potential to derail her superiors' positions. Time to broaden her scope.

Recent discoveries had also been made on her home country's soil. A dig northeast of Moscow had recently unearthed the royal tombs of two Pereslavl princes. While the find excited many who believed in the pathway to sainthood, others did not feel so enlightened. Archaic scrolls buried alongside the bodies told an alternative version of local doctrine.

Protests had erupted proclaiming that the site should never be disturbed. Certain senior bishops denounced the activity and went so far as to try to stop state funding of the project. Others pressed forward, wanting to delve deeper in the pursuit of true understanding. The situation stirred up anger to the very core of Russia's Orthodox Church. Nadya feared the fallout if the church ever turned its back on the president.

The more she dug, the greater number of redacted documents popped up. Access to materials tightened. When her screen flickered momentarily, prickles ran along Nadya's spine. She had heard of this before and it usually meant one thing. She had touched something that someone had deemed untouchable. In the upper echelons of Russian security, a tight-knit group of specialists monitored activity around highly sensitive files. They flagged anyone who accessed those files. Merely searching for certain topics got people into trouble. Mortal trouble.

Pressure crept along her temples. Not only would her derelict boss be closely monitoring her moves, but the upper reaches of the intelligence regime would also be watching. She took a drink of cool water. She had to find her own proof—a trail of whatever nefarious activities were taking place.

The possibility that the church was involved tore at her nerves. The memory of burning incense and creepy baritone chords from the last time she stepped inside a place of worship haunted her. That had been over forty years ago. Since she had moved to Malta, Nadya had avoided even walking along the sidewalk in front of a cathedral. Recent talk of building a Russian Orthodox church made her cringe. However, the thought of her own country coming after her made her recoil even further.

24

VISITOR

Carlos fell asleep after talking with James. When he woke, he lay alone inside the fisherman's hut. The moon must have been fairly full because its reflection allowed him to see reasonably clearly. Although, given the disarray around him, he felt little desire to explore his new lodgings. Besides, every part of his body ached. The mere thought of moving made him queasy.

Thankfully, the contents from the duffle bag lay within reach. Six water bottles and a Gatorade stood alongside a plastic bag filled with a pair of red apples and two cold qassatat pastries. Carlos knew he needed nutrients and liquids, so he forced down half the Gatorade and most of an apple. Semi-comforted that James was watching over Myriam, he let his thoughts return to Peter.

By now, whoever had abducted Carlos must know he had escaped. If they hadn't already done so, they would likely move Peter, fearing a second rescue attempt. Carlos cursed himself for wasting time talking to James about his archeological musings. That time should have been spent convincing James to return and try to find his friend. Their opportunity was sprinting past.

Think, what would Peter do? For one, if he thought he had cracked a potential conspiracy, Peter would have certainly made copies of his evidence. It was in his nature. Multiple backups. Peter hid data all over the place.

One time Carlos had picked up a spoon from a cup crammed full of spare utensils in Peter's office. Peter often worked late and kept a miscellany of dishes in his office so he could eat without leaving his desk. It was late. Carlos needed a snack. Except Peter grabbed the spoon right out of Carlos' hand before he could dip it into his plastic cup of vanilla yogurt. Unbeknownst to Carlos, that particular spoon had a SIM card inside its handle.

Another time, Peter ran into Carlos' office asking if Carlos had borrowed his umbrella. In fact, Carlos had used it that morning when he ran over to see the dean.

The soggy apparatus sat upside down by the door, drying. Peter practically leapt across the room and grabbed a flash drive that had been wedged discreetly inside the umbrella's handle. Without another word, he darted out of Carlos' office. Fifteen minutes later Peter yelled down the hall. "It's fine! Everything is fine. The drive isn't ruined."

Carlos never asked what *everything* actually referred to.

This gave him another idea. Unfortunately, he needed James to return in order to do anything about it.

In the meantime, he pushed past a wave of feebleness and heaved himself upright and over to the door. The handle spun uselessly. Through a crack in the door frame he spotted a thick chain and the edge of a lock dangling outside. Just to be sure, Carlos tugged on the door. Nothing budged. The frame didn't even creak. This place was sturdier than it looked.

An engine roared in the distance. Carlos crawled towards the nearest window. As he peered out the bottom of the glass, the foamy white wake of a speedboat shimmered in the moonlight as the boat curved outwards around a distant peninsula. Except for its frenzied line, the water was calm. It seemed even the gulls had gone to sleep.

Carlos slumped back down onto the floor. He felt exhausted from that short bout of activity. *Concentrate.*

Even though he had been liberated from the bowels of Valletta, he still felt imprisoned. And he didn't like it.

With a spurt of motivation, Carlos stood and took about three steps. He was aiming for the far side of the hut, but he was so exhausted he could only make it a third of the way across on his feet. Then he heard something rustling outside the hut's rear wall. Carlos froze. It sounded like someone or something was trying to burrow their way in. Whatever it was sniffed loudly, then snorted.

Darn stray dogs! Calm down. Don't overreact.

He switched his attention to an old metal cabinet that stood against the wall. Its sides were rusted and the drawers screeched when Carlos tried opening them. Inside the second drawer an old fishing kit lay discarded. Carlos opened it and found wire, clippers, various hooks and a blunt descaler. He tucked everything except the hooks inside his breast pocket. It just might come in handy.

His energy soon started to fade, so he crawled back to his spot against the opposite wall. The room started to spin, and he dozed on and off until the sound of tires jolted him awake. Footsteps approached the front entrance.

"Hey, is anyone inside?"

Carlos held still. *Who would come out in the middle of the night to an abandoned fisherman's hut?*

The person rapped on the window. "Hello. What's going on in there?" The glass was so thick with dried sea water and crud that whoever stood outside could not see Carlos inside. Carlos followed the sound of crunching pebbles as the person continued around the entire shack.

Carlos remained motionless.

The footsteps retreated. A car door opened and an engine revved to life. The car backed away from the hut.

Carlos' senses were on high alert. He needed to settle himself. The first qassatat calmed his nerves and the second soothed his stomach. The pastries had turned cold and chewy, but eating helped him centre his thoughts after what had just happened. *Who other than James knew he was here?*

25

SPARE PARTS

For the first time in years, Sasha woke to her alarm's buzz. It sounded like a helicopter was tearing off the roof of her house. She was glad her body normally roused to its own internal clock. Today was different. Her head pounded. She hadn't had any alcohol last night, but the thought of her adventure in the port and her run-in with Emanuel brought on a surge of discomfort. She rolled out of the sheets and headed towards the bathroom to grab a paracetamol. Hopefully, today would prove uneventful.

Last night had been rough. She had woken up every couple of hours, worried about her daughter. Thankfully Cristabel appeared to be sleeping comfortably when Sasha checked on her after the book reading. The Bolt driver had dropped Sasha off at the bakery. She had tiptoed up to the storeroom where Cristabel was still resting. Cristabel had pushed Sasha away when she tried to look at the wound. She said she had changed her own dressing and complained it hurt too much for anyone else to touch it. Sasha had backed off and walked home, comforted that Cristabel's vigour seemed to be returning.

After splashing cold water on red-tinged eyes, Sasha sat down to call her uncle. He answered before she even heard his phone ring.

After calming his nerves and explaining she had managed to get the sample phones, they discussed future steps. If all went to plan, they would see multiple shipments come to fruition. It was apparent that accessing the port as she had done the prior evening was too dangerous to become standard procedure.

So she had come up with a Plan B.

Once again, it linked back to her underground entrepreneurial club. Traditional fishermen were struggling. Their skills at sea had other uses, and Sasha knew one family who would be happy to diversify their catch.

It would be risky. They needed a trustworthy accomplice on the cargo ship. Her uncle would give this transport contact a special package labelled as spare parts and warranty materials. Once the freighter carrying the vehicle shipment cleared the Suez Canal and entered the Mediterranean Sea, it would be in international waters. There, her fisherman friend would rendezvous with it and pick up the special package. He would transport it along with his regular fishing haul back to Malta, where he would pass it along to Sasha. She would then give the phones to Emanuel.

The plan involved more people than she liked and would need a few unplanned payouts. But she figured her commission would cover the extra cost. Her uncle's cut would remain unchanged.

Uncle Noa confirmed he also liked the plan.

Noa and Sasha were only ten years apart. Years earlier when he and Sasha first got in touch, he had explained to her that knew he would never be able to return to his home country of Malta. His father had defected from the Allies' cause during the Second World War and fled to Japan. It meant his family could never return. Most of the family back home had rejected his father's decision and cut all ties with them. When Noa was born in the sixties, his father had originally hoped his son's name would help mend their family's discord by bridging both Japanese and Western influences. Sadly, his father's efforts failed.

After their parents had passed away, the two connected online.

When they were discussing this latest arrangement, Noa explained that it felt like he was finally regaining a semi-connection to his land and doing his part to help the local population of his family's home country get more affordable communications. Equality for all. The socialist in him craved a more equitable world. And he had to admit the extra cash helped.

Sasha hung up the phone but still felt on edge. Her plan worried her. Her wrist was throbbing. Without thinking, she wandered over to the cabinet in the living room and opened its bottom left door. The crystal flask of sherry hadn't been touched in years, but today it called to her. She poured one glass and tipped it back, slowly at first. Then too quickly. A lone droplet spread across the bottom of her glass, begging for company. After refilling her glass halfway she returned the flask to the cupboard.

Time to get going. The L&B still had to function.

When she arrived at the bakery, Sasha first tiptoed upstairs to check on Cristabel and found her sleeping soundly. From thereon, Sasha worked on autopilot. The ovens churned out sumptuous aromas. Her till chimed regularly as she filled orders and bagged take-away snacks. By early afternoon, the rush had passed.

Cristabel awoke and felt up to walking home. Sasha closed the shop for thirty minutes and helped her daughter get home. Cristabel was visibly relieved to get back to her own bed, among her own stuff. Content, Sasha left her daughter and returned to the bakery.

Raymond, her contact from the car dealership, called to say he could get away from the showroom after all. He wanted to join her so they could inspect the vehicles together at the port. She had nearly forgotten she had to go back there. A rush of excitement rose in her chest knowing she didn't have to face the guards alone. Returning to the port as an invited guest versus a rogue snoop felt much more appealing.

By the time Raymond arrived forty-five minutes later, she had served three more customers. They purchased big orders and left her shelves virtually empty. Perfect timing to close the shop.

During the drive, Sasha learned about an upcoming promotion, with the best deal on the island for a new hatchback. Raymond was ecstatic about their arrangement, especially when she handed him the signed sales documents. His fingers grazed the top of her hand, reviving a different kind of excitement she hadn't felt for years. *Not now, Sasha.*

Traffic seemed unusually heavy. Thirty minutes later, they pulled into the parking lot. As they walked up to the front gate, a guard dog ran towards them and sniffed her ankles. It started to bark—vigorously. Sasha stepped back, recognizing it as the watchman's partner from the night before.

The guard on duty stepped out from his kiosk. His brows furrowed. "Ma'am, have you been here before? Gus sure seems to recognize your scent."

Sasha answered as truthfully as she could. "I used to play around by the beaches here as a kid. Maybe that young pup is older than it looks." She gave the most innocent smile she could muster.

The watchman did not appreciate her humour. "Listen, we've had a lot of trouble lately with intruders. Gus is well trained and if he picks up a scent on someone, no matter who, I have to make a record. It's company protocol." He picked up a clipboard from the counter. "Let me get your name, address and phone number." He took down her information, then waved over a young, bored-looking colleague who was leaning against a crate. "Stewart will take you on to see the cargo now."

By the time the small group arrived at the shipping container, Sasha's heart rate had calmed somewhat. The keypad she'd used the night before looked different in the daylight. There were smudged fingerprints around its edges and on the latch of the door. Footsteps distorted the pathway around the metal box. She glanced over at the next crate, relieved to see it too was covered in blotches and surrounded by footprints. *Relax*, she told herself. *Staff work around these big boxes all day and leave their own marks.*

Raymond grabbed her shoulder and squeezed. "Exciting, isn't it? Our first shipment!"

Sasha could not help but smile back at his enthusiasm.

The metal door squealed open. Still, Stewart, their chaperone, commented on how quiet it was compared to most containers that had been at sea.

Initially, the black box looked empty against the bright sunlight. Then their eyes adjusted. Cars filled the crate, parked double-decker. Paint glistened under a dimly lit light bulb hanging inside.

Sasha circled the storage unit, pretending it was the first time she had seen her new imports.

Raymond grinned at her. As if to solidify a deal already confirmed, the two partners shook hands and agreed more vehicles were on the horizon once this first lot sold. Sasha silently hoped she would not have to wait long.

As the two drove away from the port, Sasha's phone vibrated. Emanuel had sent a text. He would be at the bakery by five.

Although tempted to keep the bakery closed for the rest of the day, Sasha flipped its sign to Open when she got back. She popped six rosemary loaves into the oven and made a fresh batch of ricotta spinach buns. They were typically popular with people who wanted to grab something to spice up their dinner plans. A few fruit pies and custard tarts remained for customers with a sweet tooth. The time flew by, nearly catching her off guard when Emanuel sauntered into the shop.

She was standing behind her till, and she braced herself against the counter as he approached. Even though she felt confident that the counterfeit phones her uncle sent would be popular, she needed Emanuel's boss to agree to the deal. Considering the next shipment of vehicles could be weeks away, her plan had cracks. She must get out her plaster and seal them up.

"Boss is happy. He wants two hundred." Emanuel gave an uncharacteristic smile.

Sasha forced herself not to show her surprise outwardly. "I knew he would like the product. They'll be here by July." Although risky, she already planned to bring in double the amount requested with the next car shipment. She could keep the spares in her cellar—locked.

Her commission would cover an entire semester of Cristabel's final year of university. Cristabel earned enough by tutoring and doing the odd casual job to cover the other semester. Then Sasha could pull out and drop these nefarious dealings.

"Boss doesn't like to wait. Your fee drops thirty percent if you can't deliver in four weeks."

***

Emanuel walked out of Sasha's bakery smiling. His boss hadn't said anything about dropping the commission. More money for Emanuel—and his boss would never find out. In fact, he hadn't felt this gleeful since the day he'd left his homeland, dreaming of a new start and his forthcoming fortune.

Earlier in the day, Emanuel had overheard that the street vendors his boss had planned to use to sell the phones had been compromised. The boss was scrambling to organize an alternative distribution network. From past experience, Emanuel knew the vetting process would take time. So Sasha's estimate of supply in six or seven weeks was actually fine, but he could use what she did not know for his own benefit.

26

LOADED GUN

———

Gerardo desperately wished he was back home in his apartment. He felt the cool tip of what he presumed to be a loaded gun digging into his back. The man had pushed him forward through throngs of people and beyond, until they reached this deserted street. Gerardo's shoulder ached, but he tried to ignore it. His right arm was twisted behind him and pressed tightly against the small of his back.

The man seemed to be about his height, for a gruff voice practically spat into Gerardo's ear. "What are you looking for? I saw you poking around the streets of Birgu."

Gerardo winced. Birgu was where Cristabel's mom's bakery was located. He wasn't about to admit anything, especially anything related to his escapades in the underground vault. "Hey, man, I'm just out having a good time at the clubs. What's your problem?"

The man did not back down. "You won't get a second chance. I heard you and your friends scheming in the club tonight. Whatever piece of the action you think you'll get in on, you need to rethink it." He twisted Gerardo's arm tighter. "Now, this is the last time I will ask. What were you doing poking around the L&B?"

A flurry of thoughts collided in Gerardo's mind. *How much did this person overhear at the nightclub? Impossible—it was way too noisy to hear details, even with a curtain for a wall.* That left the bakery. He was sure no one had seen him come or go when he and Cristabel had searched the cellar. Maybe this guy spotted him climbing up to her window afterwards. Well, whatever action he thought Gerardo wanted in on, he was clearly mistaken.

"Listen, asere, I'm a friend of the baker's daughter. I don't want any part of whatever you are involved with." Gerardo caught an accent in the stranger's voice and decided to play up his own foreign-language card. Build a commonality. He may not know asere means buddy, but it couldn't hurt to try to cut the tension.

The man tightened his grip on Gerardo's arm.

Time to gain control and get out of this messed-up situation. Gerardo threw his head back, knocking the man in the forehead and throwing him off balance. The man let go of his arm. Gerardo then grabbed the man's right wrist and whirled him around, whipping the gun from his grasp with his other hand.

In less than five seconds, Gerardo had the man pinned on the cold pavement. Gerardo recognized the once-shiny black shoes from the club. He leaned forward, startled for a second time when he saw the man's face. This was the same person Gerardo had seen trailing Cristabel's mother. "Whatever you think, leave me out of your little arrangement. Next time, *you* will be the one who won't get a second chance."

Emanuel stared into the muzzle of his own gun, stunned. He had not expected this quick use of force. This guy's moves were not the type he knew from the street. Maybe he had misread the situation. This tweed-coated meddler must be the boyfriend sneaking around, and a professional fighter at that. "Fine, I'll stay out of your way if you stay out of mine."

Gerardo smacked Emanuel's nose with the butt of the gun, knocking him out and making a point. He wiped his prints off the gun and left it in Emanuel's pocket, not wanting anything to tie him to this wacko. He walked back to the busy streets and wound his way through the crowds until he reached his car.

Clearly Cristabel's mother's nefarious meetings and stashed documents were a danger of their own. Normally, he would have been tempted to take a second look at the documents Cristabel had copied. But his superiors had made his mission clear. His priority was to track down missing agents—and to keep Cristabel safe. It was becoming increasingly obvious that if Gerardo was to succeed he needed to protect Cristabel. After tonight, that meant keeping her away from her own mother.

By the time he got home, he had formed a clear picture of his next steps. First he needed a shower and sleep. It had been a long night. Too much had transpired to dive straight in. Fragments needed to settle. He knew how his brain worked best.

The next morning, two cups of coffee with milk, a banana and five minutes of listening to the morning news helped shake his blurry thoughts into focus. His laptop purred to life, as did the dual monitors set up on his desk.

He started with police records, searching for grievances and odd disturbances reported over the past ten days. A few files caught his interest and he set them aside for later. Next, he screened all medical admissions and doctors' appointments that could fit a man in his fifties with Professor Ignacio's traits. Of course, privacy laws made such searches more difficult, but between his hacker's acumen and his access to back-channel gateways, he proved pretty adept, even without his team's help. Once again, a few patients stood out as potential leads. Their details were flagged and filed. Then he headed into the deep end.

This final step would likely drag on for the entire day, maybe longer. The records were clear; it was the humanity behind the data that proved a little more intricate. Who had come into contact with Carlos over the past six months? What folks attended his seminars and how were the Tartu Five connected to them? Although others on his team were doing similar work using their own techniques, Gerardo found it worthwhile to put multiple sets of eyes on such a broad and vague search. Each of his team members was qualified. Everyone brought their own insight and skill set, which is why their best results typically arose when they attacked concurrently.

By seven that night, his screens reeled with data. He used a handy program that compiled, sorted and cross-referenced multiple sources of data and flagged any overlap that linked to sources from other agents. Gerardo had reasonably high security clearance, so his entries should catch most levels of crossover. He decided to leave the system running while he went to check on Cristabel.

Cristabel's wounds had healed sufficiently to allow her to move from the bakery's attic storeroom back home.

She had texted Gerardo earlier in the day to say her mom would be out at a small-business meeting that evening. That gave them privacy. Still, he wasn't anxious to run into her mother's business mate again. He circled the block four times to be sure no one was lingering and then parked a kilometre away.

27

ENTANGLED

James headed towards the agreed meeting place. It was nearly midday and Friday already. He knew he could keep Carlos confined for the foreseeable future in that desolate hut on the neglected inlet. Most of the fishing industry had been taken over by larger corporations. As the small independents had faded, they'd left their derelict huts to rot along the shorelines. James silently thanked their misfortune.

But, not one to leave things to chance, last evening he had dropped an undetectable speck of polonium-210 onto the qassatat pastries. Carlos would not taste anything or have any lasting effects with this dosage. But he would feel awful and be less likely to fight his confinement for the time being.

On the southwestern coastline, James pulled into the Dingli Cemetery parking lot. A lone silhouette stood at the far end of the park. He recognized the strands of blond hair blowing, tangled in the wind. The last time he'd seen her in person, they were wound up together in a different entanglement. That was back when they were both in training.

Nadya had two years of experience on James. That mission should have been a simple surveillance, but James messed up. He lost their target and nearly exposed the entire team. Back then, he hadn't cracked his twentieth birthday. He didn't know how to admit his mistakes. He blamed bad equipment and mishandled the debrief.

Nadya was the project lead on the assignment. She took responsibility. Later, James heard she got demoted for his screw-up.

He wasn't even sure whether he'd ever apologized. Nor was he convinced time healed all wounds.

Different times, different operations. Since then he'd occasionally heard about her. Unsurprisingly, she rose quickly in the ranks and then plateaued. There were those who praised her tenacity and those who feared it.

Last week, their superiors put Nadya and James back in touch. Their communications had been brief.

They chose today's meeting place specifically to avoid getting captured in random tourists' photos and inadvertently getting posted on Instagram or Facebook. Malta was a popular travel destination, so escaping camera lenses and watchful locals was not always easy. Better to keep both of their faces unseen. The Dingli Cemetery met their criteria of falling low on most visitors' must-see lists.

The two did not speak each other's names. Nor did they engage in any pleasantries or personal small talk. Even in this field of graves, with bouquets of wilted leaves and brown-edged petals drooping against cold tombstones, words were clipped. From their first week at the academy, James and Nadya had learned what not to say. The art of subtlety had become engrained in them both, it flowed through their veins and pursed their lips.

Nadya waited, unsure whether to disclose her suspicions. Then she looked directly at James. "We have to stop whoever is behind these kidnappings. More is at stake than you may know."

She nodded towards the steeple, half a kilometre away. "We will find the core hidden behind cloaks. Old guards are losing their grip. New trails are being forged, dangerous paths bringing innocents to rise up in packs."

James recognized the code words and intended

context. The paths between religion and politics had a history of bumpy encounters and eroded trust. But clearly Nadya believed that the kidnappers had more in mind than snatching a couple of tenured professors.

She looked scared. He had heard her dedication to the motherland was profound. Today, he believed it.

"Listen, we need to talk this through properly." James glanced around. If Nadya believed what she said to be true, then they needed to get away from anything tied to the church. At this point he didn't trust the plastic bouquet draped across a freshly dug pile of dirt near them. Listening devices could be planted anywhere.

Nadya nodded towards the parking lot. Once they were back in their cars, he followed her out of the cemetery and across town. They reached a vacant parkade next to the football stadium. Perfect.

Leaning against their vehicles, James and Nadya faced one another. This stance gave them the advantage of a 180-degree view in both directions.

James elaborated on how he had tracked down Carlos and he told her pieces of the theory he had drawn out of Carlos. Nadya shared her team's work to date and Myriam's comments about the archeology club.

"We must tread very carefully," she said. "Both Carlos and Myriam suggested archeology groups to us separately. They could be trying to fool us. They could have agreed beforehand to use this as a decoy story if anything ever happened to them. What other theories do you have?" Nadya wanted to hear how much James was willing to open up.

"Carlos suspects someone is behind the latest discoveries on Malta. He and Peter must have stumbled across some evidence linked to some bigwig, which confirms your suspicions of major moves being played. But I'm not sure how it connects back to political warfare. Carlos has a muddied background and a deceptive mind, but Malta is not typically a big player in global affairs. So why here? Why now?"

Relaxing, Nadya explained her theory and the similarities she had found in recent Russian discoveries. The only explanation that made sense as to why her team was even approved to carry out this mission tied back to power. Someone with access to massive resources must be trying to topple the church, maybe even oust the government, since it relied so heavily on clerical leverage. Changing the understanding of such fundamental premises as where civilizations' underlying faiths began and how they spread would cause a massive social reckoning. If the heads of churches lost their grip, governments would lose large numbers of supporters. She wasn't sure her government would survive.

Such an uprising would stick a very sharp pin into the balloon on which global powers currently balanced.

"Do you really believe that? What sort of individual

would take on the church and try to overthrow global government stability at the same time? Faking multiple archeological finds, even on a small island like Malta, takes guts. Although, it *would* explain Carlos' interest if he still held on to his rogue military inclinations."

James poked her theory further. "But how do ancient ruins lead to a power grab and the biggest global reckoning ever witnessed? Maybe this situation is nothing more than the kidnapping of the wrong guy turned sour."

"Well, if that's all it is then great. But both ex-agent allies spoke of an archeology club and new interests. Separately. Their subconscious alarm bells are ringing and their conscious selves don't know why. This is our job now. Currently, we are half-blind and our bosses haven't a clue what's happening. You and I need to track down every piece of data we can to figure out this bizarre business."

James sensed something serious was lurking in the background. And he intended to avoid it. "Then we need to find Peter, or at the very least, learn what he knew."

James volunteered to go back into the tunnels. It was their best chance to find Peter—if he was still alive.

Nadya nodded. "I'll see who I can track down. Maybe some of our old opposition ringleaders have sprung up again."

"Good." James knew from experience not to rely on

random offers of help, even from insiders. They would work together, albeit at a comfortable distance.

James put his hand on Nadya's arm. "Thank you."

The touch was not merely to convey his thanks. A tiny microphone caught the hairs of her skin. James knew enough not to trust anyone. He also had access to minuscule tracing technology from his private company that crossed into this world effortlessly. Bugging a comrade without them ever knowing gave him an advantage. It would not last long, maybe twelve hours. Mainly, he wanted to hear her first conversation after they parted ways.

Just when he thought Nadya was about to walk away, she looked straight at him. "By the way, I sent surveillance. All was quiet at your dear friend's hideout."

James gave her a strange look. He had not told her where he was keeping Carlos.

As he wandered back to his car, the gravel underfoot crunched unusually loudly. A plane roared overhead, leaving a white streak to stain the bleak sky. Direction. Misdirection. Hints of schemes ran in various directions across his mind. None stood out as a clear lead. A lump settled in his stomach. Was the past coming back to pay tribute, or was more in store than he anticipated?

As James reversed his car, Nadya stood in the parking lot. He glanced in his rearview mirror and saw she was staring towards the old stone church that overlooked the cemetery. By the time he pulled out, she had turned and madly tapped on the screen of her phone. Like him, she probably never switched off.

At times, James wondered what life would have been like if he had chosen a different path. He also knew it wasn't his choice to make. Giving up his attachment to the government would mean he would continually be looking over his shoulder. There was no escape. Instead, his current hole had just become a whole lot deeper—and darker.

James parked near St. Augustine College. Being just off the main highway and along the bus line, this quiet suburban area offered him a convenient transition point. Twenty minutes and one bus ride later, he fell into pace with the crowds meandering along Triq Sant Anna in central Valletta.

After passing the regional police station, he cut down a narrow alley. It was close to noon and the restaurants were beginning to fill. This was his opportunity to head to the war memorials. Their popular tunnel tour of the Lascaris War Rooms would start in fifteen minutes. It took visitors through hidden rooms used during the Second World War and would lead him straight underground. With enough people to distract the guide, he figured he could easily slip away for his own secret tour.

28

FULL CIRCLE

It was Friday afternoon when Nadya looked up from her phone and out her office window. Traffic had been light on her drive back to the clinic after meeting with James. The wind had picked up since then. Whitecaps smeared the ocean into an angry expression of seething teeth, reflecting her view of the world in general. For now, the James-Yakov factor was contained. He might be a benefit if he managed to track down Peter. That is, if Peter decided to cooperate. Well, she had her ways in case he chose to be difficult. It paid to keep a veil of mistrust between her inner intentions and the outside world.

So far, Yakov was not aware of her past connection with this project. After all, it was Nadya who had first notified the authorities about Carlos' questionable activities.

At one time, she and Carlos had been counterparts, a bridge between Russian and Cuban intelligence groups. They shared everything—well, almost everything. Relations between the countries had been good at that time.

Secrets flowed both ways. Business flowed as well. But a year into their relationship, Nadya noticed a change in Carlos' messages. Individuals who weren't previously involved started to be copied on certain emails. Particular senior officers who should have been included were occasionally left off important communiqués. Of course, he conveniently explained away the "errors" as shifting internal priorities.

Nadya followed her instinct.

After months of surveillance, investigation and the work of at least one heavily entrenched spy, a pocket of ally comrades were deemed to have gone rogue. The more senior members of this network were imprisoned. Carlos held a relatively junior position at the time and was let off easy. Soon after, Nadya's commander retracted her ties with Carlos.

Cuba's military took over. Essentially, they put the crew through hell and then reassigned Carlos under the guise of re-education. They hoped that the young man would be too scared to try anything similar ever again, but they maintained oversight just in case. Myriam was tasked with the oversight role on behalf of the Cuban government. However, she developed her own bias in Carlos' favour.

Nadya's trust in the overall process eroded.

Russian intelligence was not so trusting either and sent their own on-the-ground supervision. Yakov—as James—was sent in to act as an understudy during Carlos' retraining program.

Nadya thought it ironic how they had come full circle, more than twenty years later. Her team had tracked down Carlos after James dragged him out of the subterranean dungeon. James wasn't that hard to trail and never appeared to suspect that anything was amiss. He must be getting soft over there in Canada.

Soon after, her team took a boat over to the inlet where James was keeping Carlos. The fisherman's hut appeared deserted, giving her some level of confidence in James' tactics.

While her team headed back to search Peter's office at the university, Nadya decided to take a look elsewhere. She had already covered basic reconnaissance at the family home after her team nabbed Myriam. Distrust of the Ignacio couple ran deep in her supervisor's eyes. He had pushed Nadya to get answers on the missing Carlos more aggressively than she would have chosen. The mild earthquake and resultant sinkhole made her team's job easier. When the home shook, her sniper, who happened to be outside, took advantage of the moment. He shot Myriam with a tranquilizer. Then he set off a small explosive device in the basement, amplifying the damage from the tremor and making the smashed window appear to be incidental, from the quake. All indications of Myriam's abduction were removed. The team left the place as if it had collapsed while the owners were away.

By the time the police arrived, her team had cleared out. The officers conducted a brief investigation, but without any bodies or missing person's report, they taped the scene and filed a simple dossier. Any further steps would be between the owners and their insurance company.

Likely, that action—or inaction—would not occur for some time, considering both owners were presently tied up. She laughed at her own pun, congratulating herself for mastering the language so much so that even her thoughts were in English.

Nadya parked in front of the neighbourhood park. Before leaving the car, she grabbed her oversized handbag containing a small field kit she valued more than the posh purse. She circled the idle playground before making her way towards Carlos and Myriam's sunken house. While apartment blocks dominated both sides of their home, retail shops lined the far side of the street. She could understand why none of the neighbours had called to check on the place or its occupants. No one would have noticed their absence in this congested part of an otherwise family-friendly community.

Palm trees and bougainvillea camouflaged the entryway. A patch of cobblestone bricks buckled along the driveway at the same side of the house as the living room. The sinkhole lied right below that spot. From where she stood on the driveway, the entire upper level appeared to have collapsed but she knew from her earlier visit that most of the house remained structurally intact, simplifying her endeavours.

Between the foyer and the kitchen lay what used to be a living room. Most of the room and its contents had collapsed inwards. Only the top half of a red velvet sofa remained visible, the rest tipped at an awkward angle into the sinkhole's cavity. Nadya craned her neck, trying to see more of what fell inside. The great cavern swallowed lamps, a coffee table and at least one lounge chair. No matter what else might have fallen in, she was not about to risk scrambling any closer.

Incredibly, the rim of the sinkhole must have fallen just inside the supporting walls for they still clung to their foundations, bracing the stairwell and part of the second floor. Nadya headed straight upstairs. This was where Myriam had been shot and the laptop recovered. It looked as if a tornado had planted its eye and spun around wildly. Pictures no longer hung on the wall. Shattered glass erased any artistic facade. The rug lay in shreds, masterfully splayed overtop the loose board and its secret cache. Although all that remained inside was a handful of straw.

The room's wooden door frame stood intact. The desk stood resolute, almost taunting Nadya to find whatever morsels it hid.

Pens, paperclips, random receipts and boring clutter filled the drawers. Nadya crawled underneath and stared at the desk from this angle. Her fingers slid across every crack and reached into corners. Aside from a sliver in her index finger, nothing left much of an impression. She moved on to study its legs. Three were made of solid wood. The fourth sounded hollow. She pulled out the drawer that ran directly above it. There had to be some way to explain the inconsistency.

After twenty minutes of pressing, twisting and pushing every knot and nail she could find, Nadya gave up. She surveilled the room. There, in the back of the closet lay a sturdy wooden leg in the same dark walnut as the desk. It was scarred by a deep crack. She looked back at the replacement leg. Although it was obscured by shadows, she could see that it was a slightly different hue and grain than the rest of the desk. Wood varieties were hard to come by on the barren island of Malta, and this repaired furniture simply represented the reality of the limited supply. Reluctantly, she continued her search elsewhere.

The rest of the room contained nothing of particular interest. Old photo albums and books filled half of the closet and two entire walls of shelves. Nadya decided to move on to other rooms. The kitchen was her favourite. Most people assumed it was the safest place to hide things and tended to pick obvious spots. Bags stuffed at the bottom of flour canisters or envelopes slid between "the good" dishes were the first things to look for.

But Carlos and Myriam were not like most people. Their tactics were cleverer.

Nadya then scoured the bedroom. All she located were hidden drawers in their bedside tables. They were part of the design and stored a couple of old photos and what looked to be the first love letter Carlos had written to Myriam. Entertaining, but not what Nadya was after.

She checked her watch. It was almost six in the evening. The natural light was fading. Annoyance fumed at the edges of her mind. This ex-agent lived such a normal life, doing what he loved with the person he cared most for. Few people could claim to have it so good. She stopped herself from reflecting about her own life and refocussed on her search.

Long shadows spread across the floors as she went from room to room. Finally she returned to the lower level. She sat in the small entranceway and surveyed the ground floor. It was an open-concept design, unusual for an older house in Malta. They must have renovated it after moving in. Traditional Maltese families rarely changed the bones of a building. Altering the location of walls was thought to bring bad luck. That's where she found her answer.

The Ignacios were not a traditional Maltese family. Some other culture's fear of omens would not have stopped them from shifting a wall. Here, the open area had a tinier footprint than it should have had in a home of this size. Nadya's eyes followed the tiles. The original hand-painted artistry had been maintained. Narrow grouting proved a professional had done the work.

Then Nadya noticed the tell. No professional trained to work with old tiles would have risked their reputation on wide grout lines, not even along the final row at the back of a room. This anomaly was done by someone else. *Ah ha!* She had found the hidden prize.

29

MAGNETS

James had a mental picture of the underground web. Most importantly, he knew more than certain people thought he knew. Tunnels crept all over the city, most leading out to the island's limestone lip and ultimately to the ocean. There were also random dead ends, such as the one where he had extracted Carlos. These had first interested him because they seemed to serve no purpose in the system's original design. Over time, some had been forgotten while others had become storage dens. And certain ones had a more sinister function.

A young girl working at the museum's ticket kiosk directed him to stand near a turnstile. Six other adults were already waiting. A family of four arrived after him. One teenager seemed particularly eager to step into the secret underground compartments, while her older sibling complained that he wanted to go video game shopping. The mother looked tired and gave in to a shopping trip after their museum tour. Two more families with younger children arrived, chattering continually. James tucked behind them and stuffed his cap in his back pocket.

"Ticket, please." A bored-looking attendant flashed a forced smile for a brief second as she checked the date on James' ticket.

As James turned away from the attendant, a small security camera above them caught his face straight on. Most likely, the film would get recorded over in thirty days. But if he happened to need an alibi for the forty-five-minute period of the tour, the film would cover him. And he was pretty sure it wouldn't take a month to find out that it would be necessary.

A few more couples had joined at the last minute, and he walked in the middle of about fifteen adults. Children shuffled around the outskirts of the group. Younger ones pulled on parents' hands while the elder kids hung back, unconvinced whether the next three-quarters of an hour would be worthy of their interest or would fall into the category of boring educational moments their parents liked to push on their malleable minds.

James had read about the clandestine meetings and covert operations coordinated in the Lascaris War Rooms. Without even going into the myths, he knew there was more than enough to grab the attention of most disparaging teenagers. While the Second World War might have seemed part of a stiff and distant past, walking 150 feet below the showy Upper Barrakka Gardens into hidden chambers held an element of allure. The British had once planned innumerable Mediterranean invasions from these rooms. Others sent secret messages using encryption technology that only a handful of personnel could read. Most people who attended the tour became captivated by the first room—and those who didn't certainly did by the second.

Ten minutes into the tour, the guide explained that the very same mechanism used to filter the air over fifty years ago, when more than one thousand people worked underground, was still used today. By the number of gasps, the audience's attention was well and truly held.

James took advantage of their focus and ducked under an archway. As the group wandered further along, he pulled out a small device he never went anywhere without.

The thin band of magnetized threads glided into the door's keyhole, where they moulded to its interior. He had devised the tool himself, a simple concept allowing a new key to be made effectively on demand. The filaments aligned with the grooves of any lock. The lock clicked. Quietly turning the handle, James stepped inside the next room.

He flicked on the light switch. Bookshelves overflowing with notebooks, historical textbooks and binders full of unknown documents shielded the walls. On the surface, the room looked like any other storage room stacked to the brim with stuff. Maybe the items got used, or maybe their main purpose was simply to gather dust and just be.

There was more to this room than one might suspect on first glance. James had seen the blueprints. He bent down on his hands and knees and scanned the floor. With a sigh of relief, he saw the shelving units were on rollers. For the Lascaris War Rooms were not rooms at all. A myriad of tunnels and connecting shoots burrowed underground. The illusion of walls was created by bookshelves, tables and projector screens. They could be moved around, creating small spaces or large meeting rooms on demand. The genius of the Lascaris chambers was that they always had an exit strategy.

A bookcase wobbled as he rolled it out of the way. For a moment James was sure the books on the top shelf were about to topple onto his head. He lifted his left arm just in time to push the heaviest volume back in its place. The rest rebalanced enough to hold.

When he pulled the bookcase back into position behind him, one of the thinner volumes fell. It landed in the middle of the chamber, too far for him to reach. All he could hope was that whoever found it would assume it had been inadvertently dropped by the last staff member in here. In any case, he would be long gone by that point.

Below the inner city, the tunnels took on a more sanitary nature. The odour of human excrement wafted intermittently. Elsewhere, sections had been transformed into storage cellars, with bolstered walls and locked doors. James decided to focus on these. He shone a flashlight to look for recent marks indicating someone had been down here.

Most footprints looked dusted over and months old. To be sure, he pressed his audio filtration sensor against the doors. At one door, a sound triggered his instrument. Something moved inside. Rat whiskers soon poked out from a chewed hole near James' feet. The rodent recoiled as soon as it saw him and then darted off in the opposite direction.

James continued his methodical search. Door by door. Empty dead end after empty dead end. He cursed the traitors behind this futile hunt, having dealt with them one too many times. They had tried to cut him out, blocking communication and holding funds after a minor glitch in his business's quarterly update. It did not matter. He could outsmart them. James had no problem switching allegiances—again.

He arrived at what appeared to be more of a nook than a doorway. Fresh tracks marked the damp floor. Vague notes of music flowed through a metal flap on the wall. It reminded him of a mail slot. But no mailman came to this address.

As stealthily as possible, James attached his audio sensor to the flap to better gauge what was going on inside. As he did so, he accidentally bumped the flap. It squeaked. The music stopped.

James snapped off his light and backed away. Even though he wore rubber-soled shoes, the algae grew thick on the floor and squelched with each step, giving away his position. He stopped and held still. He was about to take another step when a clicking noise pierced the silence.

It felt like a train came blasting through the darkness and slammed into his shoulder. His head smashed against the wall on the way down. The metallic ticking sounded again, but this time it came from the opposite direction. James tried to scramble away. He was not quick enough. A weight crashed into him, skimming past his ears and hitting him in the centre of his back. This time, he realized the ball was lighter than he originally thought. In any case, it felt as if a lightweight bowling ball had been dropped from above. The ticking sound returned. He envisioned a chain pulling up a drawbridge. His legs seemed disconnected, unable to move on command. He heard his own broken groan as if it came from someone else.

Where he had expected to find a dark tunnel and a locked door lurked a far more aggressive reality. For the first time in years, James feared what he thought he had once understood.

Instinct kicked in. *Get out of here.* Although his back screamed in pain, his arms still functioned. He dragged himself further along the corridor. He decided to leave his light off in case someone was watching. The ground started to get drier. His palms no longer felt the sticky goo of algae and mildew. However, whoever came looking for him would be able to follow his drag marks. This thought spurred him forward. He needed to find a crossover tunnel to get away.

A squeal pulsed through the air. The door must be opening. Someone was coming. A glow from the open door lit up the tunnel behind him. James pressed himself against the wall, half closing his eyes so they wouldn't catch the light and give him away.

Footsteps reverberated inside the narrow cavity. James prepared himself for a messy fight.

Then the steps quietened. The person was heading in the opposite direction. Maybe they were following his tracks from the Lascaris War Rooms without realizing they were walking in the wrong direction.

James took advantage of his luck. He dragged himself until he could stand and stagger forward. Finally, he arrived at an adjacent tunnel. The texture of the wall changed from rough limestone to smooth wood. A newish handle felt like velvet to his touch. He tried to turn it. After swivelling a few centimetres the doorknob stopped. A lock hung below it. He felt around for the keyhole. Within minutes he had unlatched the handle and shoved the door open enough to slide his body through.

The footsteps started up again. This time they were coming in his direction.

James spun his body around and pushed the door closed. It wouldn't lock properly but it gave him cover. He felt like a steel rod was drilling into his shoulder. Seething in pain, he rolled onto his stomach to take the weight off his back.

Seconds turned into minutes. The door handle remained still. His breathing returned to semi-normal. James tapped his watch's GPS setting to add a marker. Once back at his computer, he would be able to find out in more detail what was around this location. That might help him figure out who else had access to this section. In the meantime, he had to get out, despite being partially incapacitated.

When James turned on his flashlight, he realized he was not alone. Shadowy blobs circled him. He looked closer. Cured hams hung along one wall. Vats of wine and balsamic vinegar filled another. This gave him hope. The space was being used as a cellar, meaning there had to be another way in from above. He shone his light across the ceiling and spotted his exit.

A rope ladder with wooden slats had been rolled up and clasped to a hook in the back corner of the room. Directly above it, an access panel that looked well used sat loosely in place. A slim line of light sliced through one edge, encouraging him even more.

Pulling himself along the floor was one thing. Lugging his full body weight up a rope ladder would require an entirely different level of strength. James wasn't sure he had it in him.

As if on cue, the ceiling latch opened. "Hey, you kids can't play around—" The man stopped when he saw James. In disbelief he uttered, "Uwejja? Bis-serjetà?"

Without asking any more questions, the man leapt down. He unravelled the ladder, raced down and heaved James up by his armpits.

Pain surged through James' body, yet he tried to help as much as he could with his legs. As they got closer to the dangling ladder, James noticed a metal handhold attached to the wall. He might actually be able to make it.

Pressing through the pain, he tried to pull himself using the handhold. Together, they clambered up the ladder.

When they emerged from the hatch, James exhaled slowly, relieved to be lying above the cured hams and unlocked door.

A man with greying hair and sun-creased skin peered down at him.

30

CHILL

Carlos woke shivering on the floor, and instinctively reached for his barretina. He pulled it on low over his ears. Rarely had he felt cold since moving to Malta, even in the winter months. Mediterranean breezes normally helped to keep the muggy heat tolerable. During the summer, air-conditioned offices at the university offered respite from the claustrophobic heat. But cold, never.

Sea breezes blew in through the base of the building and swirled around him like a torn sheet. The Therm-a-Rest lay crumpled in a ball where he had tossed it out of frustration the night before. He had attempted to blow up the air mattress, hoping to get off the dank floor. In the process he had grown queasy and light-headed and had thrown the mattress aside when it became evident it had a hole. Sometime during the night he must have also kicked away the blanket James left. It lay just out of reach. But he preferred to save his strength. Even so, he felt exposed on the bare floor, reminding him once again of a prison. Alone. Trapped. Out of control.

Carlos expected more questions when James returned. Valid queries. With muddled answers he needed to sort out himself first. He sat on the empty duffle bag. It was the only dry place to sit. Resting his head against the table he let his thoughts wander back to Peter.

Peter had wanted to take a look at the latest discovery on the island in person. Carlos had heard about it through another professor on campus and understood that the excavation team was still analyzing what had been found. Peter and Carlos decided to visit the site.

Blue tarps were strung over the rocky ground. Metal poles stuck out of the ground every two metres. A grid of square plots spread across the earth, covering an area about the size of half a football field. At the far end, an ATCO mobile trailer, with its distinctive orange trim, presumably acted as the office. It would house computers, topographic maps, weigh scales and printers for the scientists. Two workers knelt over one of the plots about midway between the access lane and the trailer. Neither noticed Carlos and Peter arrive.

Five minutes later, two men came running out of the office waving their arms and yelling at Peter and Carlos. The site was reserved for those with restricted access passes. The men did not even ask for ID; they obviously knew who could enter—and who could not. Peter and Carlos were not on their list.

Carlos had not thought much about it initially, but certain details stood out as he thought back to that visit. A local construction company had parked its truck alongside the workers' vehicles. Chisels, hammers and a leveller lay strewn on the ground. Fresh cut marks lined some of the plots. He knew enough about excavations to know that such invasive tools were not uncommon. After all, test pits and trenches were often dug to survey an area.

Later, however, when he looked into the project further, it became apparent that no geophysical surveys were ever conducted of the site. Plans to do so had been logged, but no records were filed to prove it actually took place.

Carlos had decided to talk with residents who lived around the dig site. During the early days when the area was taped off, they had noticed lights and equipment working late into the night. Folks remembered the noise in particular. It reminded them of a nearby quarry that used to blast through the night until the practice was banned. They complained to the municipality, not understanding why this latest project should be exempt. Soon after, the noise stopped.

A few months later, Carlos and Peter went to another worksite. Tarps hung overtop and around the sides of the area to prevent anyone from seeing inside. Carlos noted the name of the subcontractor painted on the side of a pickup truck parked at the site, Excogitatoris Consulting. It was the same company that had been at the earlier site.

When he checked into the business, he found it had been set up about two years prior. It claimed to handle a variety of construction and architectural projects. That explained why its name stemmed from the Latin word for *inventor*. Its logo was a sunbeam attached to a hand. Carlos understood this design as a crude attempt to meld the pagan ideology of the sun—which is linked to the creation of the cosmos—with man's desire to manipulate creation through his own hands. In other words, to invent. A bold proposition.

The owner of the company was a bricklayer from the country of Georgia. Perhaps he also had a god complex.

Since their in-person visits did not uncover much information about the actual sites, Carlos and Peter turned to other means. Decades earlier, Malta's government had imposed a regulation that required all archeological documentation to be filed with the

Superintendence of Cultural Heritage. Although not directly affiliated with the university, it too was a public organization, and professors were given access to the ministry's collections management system for research purposes. All documents were scanned and accessible through an online portal.

To access *this* site, Carlos and Peter *did* have the proper authorization.

Peter spent three full days rummaging through the data. He pulled a wide swath of information and kept Carlos updated on the interesting bits.

What was it that Peter had told him? So much was going on at that point. Final exams were quickly approaching and Carlos was swamped trying to mark term papers and grade all of his students' submissions. Plus, he was supervising two master's students at the same time.

Then, just days later, Peter and Carlos learned the trajectories of the newly discovered ruts pointed towards the centres of some of the oldest civilizations on earth. The finding had not yet been made public.

Peter had handed Carlos a stack of copied pages bound with an elastic band. Carlos recognized the front page as the standard cover page used by Cultural Heritage's collections management system to ensure it was filed and tracked properly. Peter had asked Carlos to put the bundle somewhere safe, away from the university. He said he wanted to compare it side by side with another version. That night, Carlos was giving a talk and wouldn't have time to take it straight home. So he put it in his trunk with the spare tire. By the time he got home, well past ten in the evening, he had forgotten all about the documents.

Four days later, Peter had disappeared. Carlos himself had been tied up since that fateful morning. Unless someone had found them, the papers should still be buried in the bottom of his trunk.

31

CURED HAM

———

"You're not the lightest of men." The man tried not to dump James on the ground. "My entire livelihood is stored in that cellar. How did you end up inside it?" The man wiped his brow. He glared, apparently both defensive and angry at finding an injured stranger in his supposedly secured underground warehouse.

James owed this man. Without knowing the circumstances, he had rescued James from a very uncomfortable situation. Still, James couldn't be entirely truthful. "I heard rumours of strange activity taking place in the tunnels. Placed a bet with a few buddies at the pub that I could find out what was happening and ended up tripping down there on a pipe sticking out from the wall. I didn't see it. My shoulder must have knocked it when I fell. Hurt like hell. I tried a few doors. Yours happened to be unlocked."

The man furrowed his brow as if deciding whether or not to believe James. "I locked that door myself. It hasn't been opened since the city checked the stormwater drainage pipes last year, after the big storm." The man reached behind him and rummaged around until he found a small first-aid kit in the cupboard next to him. He handed the bottle to James. "Here, you should take a couple of ibuprofen tablets."

James noticed the distinct similarity between the beefiness of the man's forearms and the stocky legs of ham hanging in the cellar below. He was not someone to mess with, not physically at least.

"Are you sure those were city workers you let through? Someone else was down there when I hurt myself and they did not sound like the friendly sort. I wonder, do you know which of your neighbours has access to the tunnels?" James popped a couple of pills into his mouth and passed the bottle back to the shopkeeper.

Light glinted off the man's eyes. The man looked at James curiously, as if trying to decide whether he should trust him. "A few months back I heard noises down there.

So I checked on my stock a couple of times. Everything looked normal. *And* the door was still locked." He looked hard at James.

"Okay, I admit I jimmied your door. I'll fix it—with a better lock." He winked at the man. James figured he could do more exploring below while he installed the new lock. "But who might I run into down there?"

The man shifted a little closer, lowering his voice. "Well, most of us with dead-end tunnels closed them in when I was a boy. Some of the old-timers found things. Things they don't like to talk about. Times were different during the war. The dead ends weren't marked on any blueprints. They stayed off the record. I don't know what exactly happened down there. I've seen the stains on the walls with my own eyes—not in my cellar, but around here. And there are old chains and bolts in some places."

A light jingle drew away the man's attention for a moment. An older gentleman poked his head in and yelled that he would be back in an hour. Without waiting for a reply, the door chime rang once more signalling the friendly customer had carried on his way.

The store owner's voice turned sentimental when he spoke again. "That's my neighbour. He stops by every week for a chat, but only buys something if he is expecting company. I think his daughter is visiting this week. Now then, getting back to your question. A year ago, some bigwig executive approached my neighbour.

He offered a ridiculous number of euros to buy my friend's apartment and the section of tunnel that ran underneath it. Well, let's just say my friend now has a very comfortable house with an enviable sea view. I had to put up with construction noise for nearly a month. I was worried my shop would cave in. My friend thought the man was involved in banking, but never got any straight answers, besides a hefty deposit in his bank account. Anyway, since then things have been fairly quiet. With these rock walls and floor, not much sound typically gets through."

James stood and stretched his arms, tentatively. His back was starting to loosen up. "Have you noticed much out of the ordinary happening above ground?"

The man grinned. "You mean, besides the smoke and incantations? My friend lived in a small ground-level unit that used to be a home for clergy. The new owner rented it back to the church. You'll see the cathedral takes up most of the block."

"My friend, I have taken up too much of your day already. I suggest you pile a couple of those nicely cured hams against the door downstairs. I'll be back in a couple of hours to give you a proper lock—one that even I could not get through!" James was keen to get outside and see what he was actually up against.

Back in the bright sunshine, the street appeared harmless. Shoppers perused stores on the opposite side of the street. A car reversed into a parking stall and nudged the bumper of another parked vehicle. Then the driver pulled forward as if nothing had happened, knocking the curb in the process. At least life remained normal for some.

James' neck and shoulder still felt tender. He pulled down his hat and walked close to the wall. *Blend in,* he thought. As he passed the church he was unable to see anything through its windows. A poster covered the entire stained-glass pane. It advertised an upcoming gathering, described as a meeting of all religions. *Bloody power-hungry priests, always jostling for a larger parish.* James would have normally dismissed it as religious garble, trying to pilfer believers across faiths. Today, he scowled and carried on.

Six blocks later, James grabbed a bus to an industrial part of the city. Here, hardware, plumbing, electrical and miscellaneous contractors' shops stretched for an entire city block. Most were owned and operated by local families who lived upstairs or, at the furthest, on the next street over. James entered a hardware store and picked out a locking mechanism similar to the one he had added to the fishing hut's door.

Before returning to his new friend's store, James checked in on Nadya. The device he had planted on her sent back nothing more than static. A couple of clunks broke the hum, likely from a car door closing. He was surprised she hadn't called her office after his meeting with her. It seemed she was working solo for the day. When he synced her tracer to an app on his phone, it showed she had circled the city and then stopped in a residential area. He zoomed in. She was at Myriam's home.

She must be looking for something personal. Something that would persuade Myriam to open up. Disappointed at finding nothing of interest, he swiped the app closed.

As promised, and in less than two hours, James returned to the artisanal shop. The scent of smoked ham and zingy vinegar dabbed his nostrils as soon as he opened the door. He held up the paper bag bulging with his latest locksmith kit. His new friend was busy with a customer and nodded in his direction. James carried on to the rear of the shop and made his own way down the ladder. Thankfully, the painkiller had kicked in by this point.

Once down among the hanging charcuterie, James felt back in his element. Silence resounded from the door leading to the tunnels. Thirty minutes later, a dual-cartridge deadbolt along with a new stainless-steel keyed entry knob ensured protected access. With a sigh of relief he had safeguarded the room—and more. He did not return upstairs for another hour.

Instead, he went back into the tunnel, holding his flashlight turned to its highest setting. As he approached the door where he had been knocked down, he spotted something that he hadn't noticed the first time: a wire angled near the foot of the door. It would only catch those walking close to the entrance and miss anyone merely passing by.

Usually the depths beneath a church housed crypts and burial compartments, not anything worth stealing. It would be unusual for a church to install such sly security measures, be it for sacred texts or otherwise.

He had not anticipated this tactic. Clearly, someone wanted something—or somebody—secured more than James realized. The unexpected measures gnawed at him.

A metal slot stood a metre from the ground, allowing a narrow object to be slid into the locked cavern. Not trusting who was behind the contraption but knowing he had a safe door to retreat behind only metres away, James decided to test the situation.

He pulled a Snickers bar from his bag and slid it through the opening. It made a soft plop when it hit the ground on the other side of the wall. He waited. Almost imperceptible, but it was there—a soft rustling sound. Somebody inside was moving.

32

SUNKEN SHIP

Blue and beige rosettes decorated the handmade tiles in Carlos and Myriam's foyer. Nadya searched the section that had broad grout lines for a lever or some sort of movable piece. She grudgingly realized Carlos and Myriam had stayed true to tradition and used solid cement tiles, the Maltese way. These would be hard to crack. She shuffled along the floor, feeling for depressions or any sign of an opening.

Her right knee pressed on something. A tile clicked and released a panel in the wall above it. She stared into a storage compartment about a metre deep. It explained the lost space in the unexpectedly small room. However, it did not illuminate her quest.

A vacuum, broom, mop and bucket stood against the wall, along with a number of suitcases stacked to the ceiling. Nadya pulled each suitcase down and shook it. All were empty. She slammed her fist against the wall. Another dead end.

The living room remained inaccessible and in complete disarray.

Lost in thought, she returned to her car and almost walked into a Volkswagen parked in front of the house. She veered away, and then stopped mid-step. Palm trees towered overhead. None of the neighbouring apartment block windows could see down to where she stood. The one place she had not searched was Carlos' car. It would be a long shot.

The vehicle's security system proved harder to crack than that of most cars. But every manufacturer has a weakness. With a few extra tools from her handy field kit, she was in.

A gym bag had been tossed into the back seat. Its contents were evident from the scent permeating the car's interior. Nevertheless, she unzipped the canvas bag and rummaged through dank clothing, a musty towel and an old tube of deodorant. Finding nothing of use, she moved back outside to check the trunk.

A roadside assistance kit and a box of textbooks filled a third of the available space. Nadya hauled them out and placed them on the cobbled driveway. She was more interested in the crannies under and around the spare tire. That would be the most likely place for someone to stash something of import.

Nadya lifted the carpeted base. A pile of papers bound with an elastic band lay in the middle of the spare tire. Either Carlos had tossed them in hurriedly or he had not been overly concerned with concealing the documents. Regardless, Nadya's breathing quickened. She grabbed the wad of papers and tucked them inside her bag.

Her team would be returning to search Carlos' and Peter's offices at the university in a few hours. That gave her a chance to review this new find and decide what to do next.

She drove back to her clinic and locked her office door behind her. Myriam remained in an induced coma down the hall. Nadya was convinced there was little benefit in interrogating her again. Carlos and Peter held the answers.

Thinking aloud, Nadya stared at the piles of paper on her desk. "Carlos, what did you get messed up in? Are old ruins and archeology excavations really what this is about?" She rubbed her arm where the scratch from earlier caught on her sleeve.

Before settling in for the evening, she needed to clear

her head. The private bathroom and shower connected to her office had helped her get through many long shifts and unexpected delays. Once again, the shower's warm water wiped away the commotion of the day and reset her mental state for another late night.

Once refreshed, Nadya poured herself a tea and sat back down at her desk. Funny, a thin stream of blood stained her sleeve. She did not remember cutting herself.

She began by flipping through the stack of papers from Carlos' trunk, hoping to get a clearer sense of what they contained. Various sentences, dates, locations and names had been circled. Notes were scrawled in the margins of some pages. They meant little to Nadya on first pass. Easing back in her chair, she turned back to the first page.

A couple of hours later, when her team was busy scouring Carlos' and Peter's offices, Nadya had compiled a long list of notes. She started circling common themes and recurring names. Not long after, a more discernible picture began to take shape. Between her own suspicions and the trail in these documents, she felt her old affinity for Carlos' return.

All three of the recent archeology discoveries on Malta had been detected using the latest light detection and ranging, or LiDAR, scanning technology. The same company was used to conduct the surveillance for all three digs. The outfit was only twenty months old. Nadya also recognized the name Aram Chikadze circled in a footnote on one of the pages. He owned the LiDAR company that did the testing.

Social media chatrooms held a ream of interesting dirt on the young company. As far as she could tell, at least two former employees had filed lawsuits against the firm. They alleged illegitimate practices and wrongful dismissal. Both cases were settled out of court with their records sealed.

On the surface, Chikadze appeared to be an ideal businessman for Malta to welcome into its ranks. He brought investment money and an interest in preserving public treasures in country. From Nadya's perspective, he raised more red flags than country flags.

A very recent article commented on the ancient ruts and temple remnants found at sites tied to his company. One specialist was quoted as being skeptical of the new tactics used, explaining that they did not follow the strict regimen of proven LiDAR protocol. Given that Chikadze's company was less than two years old and he had no prior history in the industry, Nadya considered him highly suspicious.

Something smelled off. Nadya didn't trust James. Nor did she trust her superiors. She felt the pile of papers in Carlos' trunk were of extreme importance, giving her all the more reason to be cautious. Although not in her nature, Nadya had learned over the years that widening her circle of trust had its advantages. One person came to mind. Sure, she had her doubts. It would be risky. The men upstairs would never approve it.

But they did not need to know. Not yet.

33

FEEDING TIME

———————

"Now that's something worth sending through that chute of yours. How about a properly sealed bottle of water too?" The voice behind the wall sounded hoarse and weak, despite its attempt at humour.

James' pulse quickened. The man was receptive. "Hey, I'm alone at the moment. Are you Carlos' friend?"

"What? Yes!" The voice moved closer to the chute. "Is Carlos okay? Can you get me out of here?" His words tumbled fast. The man sounded desperate.

"Give me a minute. They've booby-trapped this place and my shoulder is already paying the price."

James looked left and right. The tunnels remained still, eerily so, but deserted nonetheless. He took a deep breath and went to work. Ten minutes later, a thundering crash made him stand bolt upright. The same metal ball that had taken him out earlier had fallen again, missing him by mere millimetres. He remained motionless. Then a distant rustling caught his attention. "Gotta run, pal," he said.

James darted back to the cellar where the hams looked almost welcoming. The new locks clanked solidly into place.

Catching his breath, he tenderly climbed the ladder and returned to the ground-floor shop. Its commonplace orderliness felt disconcerting compared to what had gone on below. A lady wearing an arrestingly bright red hat gave him a disapproving stare. Clearly, his arrival had unbalanced the serenity of the store. James handed the new keys to the busy shop owner and slipped out the front door.

He had been underground longer than intended. The sun reflected pink against the tiled rooftops. James pulled out his phone to check on Nadya one final time. She was now at her clinic.

He listened to his tracer's recording, adjusting the filters so it only played when voices activated certain frequencies. The sound was garbled. The device must have nearly brushed off her skin. But then he heard her words. "... Carlos ... [static] ... messed up ... [muffled] ... archeology excavations ... [unintelligible muttering] ..."

Moments later the connection failed and the transmission stopped. His device had picked up nothing of interest.

In his head, James replayed the offhand comment Nadya had made to him: "By the way, I sent surveillance. All was quiet at your dear friend's hideout." Even if he found it hard to admit, her words stung. He envisioned her gloating with a member of her crew about how they had one-upped him and found Carlos. James was sure Nadya still felt bitter about the past and the project he'd screwed up. He decided he could live with that wedge between them. At least she had not planted any surprises behind his back.

With his trace on Nadya expired, James sent out a few cryptic text messages and then considered the situation with Carlos. Returning to the tunnels for a third time to attempt to extract Peter was not an option he cared to test.

As he drove across the island, ripples of yellow meringue plummeted down cliffs. James' visor blocked the lowest rays on the horizon, but the beams still reflected across the eroded limestone. They reminded him of the baker on Fourth Avenue, a few blocks from his Vancouver apartment. He used to stop on the sidewalk to watch the busy kitchen through the wide glass window facing the street. The pâtissier would hold his bowl at an angle and slowly fold in whipped egg whites until the mixture turned into a creamy lemony curd. It was a mesmerizing display and drew in practically every person who passed the storefront. The baker's mouth-watering tarte au citrons undoubtedly sold out by 3:00 p.m. every day.

James' stomach started to growl. His thoughts of his favourite tarts led him to a more pertinent plan. He had won Peter's trust with a Snickers bar. Food erased fear. It broke down barriers.

James swung his car into the parking lot of a popular bakery. He grabbed three individual servings of take-away beef Wellingtons. Carlos would surely scarf down two of them. James hoped this would encourage him to open up. If Carlos has formed any doubts during his absence, James wanted this meal to wipe them clean.

To be safe, James trickled a wee bit of diluted polonium-210 on two of the servings before wrapping them up together. The third and safe serving he kept for himself. Enough to keep Carlos nauseated and weak. Enough to keep him contained.

By the time James arrived at the fishing hut, stars were flickering through patches of clouds.

Carlos' expression flashed with tension that quickly

dissipated as James walked inside. "Am I glad to see you. I thought I might be stuck here alone for another night."

"Sorry, buddy, I got tied up. But I think you'll agree the delay was worth it. I found where they're keeping Peter." James handed Carlos the bag of food and a bottle of water, sealing his friend's confidence. "Plus, a bakery on the outskirts of the city makes these little gems on Fridays. Figured you'd like the change."

"Well, where is he? Can you get him out and bring him here?" Carlos set the dinner bag aside and stood up. James understood Carlos' desperation to talk to Peter. If he was in the same position, he would want to get a sense of who he was up against.

"I tried. Twice. They've added security since your escape. A friendly ball of steel welcomes anyone who tries to get too close." James rubbed the massive bruise between his shoulder blades.

"Are you kidding?! Did you break anything?"

James hoped this news would convince Carlos that he was not in on Peter's kidnapping. "No. A nasty bruise, but fortunately the ball was hollow." James stretched his arms, straight out in front of his chest, rounding out his back.

Carlos stayed focussed. "We may have lost our chance, especially now that they know someone has tried to get to Peter. What I don't understand is why now?"

James watched Carlos continue to ignore the bag of

food and instead steady himself against the wall. He had probably been running scenarios through his mind all day.

"Can you pull up the website for the *Times of Malta?* And look at 'Visit Malta' and 'What's On in Malta,' too. There must be something going on to trigger our abductions. Somebody wants us temporarily muted. About what? And why?" Carlos wore the same baffled look as when he was trying to read Myriam early on in their relationship.

Perfect. James booted his laptop and searched for the websites as Carlos tucked in to his first beef Wellington.

James tilted the screen, making it easy for Carlos to scan the results.

I feed you. You feed me, mate.

Two hours later, they finished sifting through everything they could find online. Carlos crumpled to the floor, exhausted and nauseous. Minutes later he fell deep asleep.

James left for the night with about six leads to follow up on.

34

CROSSROADS

———————

After three days of being out of commission, Cristabel was finally able to sit up without pain. Besides a sore walk home on Thursday, she had done nothing but lie in her bed since the incident in her mother's cellar. BBC's Saturday episode of *Click* played in the background. The gash near her waist had stopped oozing when she moved. Its skin had begun to grow back. But as the wound dried, it cracked every time she tried to reposition herself. She tried not to scratch, but the stitches itched incessantly. To deflect her irritation, she focussed on getting herself downstairs to the kitchen.

Despite Gerardo's insistence that there was nothing to worry about in her mother's documents, Cristabel could not understand why she would be involved with car imports. Someday she would ask, but they weren't on very good terms at the moment. Her mother acted angry and tense all the time. In some ways it made sense. She was a baker. Dealing with import levies and legal documents would cramp her normal routine of kneading, mixing and spending the day among mouth-watering aromas.

Cristabel's summer semester fees were coming due. She wanted to take a couple of extra classes that were not available during the regular term since they dovetailed nicely with her dissertation topic. She and her mom had agreed to split the cost evenly. Perhaps that was too much to have burdened her mother with. Cristabel had decided to step up her contribution without giving her mom a choice. This was the real reason she had asked Gerardo to meet. After two years, she was still working at an intern's rate.

Since her mother would be out for the evening, Cristabel had convinced her to leave the door unlocked with an envelope of money on the counter for the pizza delivery person to take. That way Cristabel would not have to jump up to answer the doorbell.

***

Cristabel and Gerardo had come up with the pizza delivery idea, figuring the neighbours would be less suspicious of a delivery guy than of someone climbing in the window. As he drove to Sasha's house, Gerardo wrestled with what he should do. Pressure from above was mounting. His team needed to deliver, and he hadn't reported that one team member was down. If it had been anyone else, he would not have hesitated. But any harm to Cristabel would reflect poorly on him. Plus, he was worried she might have had enough of conspiracies and training missions after getting hurt in the process. Such an incident would undoubtedly test her resolve.

If he was honest, he did not know why she would want to carry on searching for a professor after all that had transpired instead of redirecting her energy towards her degree. Even if he managed to get a raise approved, he was not sure money alone would be enough to keep her engaged if she was in this headspace.

Rain splattered across the insulated pizza bag Gerardo carried as he approached the front door of Sasha's home. Its small entranceway opened directly into the kitchen. When he entered, he noticed Cristabel's pale skin from where she sat at a table on one side of the room. Arcs of purple shadowed her eyes. He realized how little sleep she must be getting—her discomfort was probably more than she let on. He was glad he had picked up an actual pizza to complete his disguise.

Gerardo grabbed a plate from the cupboard and slapped a piece onto it before handing it to Cristabel. "You look like you could use this."

Cristabel took a big bite before asking for an update on their search.

She listened quietly as Gerardo went through almost everything the team had found. He left out the part about his run-in outside the club with her mother's friend.

The Tartu Five clearly intrigued Cristabel. "Professors give talks outside the university all the time," she said. "I attended a couple of Professor Ignacio's speeches about trends in cybercrime and what businesses can do to protect themselves.

"Ooh, would you mind grabbing me a can of iced tea? There should be some in the fridge. Help yourself if you want one." Cristabel reached for another slice of pizza.

She carried on, barely finishing her bite. "When I went, his main talk was pretty standard. Most people came for the Q&A session. That's when he went off-script and things got interesting. Any one of the Tartu Five might have been there, or others like them. Hey, they might even have asked a question that links to whatever is going on now. We should also check which other professors might have given similar presentations."

Gerardo was amazed by how quickly her mind worked.

But he also remembered who she was related to and the risk of pushing her too fast or too soon. "Listen, don't feel pressured to come back to work. I admit, I miss your tenacity out in the field, but listen to your body. It needs to heal."

"I can feel my strength returning. Maybe I'll start back on desk research before heading back into tactical." She took a deep breath. "Gerardo, I've come a long way from when you first recruited me. I feel I contribute beyond a typical intern level."

He was glad he had given this topic some thought before she brought it up. "Rising up the ranks can be a slow process. But you've built up a strong cache of results for our team and it has not gone unnoticed. Moving into the role of a private requires certain credentials, all of which you have. I'll start the process. Quite honestly, you've made my job easy, so I expect the request will be approved."

With the administrative side out of the way, Gerardo tasked Cristabel to look into other IT professors' public engagements. He warned her not to work too much at first and said he didn't want to hear anything from her for at least a few days. The team's next meeting would be held virtually.

As he walked back to his car, his phone pinged with several notifications for updates from the team. He logged in to their secure chat site to read what they had found so far.

Ana confirmed the anonymous archeological donations traced back to members of the Tartu Five. The search had taken days.

Gerardo called her to get a more complete picture.

Ana talked for most of his drive home. The men were clever and clearly not keen to leave any breadcrumbs, no matter how stale. By working backwards she had been able to navigate their maze of links.

New company lists were typically published in public registries every six months, sometimes more frequently depending on the country. Ana started with nations that had low governance enforcement and searched back eighteen months. Considering the registries were often kept manually and not integrated into any sort of online reporting, especially for those countries with lower tax revenues and resources to automate such records, Ana had to get creative in her search tactics. After hours of combing through scanned lists, newspaper announcements, and regional registries and dumping every keyword she could think of into search engines, she finally had a breakthrough.

The maiden names of the mothers of the Tartu Five men matched with the names of new shell companies set up in Libya, Somalia and Yemen. In each country, a small local law firm was used to create the new entities.

Partners in the legal firms were named as directors. Each entity was owned by a numbered company, which was in turn owned by three more numbered companies. And so on, and so on. From there, the web got even more tangled. Once Ana mapped it all out she was finally able to trace back to something interesting.

About nine layers of companies later, she uncovered the first trace of cryptocurrency that flowed through the scheme. Eventually, the payment left the cluster of related companies and landed in a handful of charities all dedicated to archeological excavations. All the charities operated digs on Malta that had taken place over the past twenty-four months.

Just as Ana wrapped up her account, Gerardo pulled into his parking stall.

As the team chipped away at the surface cover, the threads connecting the men of the Tartu Five were beginning to reveal themselves.

35

SUPPLY CHAIN

_____

The tiny bell on the bakery's door jingled once again. Over the past two hours, it had chimed nearly continually and had started to blend into the background noise. Sasha pulled twelve more loaves out of the oven without glancing up. Her customers were a friendly bunch and generally waited patiently. The queue grew by yet another person, everyone wanting a warm loaf or still-gooey tart.

It was not worth hiring help to cover the short gaps when business got this busy. Instead Sasha concentrated on one person at a time until she cleared the line. It was for this reason she was surprised to see Raymond's face when he reached her till ten minutes later. In fact, she hadn't expected to see him for another week. Admittedly, she wasn't disappointed.

The bell had not rung again since Raymond entered. He was her last customer, leaving the two alone in the bakery. Grinning, he started talking faster than his normally controlled pace. "Over the weekend, all six vehicles sold or have offers pending approval. Customers are clambering to get such a good deal. Your lower cost makes us the preferred dealership across Malta *and* Gozo."

Considering the frenzy of ups and downs over the past week, this felt like the first good news Sasha had heard for a long time. She hardly recognized the swirl of excitement churning inside her stomach. Finally, things were coming together. "Excellent news. I am so thankful we met at our little entrepreneurial group."

"We've ordered another two dozen vehicles. Are you able to pull any strings to get them shipped quicker than the standard period? Supply is low everywhere, and the manufacturer indicated we have a three-month wait." Raymond pleaded with his eyes as much as his words.

Such a request was music to Sasha's ears. "Leave it with me. I'll do what I can. In the meantime, take this ħobża home to your wife for dinner. I just pulled it from the oven a few minutes ago." She hoped he didn't hear the catch in her voice when she mentioned his wife. A knot of guilt formed in her stomach. The thought of a glass of vermouth to dull the ache drew her mind away.

With the time difference, she would have to wait until the next morning to call her uncle. In the meantime, she sent a short text to be sure he would be free to talk.

Sasha tried not to get her hopes up. If the stars aligned, she just might be able to meet Emanuel's latest deadline and keep her full take.

The evening dragged. She finally fell asleep at midnight and woke up every hour thereafter. At four in the morning, Sasha jumped out of bed and splashed cold water on her face before dialling her uncle's number. The words flew out of her mouth. She explained the dealership's request to rush the vehicles.

She also told him about her plan to order as many smartphones as he could get his hands on. Sasha asked for four hundred devices. She was certain her fisherman friend would gladly detour during his rounds to pick up the parcel as they had discussed.

Her exuberance fizzled as soon as her uncle started speaking.

"Dear, people are asking too many questions. Two of the big bosses were in my office last week grilling me about the shipment to Malta. They have been queried about the unusually low import levies from someone higher up. I said I knew nothing about that but thought the new connection offered a good opportunity to expand our distribution network. My manager has been in a sour mood ever since." Her uncle sounded defeated. Scared *and* defeated.

"Oh, that's strange." Sasha thought for a moment. "Didn't you say your department had been given a ridiculously high sales target this year? Well, what if you focus on building the company's relationship with their new customer by fast-tracking the shipment as a way to meet that target?"

She paused before continuing delicately. "I fear we will lose our phone deal if it takes three months to get the first batch." Sasha could not imagine Emanuel's response if she were to tell him it would take that long. She felt exhausted.

Her uncle raised some doubts but then decided the idea might actually work. "Let me talk to my friend on the marketing team. I remember him complaining about losing a big client a month ago. It was something about supply chain problems and a push for home-country production. If I plant the seed that another wave of lost sales with a new customer might be on the way, he just might do the heavy lifting for me."

Sasha switched off her phone. Her eyes felt gritty. All she wanted to do was roll back under the covers and hide for the day. Instead, she turned on the shower and forced herself forward. Her morning routine at the bakery could not wait.

Around mid-morning, an old contact who had arranged the lower import fees paid an unexpected visit to the L&B. On the surface, he appeared like any other customer. That was part of their agreement. He set a lumpy paper bag on the counter. "I want to return this loaf. The sultanas were burnt."

Sasha grimaced. "Why, I am so sorry! Please take a dozen of these buns for your inconvenience."

She passed him a fresh bag and tucked the package he dropped off on a shelf below the counter, knowing the exchange had nothing to do with overcooked raisins. He was sending a message. It was not one she looked forward to reading.

Sasha's mind raced into overdrive. She couldn't think straight. Over the next few hours, she overcharged two customers and forgot to include a whole wheat loaf in another person's order. Finally, by one o'clock the shop quietened. Sasha took a deep breath and poured herself a small glass of vermouth. Once again, she needed a crutch before unwrapping whatever news was to be conveyed in the bag of returned bread.

A large thumb hole dented the middle of the loaf. Sasha tore the bread in half. There, a rolled-up note stuck out of the doughy gluten. She untied its string and unravelled the paper. The writing was typed, avoiding any personal trace in case it got into the wrong hands.

FEES TO BE REDACTED. ONE SHIPMENT MORE.

Relief flooded Sasha to her core. She could handle this. One more shipment was all she needed, then she could escape the hole she had dug herself into. That would earn enough commission to supplement Cristabel's tuition fees. Fine. Then she could return to being the happy baker she used to be. A simple life, free from conspiracies and secret liaisons. She wanted it back.

36

MEDICAL KIT

W hile most agents kept a locked drawer under their desk or installed a safe in the wall hidden behind a picture, Nadya devised her own method of cover. Two medical kits sat on a side counter. She used them regularly, ensuring no one would give them a second glance if they saw her grabbing one or the other. One of them was made of carbon steel, impenetrable by X-rays or other scanning devices. It was her cloak in plain sight.

The lid of this larger kit hid a locked compartment with her most sensitive tools. Nadya had built the system herself, adding specially made components designed to safeguard controlled substances and addictive medicines. She touched a small square patch under the lid. It looked almost identical to the rest of the box but contained a fingerprint sensor that released a tiny numeric keypad, where she typed her password.

A larger compartment slid open. Nadya pulled out her second phone. It held only five code-named contact numbers. She had not taken it out for months other than to charge the battery. *Did she dare make the call?* This question had taken over her entire weekend.

Nadya tried to warm their conversation. "It's been too long, my friend. We should talk."

***

Gerardo stared at his phone. Unbelievable. He had enough on his plate without worrying about a long-lost associate's mission. "Hello."

Although not keen to switch focus, Gerardo understood the importance of placating intergovernmental relationships. Admittedly, his curiosity also compelled him to find out what she was up to. "Of course, eight at your place?"

It was more a statement than question. Gerardo and Nadya had agreed long ago that *her place* was code for an intimate little winery and restaurant near the village of Mdina. Mondays tended to be quiet, often with half of the tables still empty by eight. Back when their two countries' operations were active, Nadya and Gerardo had worked closely together. Her skills had impressed him.

***

Nadya knew it was a long shot. But while her team infiltrated the professors' offices, she aimed to close out any other possible avenues. Considering Carlos was ex-Cuban military, it was possible that Gerardo's team either knew what Carlos knew or was trying to find him and figure it out. They might both be racing towards the same goal, just from different angles.

When she arrived at the restaurant, Nadya recognized Gerardo immediately. He still wore the same tweed jacket that she had grown accustomed to years earlier. They both had a few more grey hairs, although hers were neatly camouflaged after a recent visit to the salon.

She liked working with him. They both tended to branch wide and dive deep. Even though he was a foreign ally, she could be more honest with him than with many of her own compatriots. Although, for the time being, she was not inclined to reveal her cards fully—such as the fact that she was holding Carlos' wife captive and sedated.

The waiter poured two glasses of water and set a jug of local Ġellewża red wine on their table. Nadya preferred the sparkling rosé version, but would not turn down the variety's subtle tones in any form to start off her discussion. After a few pleasantries, she flitted around the edges of her main concern. "So, have the great minds of head office kept your team snorkelling in shallow waters?"

If she was ever going to take this leap, this was her chance.

For too many years, Nadya had pushed down her frustrations and ignored the effects of her superiors' demeaning actions. She figured eventually she would prove her worth, achieve enough to be considered equal. But lately she saw the truth for what it was. No matter the hours, the results or how much she pushed herself to do the impossible—those above her would never give her a fair chance. She needed to stop fooling herself. Today she had a chance to change that trajectory.

***

Gerardo looked across the table at his old collaborator, thankful the concierge had seated them in the private outdoor lounge area at the back of the restaurant. Trees lined the grounds and offered the added benefit of blocking inquisitive eyes.

Nadya had proven to be a trusted ally in the past. Her intel had helped him secure more than one assignment. And he could certainly do with whatever information

Russia was willing to share. Pressure was mounting on his current search for Carlos, and the murky dealings of the Tartu Five grew more complex the deeper his team delved. From what he had gathered so far, the powers that be in Russia were not behind the kidnapping or whatever strange dealings were going on below the surface.

Gerardo tested the subject matter Nadya had raised. "The science is evolving. We're certain a ship went down deep off the coast. A new breed of sharks inhabits the surrounding reef and they are starting to stretch their fins."

Nadya seemed to relax with his response. She must realize that if this relationship would last, she needed to be honest with him. "I can tell you where Carlos is. But no one must know that I was your source."

Gerardo stared across the table. He wanted to believe her.

"If I reveal this information, you need to offer me something in return." Nadya paused.

Gerardo tried to keep his face composed. Without knowing more, he nodded tentatively to indicate a certain level of cooperation might be within reason.

"Bring me in with protective immunity," she said. "I will cross over with a promise of guaranteed safety and a commitment that I never have to leave Cuban soil." Nadya's expression softened.

It was an unusual request for an agent to double-cross her own country. Gerardo would need proof before committing to such protection. But it was worth pursuing. "I'll need solid intel before anyone will approve such an arrangement. If what you say gets our man back, you may be enjoying a mojito in the lounge of the Saratoga by la Navidad. Their Christmas tree is particularly spectacular." He grinned, knowing her well enough to know that she could probably pull it off. He fondly remembered spending many evenings at the Saratoga, one of Havana's most iconic hotels.

Nadya wrote GPS coordinates on a napkin and slid it across the table to Gerardo. "He's in a decrepit fishing hut and may not respond initially. Be careful. At least one other person is involved. I cannot say more than that."

Before the main course had arrived, Gerardo was already subconsciously devising rescue missions. His team would need to be careful. This intelligence could also be a trap. He had not worked with Nadya for years. Their alliance was solid, but time can have strange effects.

For the next hour, Nadya and Gerardo batted around theories. Details emerged from both sides that the other had not considered. Neither had the manpower to cover all angles. Between Gerardo's insight into the Tartu Five and Nadya's identification of both Russian and Maltese discoveries tying to early religious beliefs, the two agreed on one thing. A rogue group seemed to be planning to knock out the legs of multiple religions and, in doing so, topple the statehoods that relied on those pillars of support. Both of their countries technically kept religion separate from politics, but in practice, strings pulled in both directions.

Both Gerardo and Nadya expressed hope that their theory was wrong. However, the risk that they were right made it critical to seek the source and eradicate it.

Together they hoped to be stronger.

37

CYBERNAUT

―――――

I t hardly seemed real that Professor Ignacio's speaking event had taken place two months earlier. Cristabel had attended to help shape the concept behind her dissertation. So much had changed since then. Closing her eyes, she tried to bring its details into focus.

At that time, her research question remained scattered and ill-defined. New technology platforms and advanced capabilities in the sector were blazing forward, making it both exciting and daunting to try to examine and be a part of its evolution. If only she could find the right path, doors could open for her to meet the top minds in the business. Contacts she would never have dreamt of knowing only months earlier seemed within her grasp. Her grand plan had been brewing for weeks. Now, she must pull together its final crucial pieces.

Cristabel had stood at the entrance of the largest hall in Malta's Mediterranean Conference Centre. Crystal chandeliers lit up the velvet chairs so they glistened. Only a half a dozen seats were occupied when she initially arrived, early as planned. Cristabel took a seat in the second row. She watched as the hall filled with men and women dressed in formal suits. Then she listened—a far more interesting part to her plan.

A cluster of women behind her discussed their start-up business. One lady expressed strong views that the only risk to their company sat squarely in the hands of the chief financial officer. She held responsibility for payments, and therein lay all the risk.

Another woman, who Cristabel figured must be the targeted finance executive, explained that corporate risk ran much broader than mere cash outlays. Customer data, email messages and operational quality control all posed risks. The company's confidential plans, supply chain linkages, data protection and even internal procedures aimed at reducing the chance of error all played a role in managing risk. As owners they had to be accountable for all of these hazards. She went further by saying that, frankly, their entire business advantage was at stake if key operational processes were not safeguarded.

Two men sat in front of Cristabel, huddled together. Their whispers were not as quiet as they must have assumed, for Cristabel caught virtually every word. They planned to create an incubator targeting existing businesses that needed help adapting to the threat of cybercrime. Their concern lay in how to keep each business's trade secrets strictly confidential while fostering an environment of idea sharing and cross-pollinating of opportunities.

Listening to this array of concerns fed into Cristabel's own focus for the evening. She wanted to understand the internal holes local companies were trying to plug. Artificial intelligence–driven cybersecurity was paving the way for the future of data security, and Cristabel planned to fit her dissertation squarely on that road.

Her theme revolved around adaptive intelligence. It blocked common threats across businesses while using the data from those threats to update and improve firewalls from unwanted infiltration. Her idea was currently stuck on identifying a unified code sequence flexible enough to operate in a variety of companies' systems while also protecting them from cross-contamination. Artificial intelligence played a strong role in security these days.

Tonight, she hoped to hear owners' perspectives. These were the same decision-makers who ultimately had to buy in to her concept—assuming her dissertation project came together as she intended.

The talk itself proceeded like a university lecture. Professor Ignacio spoke for forty minutes about fairly standard measures of protection. Then he opened the floor to questions. Cristabel sat up in her chair at this point and pressed the record button on her phone.

That's it. Cristabel's mind came rushing back to the present. Her dissertation held the key. She had almost forgotten about it during the past few weeks. The recording from that evening was saved on her laptop, along with all her other files supporting her work. With a few clicks, she located the file and clicked Play.

The first few questions offered little insight. Then one caught her attention. Someone must have handed the man a microphone because a shrill squeal pierced the recording. Cristabel recoiled. Then a man's voice boomed.

"How can business people based here in Malta ensure that we all keep a certain level of vigilance? We do business with each other all the time. If one falls, the rest of us might be exposed to the same attackers. By sharing files and opening communications with each another, are we endangering our neighbours? We are a small community and can't afford huge IT teams to monitor activities. What realistic solution is available to us?"

There was a murmur of consensus from the crowd. This man had hit a nerve.

His problem was exactly what Cristabel's dissertation proposed to solve. She remembered feeling excited that her idea had traction. It fed a real business need.

By exposing a vulnerability faced by so many businesses, this man's question broadened the discussion. Hackers could be motivated to use their power in non-financial ways—political lobbying or preferential contract terms. The web of cybercrime stretched across multiple dimensions.

The idea made Cristabel wonder if anyone had demanded a ransom for the professor. The university had not made a big deal about cancelling his classes, at least not publicly. For all she knew, negotiations were taking place in the background. The police might not even be involved. She would ask Gerardo about it. Her priority remained centred on public speaking events, most of which she had yet to track down.

Her stomach started to ache. Cristabel drank a glass of water and tried to slow her breathing. She did not want to get distracted. The cramp eased. She rubbed her eyes and returned to her search.

Most conference centre and campus theatre websites only displayed future events. It reminded her of how lucky she was to have the additional access provided by government intelligence portals. Most IT professionals with far more prestigious careers than hers did not have the level of access she held, despite her being a student. Soon, Cristabel had uncovered similarly themed speaking events given by another professor.

That professor, Peter Bustillo, had started giving cybersecurity talks almost a year earlier. She recognized his name from her department and the archeology club she had recently joined. Professor Ignacio gave his first address about four months later. Transcripts were not available for every talk. A couple of event organizers saved their recordings and used catchy sound bites to advertise upcoming functions. Cristabel spent two full days sifting through clips and details of whatever she could locate. By the end, she had compiled a dismal list of notes that led practically nowhere.

Most attendees asked typical questions at the end of the talks. She circled only one question from her list. A man with an eastern European accent—either Estonian or Latvian, Cristabel wasn't certain—asked if there was a risk for religious leaders to fall victim to cybercrime. He went on to explain his concern: "Their main assets are temples and donation accounts. Property titles and bank accounts are all managed electronically nowadays, so aren't they subject to the same cyber risk as regular companies, but also at an ideological level? Could these heads of faith be persuaded to sway their congregation to follow one thing or the other if their assets were seized and used as blackmail?"

The audience buzzed at Professor Ignacio's stark response. "Well, yes, the concept could, in theory, be applied as you suggest. However, I must admit I have not heard of it occurring anywhere. At least not yet."

This is what had been niggling at Cristabel's mind when she last met with the team. It was that advertisement she had seen in the paper the morning after she scoured the hospital looking for Myriam. A religious radical claimed to have found a revelation that would change every faith and bring people closer to the truth.

At the time, she had discounted the claim as ridiculous. Then she remembered hearing the fanatic speak on mainstream radio, calling people to attend his upcoming "ceremony." He promised proof that the world's religions were more similar than anyone had ever believed. A bold claim for a Saturday night on a small Mediterranean island.

The Big Reveal, as he called it, was scheduled for this weekend—May 14. It would be held at the Mediterranean Conference Centre. People could also sign up for smaller breakout discussion sessions over the coming weeks. They would be held at a cathedral in downtown Valletta. Cristabel found it odd that the church would condone such conversations inside its own walls. The background of this particular church raised her suspicions even more.

During the same period when historical buildings were being bought by the Tartu Five, this church effectively sold its property. Its bishop had entered into a fifty-year leaseback arrangement shortly after accepting a substantial donation from an anonymous donor. Churches rarely gave up their bricks and mortar.

Cristabel flicked Ana a message asking if she could dig up the source of the donation. Then she sent Saul a note to see if he had seen similar agreements for other cathedrals, citadels or mosques.

Cristabel doubted anyone's god ever intended them to fall victim to a misguided faith tainted by greed and ambitions for control. Sadly, money, power and religion had a habit of joining forces for all the wrong reasons.

38

EXTRACTION

───────

Saul cut the engine before they rounded the peninsula. He and Celia lugged out the oars from under the gunwale. They weren't the light fibreglass type they were used to from their rowing teams but traditional oak paddles. Heavy, but surprisingly manageable. Except for the sound of the oars dipping into water, the boat cut around the bend and slipped towards the bay in virtual silence.

Gerardo grabbed the binoculars hanging around his neck and scanned the inlet for activity. Dark shadows indicated a number of structures scattered along the shoreline. He adjusted his line of sight to zero in on the coordinates Nadya had given him. Faint lights flickered on and off inside an otherwise black box. It was the only hut on the beach showing even a speck of light.

Gerardo held up his arm. Saul and Celia slowly backpaddled to hold the boat steady.

An occasional seagull cawed. A distant engine revved as a car curved around an unseen road. Saul passed around a Thermos of tea. Ana took a tablet of anti-nausea medication after five minutes of bobbing in the sea. Forty-five minutes later, she popped a second pill.

After what seemed like hours, the light inside the hut flicked off. Nothing appeared to move for a few minutes. Then a grinding noise floated across the water. It sounded like someone was filing their nails really loudly with an emery board. Gerardo panned the beach with his binoculars.

About fifty metres behind the fisherman's hut, a mass reversed out of a dark shed and then headed away from the harbour. What they had heard were tires rolling over hard-packed sand. Its sound carried surprisingly well across the water. The lights were not turned on until the car reached the main highway.

The window of opportunity had just swung wide open for Gerardo's team.

As if on cue, Saul and Celia started rowing to shore.

They whispered their count to keep their strokes in sync and power at maximum. The bow sliced through the inlet's low ripples and skidded up onto the sandy bank. After everyone was out of the boat, Celia dragged it a little farther away from the water's edge. She then stayed with the boat, ready to propel it back out once they had their man.

Saul and Ana spread out from Gerardo. The three of them made their way towards the hut in a boomerang configuration, checking their surroundings as they went. It did not appear that any of the other buildings had been used for ages. Torn nets, dry seaweed and broken boards lay where hardworking men used to come and go. After confirming that the area was clear of any nighttime activity or prowlers, the three regrouped outside of the hut.

Gerardo shifted into stage two of his plan: contact.

"Amigo, Capitán Ignacio. Your country is here to take you home." Although Gerardo was not clear on the details of Carlos' assignment in Malta, he knew what few people knew. Carlos held the rank of capitán.

There was no response. He hoped James had not taken Carlos with him in the car. Alternatively, Nadya could be setting him up. He motioned for Saul and Ana to keep watch outside while he went in.

First, Gerardo circled the building, checking for vulnerabilities and cameras. Despite the decrepit condition of the door, its lock was new. These latest models were virtually unpickable. On his second round, he stopped by the window. Clouds of residue created a patchy and fuzzy view of the hut's interior. He decided to remove the entire window with its frame. But before doing so he made one more attempt to call Carlos. This time louder.

***

"Whhhaat? Who's there?" Carlos groaned groggily and rolled over onto his back. He didn't understand why he still felt so awful nearly a week after escaping the dungeon.

Then he realized with surprise that someone was using his Cuban title. He hadn't actually expected anyone to come looking for him. Not now. Not after everything else that had happened.

"Carlos, this is Gerardo from the Cuban military. Can you open the door?"

"No. Try the window. I saw a crack along its seal." The thorough check Carlos had done on his first day was paying off. He pulled the descaler from his pocket and gripped its handle tightly, just in case. If this person was not who they said, he would be ready with whatever tool he had available.

***

Gerardo pulled out a knife and a few other instruments from his backpack and set to work. The wood was soft, making the job easier than expected. Just before he reached the halfway point around the window, his knife scraped metal. It wouldn't budge any further.

"The frame's been reinforced. Stand back, Carlos. There might be some fumes or wood chips that get inside." Gerardo had a few backup tricks of his own.

Before proceeding, he peered through the crack that had formed around the base of the window. Carlos had crawled over to the back wall. He was reaching for a table, presumably to drag it closer and then crouch behind it.

Hydrochloric acid turns iron into a salty ash. Ever since Gerardo learned this back in his training days, he had kept a vial in his pack—and a pair of silicone gloves. He had silently thanked his course leader on numerous occasions since that lesson. Figuring the horizontal metal bar ran through both sides of the window frame, Gerardo used a third of the liquid on the side he had exposed. While it reacted, he continued cutting around the top, down to the opposite side and then applied the same amount of liquid to its iron rod.

He kept the final third just in case another surprise cropped up. With essentially no noise and only mild fumes, the narrow section of pipe disintegrated. His knife sliced through it and carried on through the remaining soft wood, up and around the window frame. For a brief second, he admired his work. It created a big enough opening to get Carlos out and through without the risk of cutting him from the inevitable shards of glass that would come from merely breaking the window. Besides, it might also buy his team some valuable time if the place looked untouched from the outside to whomever came back and expected Carlos to be waiting inside.

Once in, Gerardo turned on his headlamp. He scanned the cabin. Wood clattered against wood in the back corner. Gerardo spotted the table being shoved across the floor.

First a hand and then a head popped up from behind the table. "Is it safe to come out?" Carlos squinted at Gerardo's light, keeping one hand behind his back.

Gerardo switched his headlamp to its red-light setting, making it less blinding. Relieved to finally see Carlos fully and in person but concerned at the lethargic state he seemed to be in, he moved swiftly. "Let's get you out of this dump and into a proper safe house." Gerardo showed Carlos his military ID card and a letter from the head office. The message confirmed the mission to extract Carlos and bring him home unharmed.

"A friend brought me here." Carlos hesitated and brought his other hand out front, but not before slipping it rather slowly past his breast pocket. "But I would rather go home now."

It took longer to get Carlos out through the window than it had taken Gerardo to remove the window and haul himself in. Carlos had surprisingly little strength. Saul helped from the outside while Gerardo propped him up inside. Thankfully, Carlos' woollen hat protected his head from any rough edges. Gerardo had seen photos of Carlos in this same hat. He figured it suited him more in real life.

Once out, Gerardo sealed the window frame back in place. Clear silicone and a smear of putty made the cut marks nearly indistinguishable from the surrounding cracks.

Gerardo and Saul each took an arm and helped Carlos walk towards the boat. Ana followed behind and brushed away their footprints in the sand. When they were about five metres from the water, Gerardo whistled. A barn owl screamed back. Everyone in the group shuddered, unable to ignore the tension circling around them.

Reeds crackled just ahead. Branches crunched as Celia uncovered the boat from the layer of camouflage she had piled on top.

The fresh air helped to revive Carlos. By the time he could touch the edge of the boat, he was able to lift his legs and get in on his own. After they'd cleared the shallow waters, Carlos leaned over to Gerardo. "The other night I heard someone outside the hut. That wasn't your team doing reconnaissance, was it?"

Gerardo thought about the question. It made sense that Nadya's team had been in the area, although he would have expected them to keep more of a low profile. "Not us. It might have been a helpful ally. But if not, it's a good thing we got you out of there when we did." Gerardo did not like the prospective of another player trailing Carlos.

During the ride back, Gerardo briefed Carlos on the situation.

***

While he listened intently, Carlos slipped one hand under the opposite sleeve of his jacket. His fingernails had grown over the past week, but he needed the needle-nose clippers to dig deeper. The pain didn't bother him. It needed to be done. Minutes later, he wound the bloody metal blob up with the wire, tackle and descaler he had nabbed from the fisherman's hut. As they passed close by a boat anchored offshore, he lobbed the bundle over the side like a small ball of garbage. There was no way he wanted James to track him a second time.

About an hour later, they arrived at a little-used fishing port. It was early enough to beat the fishermen who started their day there and, more importantly, well before the owner of the boat they had borrowed would notice it missing. Saul and Celia tied it up using the same knots that had originally held it fast to the dock.

Carlos nodded, taking it all in. "I have a lot to tell you."

39

SABOTEUR

GNARLY DIVE SITE. THX FOR RECOMMENDATION.

Nadya stared at the words that had popped onto the screen of her secure mobile phone. They meant Gerardo's extraction was a success. Would it be enough to solidify her trustworthiness for the Cuban army? She hoped so. She was tired of reporting back to demeaning superiors and continually having to re-prove her worth in their male-dominated ranks. Cuba's mindset was certainly not perfect, but at least women had a strong voice up the chain of command. She wanted to be respected for her work, and lately she had realized the never-ending blockages put in her way would not go away.

She and Gerardo had agreed that her extrication by the Cuban military, if it were approved, should not happen straight away. It would raise too many questions and possibly tie her back to Carlos' extraction. It had to appear as if she were supporting James, even if she did not trust that he was fully supporting the Russian cause. She also fully expected he would be furious when he realized Carlos had slipped through his fingers.

At the moment, she had more pressing concerns. Her team had finished their sweep of Carlos' and Peter's offices in the wee hours of Saturday morning. After mandating Dominik and Dmitri to take a couple of days off to decompress, she was eager to hear their front-line perspective. They had sent her a detailed report of what they had found, but there were gaps she wanted to talk through in person. By Tuesday morning, they were both headed to her office for a debriefing.

Dominik, who had searched Carlos' office, started the discussion. Carlos' office phone had received only three voicemails since he'd disappeared: two from a student named Cristabel, who wanted his advice on her dissertation, and a message from the dean asking him to call immediately. Carlos apparently kept no handwritten notes. Even his lecture notes were typed and filed according to class and year.

Yet he had found one thing he deemed photo worthy—the only thing at odds with the rest of Carlos' space. While everything else in his office was neatly stacked or filed based on lecture or research topic, one pile of brochures lay in disarray. The pamphlets related to off-campus speaking events from the past year and had been tossed haphazardly on the back of a cabinet shelf. Dominik knew to concentrate on the overly normal, or in this case the overly abnormal.

Dmitri's search proved significantly more fruitful. He found USB drives and files hidden in creative places all over Peter's office. A modified metal detector helped him locate crystal oscillators, a key component in USB drives and watches. He found them planted in the most obscure locations. Dmitri dumped eight USB sticks onto Nadya's desk; one had been embedded inside a piece of cutlery and another in the handle of an umbrella.

Like Carlos, Peter had a stack of pamphlets from conferences he had spoken at. His were lying on the top of the filing cabinet. Still, Peter's notes proved more interesting. Using carbon flecks, Dmitri was able to recover the last sentences of handwriting in Peter's notebook. He must have been pretty passionate when he wrote it, because the pen went through three pages and left a remarkably clear imprint. Dmitri slid the paper he had recovered across the desk.

Nadya read Peter's bold scrawl: *Modification residual and cherry-picked metrics—Religious unification event—Excogitatoris Consulting—Global election schedule?*

Nadya's hands shook as she placed the note back on the desk. Peter's suspicions mirrored her own. Russia's next election was scheduled for eight months from now. Iran's president had committed to hold an election before year-end. The American election stood a few years off; however, polarized dissent and radical groups were already eroding public trust in the country's most fundamental systems. That blazing fire didn't need more kindling. She feared another fracture in the thin bands of order could collapse the nation.

Whoever devised this scheme had given themselves enough time to sow seeds of discontent across both the religious and political worlds. If leaders lost the trusting ears of their followers, their persuasive capital would disintegrate. The power of persuasion wasn't called that for nothing.

Nadya shared her concerns with Dominik and Dmitri. They spent the rest of the morning trying to punch holes in her theory and develop alternatives. By midday, Nadya directed the men to go home and get some rest. It would be another full week.

Nadya scanned the various speaking events linked to

the professors. They generally related to technology breakthroughs and data security, whether about trends in cybercrime or misinformation tactics. These were normal themes for IT professors. Her thoughts carried her back to Peter's message. Religious unification event. Singular. Event. The prospect haunted her.

History had proven that once a malicious message was disseminated to the public, it was very difficult to rein it in. She started searching upcoming concerts, religious gatherings, far-right and far-left chat rooms, and anything else she could think of. A mess of notices filled her search screen, but nothing jumped out as relevant. They all appeared either too small or too self-absorbed to be the type of event that fit. It needed to be about a cause. It needed to have a hook that attracted people. Folks already inclined towards conjecture and contradiction.

She sank into her chair and closed her eyes. A knock at the door broke her thoughts. "Yes?"

Eva opened the door and dropped the day's newspaper on top of a pile on a bookcase by the door of at least a dozen other papers Nadya had meant to look at. "Take a break, Nadya, you look exhausted." She smiled and closed the door quietly behind her.

Of course, it's right there in front of me. Nadya dashed over to the stack and started flipping through it. A grandmaster would want to appeal to a wide audience.

They wouldn't merely call on people already listening to them. They would want to build an audience. To tear apathy from the masses.

She stopped. The bottom third of the front page of a paper from a week ago stared back at her.

The advert promised groundbreaking evidence that would change the basis of every major religion. Nadya leapt to her computer and typed in the website address given in the advertisement. It opened with an image of gridlines flowing outwards from a central point like the spokes of a bicycle wheel. Then a fireball took over its hub. Flames moved across the screen, drawing the eye in an uncontrollable frenzy. They leapt in multiple directions, seething and snapping towards the outer edges of the screen.

Nadya's pulse quickened just watching the home page. Whoever had created this design understood how to engage viewers. They also knew how to exploit emotions and lead people down a path they may or may not want to follow.

A message popped up on her screen: *Event delayed. More evidence uncovered that you must see! Purchase your ticket here.*

The revised date fell in four days' time. Nadya still had a chance to catch—or stop—the big show. Oddly, the pop-up was dated less than a week ago, meaning whatever had caused the delay had occurred quite recently. She would have thought Carlos' escape, with James' help—would have the opposite effect. Moving up the date would have nipped any chance for Carlos to speak up. But delaying it didn't make sense. Something else must have either scared the organizer enough to hesitate or prompted them to regroup so they could ramp up more. Neither option comforted Nadya.

Nadya left the office to mull things over. Walking always helped her to separate distractions from critical points. She would have preferred to follow one of the rarely used paths overlooking the ocean, but temperatures were already scorching this May. The air-conditioned gym with its treadmill won out.

By the next morning when she returned to her office in the temporary clinic, Nadya had accepted the unavoidable next step she must take. She reached for her phone.

Before she picked it up, it vibrated and interrupted her train of thought. "Hello?"

"You conniving bitch, what have you done? Where did you take Carlos?" James' voice shook through the phone.

Nadya recognized his self-serving impulsive trait shining through as strong as ever. "What do you mean, he's gone? You said the hut was secure." Nadya played up her innocence with an offensive return serve.

"Your team were the only ones who knew he was there.

I saw tire tracks, Nadya." James blatantly charged his fellow agent with sabotage.

In Nadya's mind, his bold antics were yet another example of the low-level disdain her colleagues felt towards women in general. "My dear James, when my guys surveilled your little hut, they went by boat. They left no tracks."

She hoped her words slammed into James as if she had physically struck him.

Nadya closed her eyes as a dial tone buzzed back in her ear. He did not even have the backbone to finish their conversation. Just like his younger self, he could not face his own misjudgement.

What interested her more, however, was his statement that another player had entered the scene. She knew Gerardo would not have been so careless as to leave tread marks. Had the master planner made an appearance to reclaim his lost victim?

40

SAFE HOUSE

———

The fourth-floor view caught every cruise ship entering and leaving Valletta's waterfront. No neighbours, traffic cameras or other prying eyes could see what went on inside the apartment. A well-stocked kitchen, a laptop connected to a secure network, and a closet full of clothing—correctly sized—assured Gerardo that this safe house lived up to its hushed reputation.

Carlos entered the kitchen, straightening his freshly washed barretina. He appeared revived after taking a shower and pulling on a fresh short-sleeved shirt and cotton pants. The scent of coffee and chatter must have drawn him in.

Sometime through the night or early morning, everyone from the boat had taken turns to clean up in the apartment's second bathroom. They looked full of energy as they stood around hashing out the events from the night before.

Carlos grabbed a banana and caught Gerardo's eye. The team needed direction. Gerardo stepped up.

Going forward, all communications would pass through an encrypted internal system that was invisible to all except a niche group within the Cuban military. In-person visits increased the chance of being discovered and were highly restricted. No one wanted to jeopardize control over an already precarious situation.

Everyone stood eager to move forward while Carlos sat down on the nearest chair.

Before the team cleared out, one question hung in the air. Carlos' lethargy and nausea should not have dragged on for so long. His unexplained symptoms alarmed Gerardo. Even Celia and Saul had pulled Gerardo aside to voice their concerns. Like many safe houses, the apartment was fitted with an array of hospital-grade equipment. The team conducted a number of tests. Their results caught everyone off guard—they pointed to only one country.

Gerardo could not help but wonder if this might have

been one of the reasons Nadya was so keen for him to extract Carlos. He knew in the past she had voiced reservations about the Russian intelligence agency's propensity to use the radioactive chemical as a poison. They did not tend to welcome criticism, light or otherwise, so it might also explain her motivation to shelter under Cuba's protective wing.

"We found traces of polonium-210 in your urine," Gerardo told Carlos. "It's an extremely low level, but it likely explains the nausea and dizziness you have experienced lately. Do you remember when exactly these symptoms started?"

Carlos' mouth gaped. "Radiation poisoning? Those bastards! I first felt ill after eating food they shoved into my prison cell, not long before James arrived and got me out. Now every time I eat something a wave of nausea takes over."

Ana dissolved a sachet of electrolytes into a glass of water and passed it to Carlos. "Try drinking this with a slice of buttered bread. Mild foods should be easier on your stomach."

They decided to stay in the apartment to monitor Carlos for the next twenty-four hours. Spare laptops and phones stored in the unit would allow the team to push forward. Gerardo pulled in Cristabel to work remotely. When he told her who was sitting beside him, she nearly choked on a mouthful of water.

"I am so relieved. And I have so many questions." Cristabel started talking faster than the video technology could handle. Her words cut in and out when she updated the team on her latest suspicions.

Celia ramped up the bandwidth.

Carlos suggested they check whether the consulting company he had noticed at the archeology sites was linked to any of the data they had found to date. Ana ran Excogitatoris Consulting through her program, looking for hits. Celia searched the registries of all churches on Malta for significant donations. Saul began downloading recent lease agreements taken out with temples of faith. After a great deal of discussion, it was decided not to send a blanket message to attendees that the event had been cancelled. That would give the conspirators advance warning. Instead, Cristabel signed up some of the team members using false names to attend the Big Reveal and several of its breakout sessions.

In the meantime, Gerardo and Carlos strategized about how to extract Myriam, find Peter and infiltrate the upcoming grand event.

Carlos admitted he had an uneasy feeling about his friend James, despite having been rescued by him. "I know it doesn't make sense, but I feel more relieved about being pulled out of that hut and being here with you now than I did after James rescued me from the pit. Something was wrong with him. He tried to hide it from me but his eyes gave it away. His answers were evasive, just partial responses with no clear plan."

Colour drained from Ana's face. She caught Gerardo's eye, and he moved over to her side of the room. "What's up?"

"My last approval came in this morning to access the investing regulator database I had wanted to check." She swivelled her screen so he could read the condensed background report she had pulled together on Carlos' friend James:

> The "James" who went to school with Carlos and Myriam and who now lives in Vancouver has ties to Russian intelligence. His real name is Yakov. Funding for his company came from private investors. On the surface, they appeared to be concerned citizens looking to propel a well-intentioned technology start-up forward. Financial benefits sealed the investment case. Deeper, the men also had ties to military contracts and attended Komsomol together, Russia's Communist youth league. They went through the program at the same time as Yakov.

> Even more concerning, three years ago the military cancelled all contracts with these men and added their names to a blacklist. Cuba was given a copy of the rebel list. The Russian government no longer wanted to deal with these people, nor

did they want any of their allies doing business with them either. Typical for such denunciations, the explanation was kept brief. The read-through of two poignant words—*unreliable contact*—really meant "individual gone rogue."

Ana then switched to another page of the document. These men had stayed active. At least fifty companies tied back to them. Ana moved her cursor over one name about a third of the way down the list: Excogitatoris Consulting.

The same men who had been declared enemies of the Russian state were funding James' company. And James was supposed to be an undercover agent for Russia.

On the team's portal, Ana opened a folder of work Saul had been investigating.

It turned out Excogitatoris Consulting had also signed contracts with multiple churches across Malta, all for miscellaneous construction work. In the past twelve months, these churches received substantial donations from entities that traced back to the Tartu Five.

Not so coincidentally, it was at one of these churches that the Big Reveal's breakout groups were scheduled to be held.

When they updated Carlos and the rest of the team, another missing piece fell into place. "The so-called construction work done by Excogitatoris Consulting was likely carried out underneath the church," Carlos told them. "I bet they turned the old tunnels into the dungeon where they kept me. They removed door handles from the inside and closed off access."

Then his face turned ashen. "That means James, or Yakov, is involved in this scheme. He intentionally kept me ill and weak. Damn, he knew where Myriam was being held. I bet he never planned on actually rescuing Peter. He just wanted information."

Gerardo quietly put together another connection. Nadya also mistrusted James.

41

RELEASED

———

"She is of no use to us. Let me release her." Nadya explained her plan to her superior for a third time. She kept it succinct. Myriam would gain consciousness sitting at a park table near her home. Short-term memory was malleable. Nadya understood how to modify and erase those recollections that led back to her. Though her true intention to separate herself from their experiment remained hidden, her outward story focussed on what little she had gained from Myriam. It was time to end the operation.

Her boss felt she should try to push once more. If that failed, release was not the end game he envisioned.

She tried another tactic. "If I do that, my fate is in jeopardy. She is an ally. We cannot do this to each other, regardless of past decisions. There will be consequences. My plan allows us to duck out from this problem without anyone ever knowing we were involved." She emphasized *we*, not wanting to highlight that it was her own face Myriam would recognize.

"Stop antagonizing me. Make this disappear completely, no placid waking up on some park bench. Do what we trained you to do." He spat the last words into the phone, disconnecting before Nadya could utter a response.

She contemplated calling Gerardo once more. She could run to the Cuban government's protection immediately, hand over a second agent and then defect. The risk would be immense. With what she had already done, she still had an out. *Let some time pass.* Maybe she would cross over to Cuba, maybe not. That way, there would be no clear link between her and the events about to unfold. Plus, she could carry on knowing she had helped a friend. *Carlos is a good man.*

But if she handed Myriam over to Cuba, there would be no hiding. No matter what precautions she took, Mama Russia would eventually track her down. This reality crumpled all hope, smashing the bewitching temptation she had shaped so dearly over the past few days. Her life would not change. Sadly, she had made her choice years ago.

With this realization, Nadya picked up her medical kit. Her footsteps clipped against the tile like the metronome that had impelled her as a child to practice piano for one more painful hour when all she wanted to do was run outside and play. If only she had known how light a sentence that charge was in comparison to what she would face as an adult.

She opened the door. A smooth cotton sheet and plump white pillow made the scene look almost pleasant. The sheet obscured the woman's face, but its movement confirmed that she was breathing. Gently. Evenly. Underneath, an oxygen mask pumped filtered air mixed with a sedative. The other monitors had already been unplugged. Nadya would miss Eva's efficiency after this mission ended.

Nadya knew how much to increase the dose to make the shift painless. She knew what to add to the solution to ensure the result was permanent. No further inquisition would be held under her watch, no matter what her boss wanted.

She never wanted to look into those eyes again. Even sedated, they spoke too many words and conveyed too much lost emotion. She left the sheet where it lay.

When she left the room this time, she had no need to

lock the door. Her trusted Dmitri would handle the rest. Deep oceans and weighted cargo made for the cleanest disposal.

Nadya made one more call. It was the first time that she had spoken to her boss twice in one day. "Bring me back. I'm done."

***

After the team cleared out, Dmitri made a final sweep of the floor. He did this job for every assignment, checking desk drawers and behind doors to be sure they had removed all traces of their operation.

Since rifling through the professors' offices, he had developed his own theory. He knew times had changed since he'd gone to school, but these instructors seemed to be involved in way more than just teaching. It felt off. And packing up and leaving today left the job half done. He expected to hear about it at some point. Some other division would likely be assigned to carry out the final steps.

Dmitri was certain the professors would not live to see their students graduate. People went missing for a reason. In his mind, it meant one of two things: either they were involved with something shady or they had made friends with the wrong folks. Dmitri bet on the former, considering the hidden files and articles the professors gravitated towards. He suspected the two men were developing some high-tech infiltration system they planned to sell to the highest bidder. Their interest in and ability to tap into secure data sites around the world and then filter and connect whatever they found only proved his point. Confidential communications would garner a very high price from those seeking inside knowledge of foreign powers' strategies.

Frankly, Dmitri wished he was on the team tasked with ending their charade. Instead, he got stuck disposing of a lifeless body.

Nadya had not told him directly, but he was pretty certain she had not extracted any more information from the professor's wife. When he entered the last room of their rented third-floor clinic, Dmitri checked the cabinet shelves to be sure they were empty. The rental company would pick up the medical equipment sometime over the following week, so he wrapped their power cords and left them where they sat. He glanced at the closet, knowing no one had used it. The orange *Sanitized* sticker that had been there when the team first moved in hung limply on the edge of the door.

Turning away, he grabbed the handle of an extra-large suitcase he had left in the corner over two weeks earlier. Luggage had become his signature tool. Dmitri knelt down, unzipped the flap and unclipped the interior straps. They would come in handy. He cleared his mind, intent on making no mistakes. The bedsheet would only take up space, so he pulled it and the blanket aside. He gaped at the bed. Except for a pile of pillows and the strewn bedding. "Damn. She is such a control freak."

Dmitri kicked the bed. It rolled half a metre before its wheels rotated inwards and stopped. He couldn't believe Nadya had done this again, not trusting anyone but herself to do something important. She had seemed to be learning how to lead a team but then, just the other day, she took off by herself without talking to anyone for over twenty-four hours.

Frustrated, Dmitri zipped the suitcase closed and decided to use it to pack his own gear before heading to the airport.

***

At two in the morning, five passengers boarded a jet parked on a private airstrip on the west side of the island. Nadya selected a seat at the opposite end of the cabin to the other doctor. She considered his involvement an imposition on her team. He was one of her supervisor's minions who occasionally dropped in unannounced. Although a shrewd medical specialist, his ethical line in the sand had blown away years ago. He proved more pawn than practitioner. Dmitri and Dominik sat in the centre of the plane, arguing intensely over which pursuit took more physical strength: climbing K2 or skiing to the South Pole. They did not even pause as she walked past.

Eva, Nadya's favourite nurse, sat across from her and glanced over with a brief look of knowing relief. This was her final mission. For the past week, all she had spoken of was how she couldn't wait to head to her small house in the mountains after this assignment wrapped up. Her retirement had been agreed to long before the project began.

A steward passed around full glasses of vodka. Nadya tipped hers back. It was the first of many. No matter how much she tried to mute the screenplay of her own reality, scenes kept flashing through her mind. Only hours later did darkness creep in.

42

DISARRAY

————

If it had been possible to turn the room into more of a wreck, he would have done it. James ripped doors off cupboards and yanked up floorboards. The fisherman's hut looked even more dejected and rundown than when he had first found it. Only now, it offered him nothing.

He could not figure out how Carlos had escaped. The lock on the door remained untouched.

Outside, James peered at the tire tracks that approached the hut. At first he thought they were fresh since he hadn't noticed them before. But looking closer, he saw that tiny plants had sprung up through the ridges. Sand had blown into the grooves. Last night had been calm. Whoever came must have been here at least a day ago.

Furious, James cleared out all of his things from the hut. He removed the lock, replacing the door to its previous state. If Nadya was not involved, there was someone else he needed to see. This time, he would not call ahead.

James headed towards the shed at the far end of the beach. He revved his car's engine before slamming it into gear, kicking up sand as he left the inlet. He didn't care what tracks he left.

He drove towards Valletta and parked near a small port at the edge of the city centre. From there, he walked the remaining distance.

The more he thought about the situation, the angrier he became. Fresh air did not help clear his head.

He stormed through the doors of the bank.

A security guard stepped forward. "Excuse me, sir. May I help you?"

"Yes. Tell Mr. Ast that he has a visitor." James enunciated each word with precision, trying to contain the turmoil roiling beneath the surface.

The guard pressed him. "Mr. Ast is a very busy man and does not take walk-in appointments."

James looked the man in the eyes. "Tell Mr. Ast that

Mr. Glacier is in his lobby." After he'd launched his business operations in Canada's north, he'd been given that nickname as the investor group's gateway to the Arctic.

"Certainly, sir." The guard nodded at James to take a seat. Then he walked to his post and picked up the phone.

James avoided opening his phone. Instead he stared at the old-fashioned clock hanging above the tellers. Its second hand seemed to click forward in slow motion.

"Please follow me." The guard led James to the elevator bank and escorted him to the fourth floor. The executives and investment advisors kept their offices on this top level. A receptionist greeted the guard and told him to take James to the second meeting room.

Once James was alone, Mr. Ast entered the room. "I am surprised to see *you* here. We were not to meet again until next week. Although, I must say, your recent visit to my asset's headquarters gave me a clue you were in town. No worries, though. I simply intensified his treatment. It's a wonder what twenty-four-hour therapy can achieve."

This news only fuelled James' already sour mood. "You would have sent me in blind! Next week I was supposed to sweep the place and ensure all traces were gone. Did you really expect me to do that without any advance reconnaissance? Or did you intend to keep the location from me, hoping I would hunt it down, unaware of your little toys, so you could knock me off and avoid paying me?" He rubbed his shoulder.

Tossing in a Snickers bar may have gained an ally in Peter, but the experience killed any remaining trust James had in his associates. They seemed to be throwing him a not-so-tasty treat of their own.

"Well, it seems you have a propensity to arrive prematurely. Besides, that little welcome gift should not have slowed down someone of your calibre." Mr. Ast looked at James grimly. "Now, as for today's visit, it is rather untimely. I trust you are bringing critical news you could not tell me by phone. Are you hand-delivering the revised report that you messed up last quarter?"

"Last month's mishap was weather related. Nothing has changed in military positions since the prior report. I kept my side of the bargain. Then you stole my asset right before it yielded results. Big results. Our arrangement is off, both here and at home." James glared, unsure how the situation had fallen so far out of his control.

"I have no idea what you are talking about, Mr. Glacier. I am sure you are aware that games are useless at this point in the transaction. Nothing has changed. I don't care how you do it, but get out of here and do your job—as and when agreed." Mr. Ast glanced up at a point high on the wall. "And don't try anything stupid, this room has video. I have security."

James smirked. "Your threats are thin. Perhaps I'll have

to make another trip to your asset's headquarters and start its cleanup sooner than planned."

"Well, I am sure you recall that such an unapproved act would nullify all future payments. In fact, my next capital injection into your Canadian venture has been delayed for an indeterminate amount of time, until you deliver what was promised. Last quarter's report is overdue."

James left the building without saying another word. Incoherent thoughts raged through his mind.

He drove to the university and parked outside the building that housed the IT department. Students wandered carelessly, and James had to swerve on two occasions to avoid running into them as he walked to the main door. The hallways inside the building were quieter.

The upper floor, however, proved more difficult. Professors worked with their doors ajar to counteract the poor ventilation and muggy weather. James wasn't even sure what he hoped to find. Obviously Carlos would not be hiding in his office.

Frustrated, he pulled his cap low and walked directly to Carlos' door. It was locked. A few newsletters stuck out from under the door, suggesting no one had come or gone recently.

James quietly jimmied the lock and slipped inside. He stepped over the papers on the floor. As he closed the door, one sheet caught the breeze and blew across the hall. *Shit.*

The office looked as if Carlos had just left for the day. Two stacks of papers sat on top of his desk, one already graded, the other awaiting review. Pens stood in a cup on the corner of the desk. The bookshelf brimmed with neatly arranged books, aligned in alphabetical order. Even the drawers were kept tidy with little trays and neatly clipped notes.

James gave up and left. He shoved the newsletter that had blown into the hallway back under the door before returning to his car.

Cursing himself for not thinking of it sooner, he pulled out his laptop. He should be able to find Carlos the same way he always did—the GPS tracking system. James entered the codes he had memorized so many years ago. A red dot blinked offshore from the fisherman's hut. *Bloody hell, he's gone and holed up on a boat. I bet he was watching the whole time I ransacked the place.*

43

FULL CLEARANCE

Gerardo switched off his phone at 1:00 a.m. Head office had given him full clearance to close down the mounting situation. Initially they had wanted to send in more support, but they eventually agreed to a smaller team. The ability to be more nimble and less noticeable clenched the decision.

Nadya's request would be handled separately, and only after this mission was over. Too much remained at stake. The threat posed by a rogue group of an ally's ex-intelligence agents reverberated up a narrow band of senior Cuban officials. Sleep would most likely elude them all that night.

Gerardo sighed. The approach head office eventually approved was precisely the assumption his team had been working on for the entire day.

They had branched into subgroups. Divide and conquer.

Cristabel and Saul focussed on finding Peter. Cristabel forged ahead in the background, frustrated that she still wasn't strong enough to get out into the field. Instead, she used her skills to find a back route into the city's CCTV records. The cameras did not capture the location where Carlos was taken, but something might be recorded related to Peter's kidnapping. Knowing the precise time Carlos had been abducted allowed her to work backwards.

She focussed on the fourteen-hour period between his disappearance and the last time he had spoken with Peter. Zeroing in on the streets near the churches that had recently received large anonymous donations, she downloaded a short list of video clips and sent them to Carlos. He would recognize Peter more quickly than anyone else on the team.

In the meantime, Saul scrutinized blueprints. He scoured construction permits and noise complaints near the historical buildings purchased by the Tartu Five. Not only could the old tunnels be transformed into prison cells, but the team decided they might also be used to stash supplies or bury evidence. Artifacts that are hundreds of years old are not typically easy decoys to hide.

Carlos reminded the team that he and Peter had found links to three major ancient civilizations, but there could be more. He explained the idea he had been mulling over for days and it was finally starting to fall into place. It helped to verbalize the concept aloud so they gathered around the dining room table to talk it over.

Laptop fans wheezed from running for most of the morning. Someone's device played classical music at a low volume in the background. Gerardo was sure it had started out as a lounge-funk mix and appreciated the switch to the current selection.

"The ruts that were recently discovered are similar to other findings on Malta," Carlos said, "but they're unique in their own right. Like on other sites, the depth and width of the grooves vary. There's enough variation that even experts disagree on what the ruts were used for. In that sense, the latest locations echo other archeological mysteries around Malta. However, instead of curving like bendy roads, these latest tracks spread out like spokes from one central point."

Carlos paused to drink more of the ginger tea Ana had recommended. "On top of this strange design, when Peter fed the data from the new discoveries into a program he designed, it kicked out some odd readings. Certain sections fell outside normal parameters for archeological carvings from around the world. While other ruts eroded irregularly and contained naturally explainable markers, parts of these latest grooves didn't have such tags. These segments ran too straight to have aged naturally."

"So what does that mean?" Saul asked.

"Essentially, Peter's program raised the alarm of potentially falsified data. When we extrapolated the directional trajectory of three of the straightest portions, they pointed directly towards three historical powerhouses: the Great Pyramids of Giza, the Maya city of Tikal and Persia's royal ruins of Persepolis. These are all pinnacles of massive civilizations from a historical perspective. Regrettably, we didn't get the chance to analyze any other segments that fell outside normal parameters."

"Gotcha!" Celia's excitement caught the group off guard. She had been quietly working in the corner. "Sorry for interrupting, but this could be relevant. I dug up a dropped criminal charge on Man D. He was caught smuggling relics from the site of Persepolis out of Iran. If he were to bring such an illegal cache to Malta, the tunnels would be an ideal place to hide them. At the very least, this ties a member of the Tartu Five with one of the archeology sites that Carlos and Peter identified." Celia scooped a handful of almonds from a bowl sitting at the edge of the dining table.

Carlos picked up on her point. "Nice work. If antiquities that match younger civilizations from around the world were found on Maltese sites, it would put into question the generally agreed-upon expansion of humankind. That's all fine if the process adheres to scientific ethics. After all, science evolves by exploring new information and testing alternative theories. But this situation reads more like a crime scene filled with manipulated data and planted evidence."

Ana leaned forward. "If someone wanted to change the narrative, altering the underlying facts would certainly send them well on their way."

Carlos nodded enthusiastically. He stood up and started pacing the room. "Let's carry this idea forward. If it emerged that a newly discovered civilization came before all others and actually fed the belief systems of what we previously thought were independent ideologies, people around the world would be impacted significantly. The source of various religious ideologies might flow very differently than how their stories are told today."

"I am starting to feel more like myself." Carlos broke momentarily and rested his arms on the back of his chair. Still standing, he then launched into another whirlwind of facts. "Malta offers the perfect place to lay the groundwork for such a conspiracy. It's already been proven that life on Malta predated many well-known ancient civilizations. Since 1980, UNESCO has recognized seven megalithic temples in Malta that represent the world's earliest free-standing stone buildings. The Ħaġar Qim, Mnajdra, Skorba, Ta' Ħaġrat, Tarxien and the two temples of Ġgantija on the island of Gozo were all constructed between the third and fourth millennium BC—before Egypt's pyramids, earlier than the Maya temples and even predating Persia's great Persepolis."

"Hold that thought, Carlos. We need more to drink." Ana hopped up and went to the kitchen to refill and turn on the kettle.

"Yeah, and we need energy for this conversation. Carry on, we can still hear you from the kitchen." Saul got up and searched the kitchen cupboards for more snacks, bringing back bags of mixed nuts, raisins and small Snickers bars.

Celia switched the music again. She started to groove in her chair.

Gerardo felt the group getting distracted. He swivelled his finger at Celia, motioning for her to change the station. She made a pouty face, but quickly tapped her device to play a relaxing-music station. Sounds of waterfall splashes mixed with the occasional call of a tropical bird played in the background. Her grooving continued but at a more subdued rhythm.

Carlos looked across the island into the kitchen for a moment and then returned his focus to the group in the dining room. "Imagine if you were told that irrefutable evidence exists showing Jesus, Mohammed, Vishnu and Buddha were actually directed by an earlier civilization and not by divine intervention. Relics mimicking these diverse faiths found on an even older site, like here in Malta, would set the stage to rupture the most basic assumptions behind the dogma. People would revolt. Religious wars could erupt."

Gerardo sat forward. "So, who would gain from this type of mayhem? Why would anyone devise such a hoax? If the various facets of faith actually crumbled, think how much political power would be lost in the process. Someone out there with a massive chip on their shoulder is trying to destabilize the global balance of power. And it appears they don't care what they destroy in the process."

Celia jumped in. "I think this might answer the question of who. Remember all those donations to fund digs around Malta? The ones made through multiple shell companies? Well, at one level of the many layers of companies, there's a group of entities that appointed our Tartu Five to act as directors. This shows another concrete tie that binds them all!"

Celia let them absorb that information before she

dropped another bombshell. "I also found direct communications between Man A and Man B. Remember, Man A lost his parents to the Soviets? They were rebels who tried to lead a siege on Saaremaa, the Estonian island that was made into a military restricted zone by the communists. Man A has money. Lots of it. So he could be motivated to destabilize governmental power, especially Russian power, if he holds a grudge."

Ana returned with a full kettle and a few cans of iced tea on a tray. Carlos dropped a new tea bag into his cup and filled it with hot water. Saul was tearing open his second Snickers bar. Gerardo smiled inwardly; his team was revved up and no one had complained about the extended stay at this apartment.

Celia checked her screen before continuing. "Man B is the one whose parents gave all their money to their church while he was broke. He later went to jail for defrauding that same church—clearly he has a bone to pick with at least one religion. Well, five years ago, Man B called Man A. I traced the call to the same harbour where Man A stores his yacht. Records show his yacht was signed out that day. I think we just found where they first started to plan their scheme."

She skipped forward on the music track as the sporadic bird calls had turned into a cacophony. Quiet raindrop sounds took over. "Telephone coverage is only available from one provider on that part of the island. I ran a search through all the call records on its network around that time. Over the span of a month, Man A phoned each of the other four men *and* took out his yacht on the same days that he made the calls."

Celia added that she had summarized most of what she said and they could reference the file anytime for live links to her sources.

"We're lazy, Cel, and love to hear your voice!" Saul joked and encouraged her to keep talking.

"Okay, you asked for it." Celia resumed. "Man A may be the money man, using his own plus convincing the others to chip in. Man B probably came up with the idea. He's got a criminal mind and a score to settle against the church. Man C owns Excogitatoris Consulting and must provide the physical labour and equipment to carry out the rough work—like building prisons in underground tunnels. He maybe even altered the archeology sites to point towards ancient cities around the world. Man D smuggles relics. I'm sure we will find some planted at the dig sites or hidden in the tunnels beneath the historic buildings they bought."

Ana set her mug down. "So, it looks like the fifth man is kinda a bore compared to his friends."

"Yeah, no kidding. Man E's link is less clear. He owns a bunch of properties on the island, most of which are under development and way behind schedule. Maybe he's simply tagging along with his old buddies from university, hoping to make some money and dig himself out of a whack load of debt."

The clock hanging on the wall ticked a full five seconds before anyone spoke. Gerardo was the first to break the silence. "Well, that's some group of antagonizers we're about to take down. Our next goal is to infiltrate and stop them before the big event this weekend. And, of course, to get our people back safely."

44

NOISE COMPLAINTS

———————

"Oh, gracias a Dios!" Carlos waved Saul over to the computer where he was scanning the videos that Cristabel had sent him. Already he felt his strength returning after rehydrating and eating the food supplied by the team. "There, that's Peter. I recognize the shaggy hair and brown jacket. It's a block from the corner where I was taken."

Saul grabbed the maps. "One of the churches is along that street. They had a contract with our friendly neighbourhood Man C through Excogitatoris

Consulting. And several noise complaints were raised by tenants soon after. Residents reported banging in the middle of the night when noise restrictions were supposed to be in effect. I think we just found the location of Peter's prison."

Carlos tried to think of how he could help Saul. "James talked about a city maintenance crew leaving the manhole where he entered the tunnels on the morning he found me. Keep an eye out for them. They might be in disguise and somehow involved. And be careful, James also said Peter's cell was rigged with a swinging steel ball to keep out intruders."

Saul checked Valletta's public works notices. "According to the announcements, no maintenance or construction is scheduled for the area. I'll keep an eye out for any workers. Their safety vests should be pretty easy to spot."

Gerardo fitted Saul with a tracking device hidden under his clothing. Earpieces, bodycams and backup communication lines ensured the team members could stay in constant contact. "We'll get a vehicle there when you need it. Take care of yourself."

Not long after Saul left the apartment, Ana called in. "I'm at Carlos' house. The place is surrounded by police tape but no one is around. I searched the trunk of Carlos' car. It's empty except for a box of books, the spare tire and a dusty ratchet. I pulled everything out. Any papers that were here are gone."

Carlos' face sank. He chastised himself for leaving them there. "I didn't even get a chance to look at what Peter gave me."

Then he brightened. "Peter might have kept a duplicate in his office. He lived there more than at his apartment. But that's the first place James would look for me. We can't risk going there."

Gerardo told Ana to move on to the next phase of her assignment: extracting Myriam.

Celia left to meet up with Ana. The two would then head towards the Xewkija Industrial Estate, where James had told Carlos she was being held.

Gerardo stayed with Carlos so they could follow the team's progress together. As people spread out and left the safe house, all remaining work and communications would continue remotely.

***

Even though they had agreed to cut contact for now, Gerardo dialled Nadya's private line. Her team might have dredged up some insight she would be willing to share. Odd. A recorded message came back saying the number had been disconnected. Well, he had enough to deal with without worrying about tracking her down. He had what he wanted—Carlos. If she didn't want to be found, it made his part of their deal irrelevant.

A notification buzzed on Gerardo's laptop. Saul had activated his tracer. Gerardo pulled up a chair next to Carlos and set the computer on the table so they could both follow.

Saul's mic picked up his voice clearly. "I'm going underground at the corner of Melita and Il-Batterija. CCTV cameras don't cover this intersection, and there aren't many people around at the moment. Some pub nearby must have a hell of a Thursday Happy Hour deal. I can hear people hollering from here."

***

Saul slipped a narrow crowbar through the holes of a manhole cover and slid it to the side. After dropping down, he yanked the cover back, leaving it ajar by a thin crack. There was a chance it would fall back into place, but he had a backup plan. Excited to be back in operation mode, he whispered, "Go time."

In the city drainage canal, a slick layer of algae covered the floor. Saul slipped a pair of Yaktrax cleats over his shoes and followed his planned route for the next five minutes. Two crossings appeared, as per the blueprints. Two metres after the second turn, he shone his light around a cavern. There should have been an access panel to get down one more level into the older tunnels.

Nothing. Beyond black mildew, the walls appeared smooth and inaccessible.

"I'm going to have to do this manually," Saul said. "The maps don't match what's down here." He opened his pack and pulled out a hand-held metal detector. It was a small device, but effective. Where his eyes failed, it would see.

Saul ran the device over a three-metre section where the entrance should have been. Its silence said otherwise. Hitting nothing, he extended its range beyond his initial target. Trying not to get frustrated, he took a slow breath of the dank air. Then as if the wand heard his thoughts, it pinged. The spot was precisely two and a half metres off the access location shown on the city plans. Using his fingertips to wipe away the gooey mildew, he discovered a metallic cover underneath.

He grabbed the handle, twisted and pulled. Like the mouth of a giant beast, the door creaked open, exposing a dark, gaping hole. Saul stepped inside.

Besides the occasional rumble of a bus overhead, the tunnel was devoid of sound. Saul retraced the route he had planned from the drawings. Out of curiosity, he detoured to check one of the unmarked dead ends that Cristabel had originally pointed out. Sure enough, it existed, leaving him with even less confidence in the city blueprints' accuracy. A fairly recent-looking lock barred further scrutiny.

Saul spoke into his microphone. "I'm five metres from the target." He stayed close to the wall, feeling for any changes in its texture. His wrist grazed something dangling from the ceiling. Without taking another step, Saul eased his opposite hand across his body until he found what he had bumped into. A thick chain hung just out from the wall. Saul followed it up to a hook, where it then continued along the ceiling. He then followed the chain down the wall to see what lay at its base. About four centimetres off the ground, a wire had been tied to the chain and stretched partway across the tunnel shaft.

"I found the tripwire. Someone definitely doesn't want visitors poking around." Saul carefully stepped over the wire. He stopped to listen. For a moment he thought he heard something dragging against the rock, but it was distant and unclear. Seconds later, it disappeared.

Gerardo piped into his earpiece. "Stay quiet if there's any risk of someone around. We can see most of what you're doing through your bodycam."

Saul reached up and traced the metal links running along the top of the tunnel. He ran into another hook. As he pulled away, his fingers got caught in another thin wire but this one was looped around a pulley. He tugged them free. Then a massive ball of metal came flying out from the dark. It collided with his palm, just missing his face. "Bloody hell!" On instinct, he ducked down and shielded his head with his forearms before the next attack.

The projectile swung back, brushing his knuckles. Its chain creaked. Saul held steady.

After turning his light to its brightest setting, he checked the rest of the space for any more unwelcome gifts. It appeared clear. Other than a bruised hand, the ball had not caused any serious damage. The wire had gone taught. He reached out until his fingers brushed the cool metallic sphere, secured in probably the same place it had been before he had triggered its wire. *Thank God that thing is hollow.*

Saul had almost forgotten Gerardo and Carlos were listening and watching. "Leave the ball. We'll disable it another time. Just don't hit those wires again." Gerardo's instructions stressed the primary purpose of Saul's mission: extract Peter.

Carlos had explained about the opening in the wall his food had been sent through. Hoping Peter's cell might be set up the same way, Saul had devised a bendable scope before leaving the apartment. It could slide inconspicuously through small openings to give him a visual of the interior. He'd named it the Panther.

As he knelt on the rough limestone, a damp coolness spread across his knees. He opted for an easier approach. With a click, his metal detector whirred into action. It took thirty seconds to locate a thin metal rim. He then eased the Panther, as stealthy as its namesake, through the narrow gap.

The scraping sound returned. This time, it sounded like it was right in front of him.

45

OLD FLINGS

———————

T he side street near the Xewkija Industrial Estate was littered with crushed paper coffee cups and used medical face masks. One rusted-out brown sedan sat beside a half-clogged street drain. Neither looked as if anyone had checked on them for weeks, maybe months. A cat screeched from inside a dumpster as Ana and Celia pulled up beside it in their borrowed courier van. When Ana opened her door, a raggedy calico cat jumped out.

Ana had briefly dated a guy who worked for a delivery company. While the two were dining out one evening,

Cristabel discreetly borrowed his key card, made a copy and returned it to his jacket pocket without his realizing it was ever missing. Ana broke off their relationship soon after. She told him she'd lost interest. The courtship had served its purpose.

The team rarely took advantage of the courier company's access card. But when the need arose, cargo vehicles offered the perfect cover.

Celia was never sure whether her teammate ever had any real feelings for the guy. In any case, today was not the day to ask.

The white van gleamed against the dinginess of the street. Celia and Ana stepped out wearing standard-issue overalls, a natural-looking disguise. City inspectors often arrived unannounced.

Tinted windows covered in a layer of dust ran along every floor of the industrial grounds' central building, making the interior indiscernible. Celia and Ana approached opposite ends of the three-storey building and each raised a pole that reached the top floor. They both inched along the building in five-metre sections. The tips of the poles held sensors that looked like those used for testing structural integrity. In fact, they were optical sensors that fed visual readings down to the women's hand-held devices. Essentially, they acted as eyes into the building.

After circling the entire structure, Ana and Celia

knocked the first two floors off their list. The first level housed a cafeteria and a maze of administration cubicles. Half of the second level was filled with printing equipment. The other half contained a multipurpose design centre for architects and surveyors. Most of the top level belonged to a private medical practice. Its nursing station stood empty and the computer screens were blank.

"Let's make our delivery. It's unfortunate no one will be there to collect." Ana grinned slyly at Celia.

From the rear of the van, Celia grabbed a collapsible stretcher and a clipboard. Ana picked up a box full of rope and other tools. They weren't sure in what state they would find Myriam, or if they would find her at all.

The main entrance to the building was unlocked. For the moment, the hallways remained vacant. Taking the first door, they climbed a staircase up to a foyer on the third floor. A note outside the clinic's reception area indicated it had been temporarily closed as of that morning. Emergency lights lit the reception area and glowed eerily through the glass doors. Celia went to work on the lock. She glanced at Ana, hoping they were not too late.

Extra bars had been added to the mechanism, making the lock particularly difficult to break. Celia ended up smashing the glass and reaching inside to unlock the last bolt. Once they were in, a faint click sounded at the far end of the hall.

Hallways on either side of the reception desk ran to the back of the office, connected by a third. Celia took the hallway on the left and Ana darted to the one on the right. They progressed forward simultaneously, checking each room and closet along the way. Cabinet drawers had been left partially open and pictures hung askew. It looked as if the clinic had been abandoned quickly.

Celia arrived at the last room on her side. Ana joined her soon after.

Tangled sheets were draped across a medical bed. A couple of expensive monitors sat dormant on a side table with their wires neatly wound up, no longer connected to a patient. Ana stayed back, covering the doorway as Celia approached the closet. Its folding doors ran along a roller track covering the full length of the room. She slid the first door open. The click of its latch matched what they had heard earlier. Celia made an almost imperceptible nod in Ana's direction.

Celia crouched down and crawled into the tight space. Two eyes reflected back, glinting from a sliver of light that made its way to the back corner of the closet. Celia could see enough of the woman's face to know it was Myriam. She whispered gently, "Myriam? Hola señora. We are here to help. We want to take you back to Carlos."

***

Myriam whimpered, "Who are you? Carlos? Is he alright?" Myriam ached for details, but feared another set of strangers.

"He's fine. My colleague and I are with the Cuban military. We want to help you." Celia reached deeper into the darkened closet, holding out her special-clearance ID badge lit up by a small flashlight.

"They think I'm dead. I watched the doctor increase an intravenous sedative into what she thought was my arm. She didn't check under the sheet. But I was right here, watching." Myriam's voice shook as she explained that she had remained hidden as everyone else left.

She started to crawl out from the closet and collapsed into Celia's arms. "I should be dead. They wanted me dead."

"You're safe now. Who are they?"

"Russian intelligence. I recognized their tactics." Myriam's whole body tensed.

Celia coaxed Myriam further out of the closet. "You're okay. Let's get you out of here so you can see your husband."

"Are you able to walk?" Ana's voice floated gently through the air.

Myriam leaned on the cabinet to heave herself up,

pushing with every ounce of strength she had. She managed to stand up, her legs shaking with the effort.

Light flowed into the room through the window, its thin cotton curtains partially open. A pigeon stared at its reflection in the glass, cooing and dancing from one leg to the other. Myriam smiled. It felt good to see that messy little bird again.

46

PANTHER'S EYE

Through the Panther's lens, the room appeared more like a wavering crystal ball than the stone cell it truly was. Saul adjusted the focus. As he twirled his scope around to get a rough sense of the place, he saw little except for a bulky shadow at the base of the far wall. Elsewhere, the room appeared empty. He returned his focus to the dark area. The shadow twitched. Every time it moved, the same scraping sound he had heard earlier grated against his ears. It sounded like fingernails clawing at stone.

In the dim light, he could not tell who was lying on the floor. It could be Peter or someone else altogether.

Saul decided to take a risk. He would activate the Panther's night mode. Hopefully, the person wouldn't even notice it unless he happened to look up at the same moment. Saul twisted the lens and aimed it towards the opposite wall. A burst of light flashed when it was initiated. Then the mode's backlight allowed the lens to pick up additional detail without adding the glare of an obvious spotlight.

He waited. Nothing moved. Presumably whoever lay inside had not noticed the flash. Relieved, he panned the Panther across the walls that had appeared bare.

Posters of archeological sites covered every available space. A map of the interior of an Egyptian tomb was tacked beside a rough sketch of the cliff tombs bordering Persepolis. Someone had used a red marker to circle altars and highlight where guards stood and weaponry was once stored. They were placed in precisely the same configuration at both sites. Saul scanned the posters further along the wall. Red ink marked endless ancient motifs and exposed more and more parallels between civilizations and eras.

Maya royal temples gleamed from maps revealing imprints of hieroglyphic panels lining burial chambers. Arrows linked Maya and Egyptian artistic panels, with an added equals sign for any viewer who might not see the similarity. Further below, photos of Egyptian sphinxes next to images of Persian falcons exemplified more commonalities between the ancient symbols.

The Panther scanned the next wall. Enlarged images of geologic cross-sections showed corresponding cut lines in the limestone used in Egyptian pyramids, Maya temples and Malta's ancient monoliths. Persepolis differed with its sun-dried mud bricks, yet their crumbly silica had a similar composition to the rock used at the other sites. The carving technique also matched, or at least appeared consistent. Saul moved the scope along. He could hear Gerardo's gasp at the images he was livestreaming on their closed-circuit network.

On another part of the wall, clips of scrip taken from a Harappan site in the Indus Valley were taped beside sections of ancient Egyptian hieroglyphics. In such an isolated context, blatant similarities stood out. Further along, photos of old irrigation channels mimicked one another. From the Indus Valley civilization to ancient Egyptian, Persian and Maya communities, all used hand-carved rectangular channels to distribute water over great distances. A particularly large arrow pulled Saul's eyes to an even larger collage of posters displaying parallels between Malta's eroded rut lines, ancient monoliths and miscellaneous artifacts and similar images from other ancient sites.

Saul knew the connections were rigged. He also knew

how easy it would be for an uninformed bystander to fall prey to this sort of misleading doctrine. The world was overrun with fake news and conspiracy groups. He was convinced this portrayal was indeed intended to manipulate rather than educate.

When the Panther's eye finally reached the dark shape huddled on the floor, the person had begun to move around. Saul could see it was a man. The man turned his head from one side of the room to the other. His legs were stretched out in front of him as if he were barricading himself against the wall. Clearly, he sensed something in the room had changed.

Carlos' voice rang through Saul's earpiece. "That's Peter. He looks crazed and thin, but that's our guy. Let's get him out of that absurd room of hoaxes."

Saul spoke smoothly and quietly through the chute, hoping to calm Peter. "Peter, I am here to help. Will you let me help you?"

Peter swung his head towards the chute. He looked around the rest of his chamber, as if questioning what he'd heard or checking who else might be listening. "The lines are the key. Follow the lines." Peter's eyes were wild. They darted around the room, seeking a response.

A third voice boomed into the room. "Everything is connected. The source is proven. The source is on Malta. Look at the data. Follow the lines."

Saul pulled his scope out. His side of the tunnel still

appeared silent and empty. He pressed his ear against the slot.

"Everything is connected. The source is proven. The source is on Malta. Look at the data. Follow the li—" Static corrupted the last word.

It was a recording, being played over and over. No wonder Peter looked as if he had lost his mind.

Saul reinserted the Panther and tried to get Peter's attention. "Peter, show me the doorway."

"The lines are the key. Everything is connected. We are connected—in the far corner." Peter nodded his head at an angle.

Carlos' voice interrupted Saul's thoughts. "He is being watched. Listen to his words, they meld into the recorded message, but he added a phrase. That's his message to you. Keep out of sight. Someone is watching him."

Saul pivoted the Panther's eye to the opposite wall. Strips had been torn from the bottom edges of posters, leaving an image of what looked to be part of a compass. Saul moved his line of sight lower to the floor. A pile of urine-soaked paper shed light on what had happened to the shredded pieces. Halfway up the wall, a metallic ridge stuck out from one of the bulletins.

Inching along the tunnel wall, Saul waved his metal detector up and down until he found a second hinge. He then carefully crept over the wire release on the floor to prevent the cannonball from dropping in for another visit. Beyond the wired contraction, he found a door handle—double-locked with a deadbolt and coded entry pad.

Even for a highly trained agent, these latest locks were virtually impenetrable. Saul would have to clear the door in the traditional manner. Explosives.

He carefully returned to the gap in the wall and whispered loud enough for Peter to hear. "Wait four minutes. Then come to the far wall."

Dodging wires, Saul rushed back to the door and set the required pieces in place. He grabbed a screwdriver from his pack to tighten the wires and then shoved it in his back pocket. Nearing four minutes, he heard a muffled request from the other side.

"Bathroom, have to go to the bathroom. Two minutes. Please, give me two minutes." Peter motioned as if he was about to crawl towards the far corner. The recorded voice paused.

Saul ignited the filament and jumped back. As he did, he inadvertently knocked the wire along the floor with his elbow. The steel ball thudded into him, but it sounded worse than it felt. It glanced off his pack and he heard something crack. Saul's shoulder took the rest of the impact.

What worried him more was the piercing alarm that went off as soon as the explosive detonated and smashed the door lock. He estimated he had about three minutes to grab Peter and get out of visual range.

Gritting his teeth, Saul slammed his shoulder against the door. It fell open and almost landed on top of Peter. Saul grabbed Peter's arm. "Which way will they come from?"

"From the main tunnel. They never enter through the cell." Peter scrambled to his feet.

Footsteps echoed down the cavern. Saul couldn't tell which direction they were coming from. He knew heading back the way he'd come would lead outside. He listened a moment longer. *Damn.* Whoever was approaching had chosen the same route. He tugged on Peter's sleeve to move in the opposite direction. "Come quickly, we need to go this way."

Saul kept a tight grip on Peter. The layout of the blueprints was engrained in his mind after studying them for so long. An access point should lie ahead after about three left turns. He took the first left.

The alarm stopped. Somewhere behind them, a voice swore in the dark. The footsteps started again, heading toward them.

He and Peter needed to get out of these tunnels fast. By the third junction, Saul had to nearly drag Peter. The man's legs were weak after being confined for so long.

Saul heard heavy breathing behind them. The person would catch up with them in about five seconds. It did not give him enough time to open the access door and get them outside.

He pushed Peter around the next bend. "Stay there."

Saul turned back. It was time to face their pursuer.

47

GUEST LIST

———

Cristabel sat hunched over the desk in her bedroom—oblivious to the barking dog in the back alley and muffled voices from pedestrians greeting one another on the sidewalk beside the house. Her laptop's screen flickered black. Eventually a white cursor began to blink in the top left corner. Moments later, strings of text filled the top third of the computer monitor. Cristabel took a deep breath. She hated being on the outside of the action and wished she could have gone with Saul. Considering it still hurt to stand up and her stitches pinched at the slightest touch, she knew she offered more help to the team by doing exactly what she was about to do. Still, it irked her to be stuck inside.

A wave of apprehension snapped her attention back to the computer. Cristabel knew how to hack sites. But dancing in the dark web came with its share of shady commerce and slippery corners. She had learned how to do so in courses meant to teach cybersecurity governance. Universities wanted to get in front of an ever-growing underground training pool of amateur illegals turned pro. It was a lucrative career. Companies paid professionals to test their systems and recommend how to close any holes they detected.

Cristabel found the work tedious. She hated looking backwards to fix weak links—she would rather be creating new technologies to move the bar forward. But she realized the work had its benefits, especially the chance to stop a nefarious criminal from destabilizing world superpowers. With that thought in mind, she played her first move: attack.

ACCESS DENIED. AUTHENTICATION INVALID.

She swore. The cursor winked, daring her to make a second attempt. She grabbed one of the three bottles of ruġġata she had lined up along her bedside table, expecting today's challenge to be tiresome. The drink still held its chill from the fridge. Condensation on the glass cooled her fingers and helped to focus her attention.

Unfortunately for the system, Cristabel knew it could be broken into using one of two techniques. She had one more chance—if she chose the right steps. A decision tree thick with options formed in her mind. Each keystroke performed a crucial role. The branches might have looked a tangled mess, but she understood how to prune her choices back to a workable number. From there, she hoped to pick the correct sequence.

She typed several characters onto the command line and then paused, carefully considering her choice. Satisfied, she gave the Enter key a decisive tap.

Hold your breath. Hope. Wait.

She was in.

Exhale.

Her first task was to access the administrative side of the website. On a second laptop, she kept the Big Reveal's home page visible. She wanted to monitor it while she worked. Websites often hid pre-set "bombs" designed to detect and prevent infiltrators. If activated, the bomb would splinter into an entirely new set of web pages with an impenetrable firewall to blind the hacker. It was a safety measure recommended by many software developers. Still, a lot of companies did not bother to deploy it. They figured the upfront effort would not pay off. She hoped a similarly naive mind was behind this particular website.

Because attendees could register for the Big Reveal

through the website and sign up for text notifications, Cristabel's first goal was to download the guest list. If she could figure out who was attending, she could notify those customers that the event had sadly been cancelled. Unforeseen circumstances and new evidence would be the culprits. She grinned, looking forward to devising the regrettable message.

Layers of security and encryption made the next steps cumbersome. Too many attempts would raise alarms. Cristabel pulled from the most advanced techniques of infiltration available. Her favourite maneuver took time to set up, but when run it would cut to the core as easily as a knife slicing through sun-warmed butter.

Eventually, the fiery image on the home page faded away. Names, emails and phone numbers streamed onto her screen. Cristabel sighed with relief, hardly believing she had broken through. Using the website as a portal, she had accessed their entire system. She quickly uploaded a copy to the team's safe server.

Step two was more a hide-and-seek game. She was not entirely clear what she was looking for or where the evidence might be tucked away. It was likely stashed in layers of folders or encrypted files. A cursory sweep of the hard drive proved fruitless. From talking with Carlos, she expected the key to be lodged somewhere in geological data readings from the three Maltese sites.

The empty ruġġata glass started to leave a ring on the

wood. She grabbed a sock from her laundry pile and wiped the desk dry. Sniffing the damp cotton, she decided she better do a wash later that day. In the meantime, she set a clean T-shirt beneath the remaining bottles. Her mom kept coasters, but they were all the way downstairs in the living room.

The sidewalks had quietened. Even the dog stopped its yapping. Cristabel turned the air conditioning up to medium as the sun beat down on the roof.

She wanted to find the original data. They needed proof that somebody had actually manipulated the inputs to make it appear as if the ancient ruts followed trajectories corresponding with specific compass readings. This trickery laid the groundwork to claim an ancient civilization on Malta knowingly shaped subsequent civilizations—the Egyptians, the Persians and the Maya. If the Maltese lines pointed directly to the location where cities were later built, it proved intent. Planting evidence of civic planning on a global scale from nearly three thousand years ago was a gutsy ruse. One designed to grab headlines.

As Carlos had advised, Cristabel searched for LAS file extensions—the file format used for LiDAR data. She found thousands of such files saved in five main folders. Cristabel drilled deeper. Her fingers flew across the keyboard. She hardly knew what the metrics meant, only that they drove the story behind the data. Over and over, terms like *data pulse range, point spacing* and *intensity* jumped onto her screen.

As she skimmed the results, a clear trend emerged. Consistently, files saved at later dates held a broader range of figures across all of the key criteria. The bandwidth of the readings was growing. One thing she did know was that a wider array of data points allowed for a wider interpretation. And a tale could be strung together far more easily when the storyteller had room to wiggle.

When she compared the sites' final digital elevation models to versions run using earlier inputs, the results differed dramatically. Straight trajectories appeared instead of the bendy patterns of the original, tighter metrics. Cristabel would need Carlos' guidance to confirm, but it certainly looked as if readings from the stone ruts at the three archeological sites had effectively been stretched.

The mastermind behind this scheme presumably wanted to prove that a predetermined global expansion had begun on this small rocky island in the middle of the Mediterranean. Even knowing it was a farce, Cristabel shivered at the thought of a master design *directing* some of the most unique civilizations on where to settle. This snake wanted to unravel human history.

In its place, the Big Reveal stitched a new directive out of deception and disinformation. Its intent was clear: the

Tartu Five were fuelling mistrust and spurring revolts in the hopes of toppling leaders around the world.

Cristabel's mind spun. The implications her team had spoken about felt heavier with the weight of hard evidence. People rely on their faith. Political heavyweights rely on religious groups' support. With that shattered, most nations would face at least some level of unrest. It would hit the most powerful countries the hardest.

In Russia, the Orthodox Church supported a large group of high-ranking officials. Even democratic American politics could be swayed by zealots who lobbied the government, gifting hefty donations to favoured candidates. China's leaders might try to minimize religion's grip, but in doing so they validated the very potency it holds in the political arena. Middle Eastern governments tended to be more transparent, openly basing law and policy on their beliefs.

In all of these countries, religious support equated to power protection. In its absence, global instability would likely erupt.

Like most big disasters, all it would take is a series of small events to create a massive crisis. With the files Cristabel had found, her team could start to chip away at the edges of this carefully planned tinderbox. She hoped today represented the beginning of its demolition.

Cristabel cracked open another bottle of her almond-lemon beverage and turned on a mix of techno-punk tracks for background inspiration. She would need it for the next stage.

Her third step focussed on the administrative portal. Initially, it looked normal. Program files and system controls appeared as expected. But when she checked the source code, things turned more opaque. Batches were stashed all over the place, in multiple folders. Duplicate information cluttered directories. Updates seemed random and often incomplete. An incoherent farmer thrashing through a hayfield and tossing bales in every direction, including a neighbour's pond, would create less of a mess than the files in front of her.

She needed to embody the mental state of an unstable warrior to decipher this jumble.

Then she had an idea. Her mother's recent bout with what Cristabel referred to as scattered mind syndrome had led her to the safety of her old haven in the cellar. Maybe whoever created this database had a similar safe space they defaulted to.

Cristabel recalled an introductory IT class that compared the history of technology across countries. For example, while the World Wide Web had been developed at the CERN scientific facility in Meyrin—just outside of Geneva, Switzerland—to meet the need for disseminating information laterally between universities and research facilities around the world, other countries pushed for a more hierarchical structure. The Tartu Five would have been trained using Soviet techniques.

Cristabel considered how the Soviet curriculum would have shaped their fundamental tendencies. In the early 1970s, Soviet cybernetics relied on layers of approvals. Rumours suggested that their mainframes bogged down to a near standstill under tedious approval regimens. If the designer of the Big Reveal's system had defaulted to these basic principals, the evidence Cristabel wanted to find would lie in those files with the most access restrictions.

It did not matter *where* they were stored but *how* they were retrieved.

Cristabel pulled a sample of files from the administration site and began to devise a program that ranked them by security level. By the time she finished, the sun had begun to set. A mauve veil blanketed everything outside her window. She had been sitting for over five hours and still needed to test her work. Stretching her legs, she let out a loud sigh and then hobbled into the kitchen to make a sandwich.

Her pilot program's first attempt spit back an error message. *Ah, typical.* She started to dredge through the code, searching for the delinquent character or miscoded instruction. Twenty minutes later, Cristabel ran another test. Five files popped onto her screen. Success.

The chosen files' authentication levels blew her away.

They ranked sixty-five percent more secure in password complexity and double the number of security patches compared to an average file. A promising sign. Would their content confirm she had actually penetrated the designer's safety shield and struck gold?

The first two files contained contracts for technical studies. One agreed to a reduced LiDAR scanning protocol at Malta's recent dig sites compared to industry practice. The second agreement sought to clean the data and make it usable as per the researchers' goals. These goals were left undefined, making this agreement a blatant red flag to standard scientific integrity. She found a hidden sheet inside a spreadsheet, which raised additional alarm bells. It outlined the flow of funds across more than fifty companies—some of which matched names her team had already identified. The fourth document contained draft speeches for the main event, highlighting keywords described as crowd agitators.

The fifth document proved to be another gold mine. It laid out specific artifacts pilfered from Tikal, Persepolis, the Khufu pyramid of Giza and the city of Harappa, all cross-referenced to locations where they were "discovered" on the new sites in Malta. It even boasted how to buff and shave them to appear slightly older and more worn than they actually were.

The five files alone proved beyond any doubt that the Big Reveal was completely manufactured. Fake news.

Cristabel anxiously wondered what else her program might stumble upon when she set it loose across the entire server. Before running it, she scanned the Big Reveal's live website to check for any changes or anomalies since she had started to play around in the background. A new blog post had popped up. She skimmed its content. The article advertised the upcoming event, reminding people they had limited time to buy tickets. It tried to suck them in by claiming to be a "once-in-a-lifetime" evening. Cristabel figured the advert had been written days earlier and was posted on a pre-set schedule. Relieved, she moved back to the main laptop.

The pilot program integrated easily into the full administration portal. With a few more clicks, Cristabel launched her program.

She watched both screens.

The system hummed. The web page flashed its attention-seeking flames.

Cristabel waited.

Twenty files flooded her screen.

48

SCREWDRIVER

Saul saw the glint of a knife from the corner of his eye. The attacker had caught up with him quicker than he'd hoped. Avoiding a direct fight, Saul dove at his aggressor's feet. He preferred to add an element of surprise.

Saul snatched the screwdriver from his back pocket. Right now, it was his most accessible weapon. He shoved it through the man's shoe and deep into his foot. The arch of the foot holds one of the weakest bones in the human body.

"Aaahhh!" The man's blood-curdling scream bounced off the tunnel walls. He tried desperately to pull away.

Saul pressed down with all of his weight.

The man managed to swipe at Saul with his knife. It only caught the canvas of Saul's backpack.

Saul drew the screwdriver out of the man's foot. Adrenalin pumped through him, overriding the pain in his shoulder. Focussing on the curve where the man's neck met his jawline, Saul plunged his arm upwards.

Blood exploded from his target. The man's eyes bulged in surprise as the thin metal tip of the screwdriver disappeared into his skull. Seconds later, those eyes turned blank.

The man crumpled to the ground. His fingers relaxed and the knife fell. Its metallic finish glistened, unstained.

Saul reached under the man's jacket, searching for any shred of information. Even the innermost pocket lay flat and empty. A leather holster around his waist held two handguns, but the front pockets of his pants were bare. Saul stretched around to feel inside the back pockets. He pulled out a business card with a phone number scrawled in blue ink.

Saul was about to turn away when he thought of an additional place to look. He removed the shoe that was still intact and pulled out its insole. A single key and a white access card slid down to the heel. Saul grabbed them and ran to Peter.

"Peter?" He looked in both directions. Nothing but empty blackness peered back.

"Over here."

"Are you okay?" Saul helped him up.

"I'm okay. I thought it best to get far away from the action."

"We have two options," Saul said. "We can continue on ahead, but I'm not sure what we'll find. Or go back the other way and get out of the tunnels the same way I came in."

"I don't want to get anywhere near that prison again. They might send in more muscle." Peter's voice shook.

While deciding, Saul swung his backpack off his shoulders. A wide gash split the front of it. Inside, a crack ran the entire length of his metal detector. It was likely completely ruined. Better the device than him, but it certainly didn't help their situation. "It's going to be difficult to find a way out with broken tools."

Gerardo's voice chirped in Saul's earpiece. "We've located you on our maps. Continue ahead for about thirty paces. There should be a door on your left that connects with an old water reservoir. I'm sending Ana over. She'll meet you at street level with a car. She and Celia got Myriam out and are on the ferry back from Gozo."

As Peter and Saul started to make their way forward, a

staticky voice rang through the air. "Tüvs. Tüvs. What's your status?"

"Our friend must have a walkie-talkie on him. Wait here. I'll deal with it." Saul edged back to the body and felt around for a hard plastic device. He found a rough canvas cap instead. It wasn't until the voice came through a second time that he noticed the thin rectangular receiver clipped to the brim of the hat. Saul grabbed it. He pressed the green Talk button and spoke gruffly into the receiver. "It's taken care of."

With that, he pushed the red power button into its off position and tossed the radio onto the ground.

"That'll buy us some time. Now, let's get moving." He led Peter towards their exit route.

A bucket of rubbish and a broom marked the spot where the door to the water reservoir should have been. Saul stared at them, unable to process why such everyday items were sitting in the middle of this unused tunnel. His first hint was a sliver of light where the door met the wall. He pushed the door with his good shoulder and nearly fell into an enormous room.

Saul and Peter glanced at one another, unsure if this luck would quickly turn sideways. Purple and yellow lights lit up the voluminous cavern. They stepped inside, tentatively. Yellow arrows pointed up along a ramp towards red exit signs. The walkway led directly to ground level. They started to run up it when they heard a voice approaching.

"Yeah, I'll clean that up right after I finish the knight's cistern. There's another group coming in five minutes and I need to finish sweeping from the last group. Someone brought popcorn!" Footsteps reverberated across wooden scaffolding that wound around the upper reservoir overhead. They continued running up the remainder of the ramp.

Peter pointed to a sign. It read, "Heritage Malta: Discover Underground Valletta's Lost Cisterns."

He laughed. "I hadn't expected to catch their latest tourist attraction, but I must admit it is a pleasant surprise. Now let's get out of here and find your friend's vehicle."

49

ANCIENT CONNECTIONS

The scent of burnt coffee teased the air. Laptops and blueprints camouflaged the shiny maple of the dining room table. A printer and multiple screens took over the side buffet. Dark smudges in varying shades of purple curled under everyone's eyes as they stared at their computer screens. Over the past twelve hours, nearly the entire team had squeezed into the safe house apartment's adapted workspace.

In the adjacent living room Carlos and Myriam sat on a leather couch, leaning into one another, not wanting to lose contact for even a second. They had so many questions for each other, trying to understand exactly what the other one had gone through. Both felt a mix of relief and angst as they replaced their imagined worst-case scenarios with the truth of what had actually transpired.

Myriam sipped a solution of electrolytes and protein in an attempt to build back her strength. She could not explain how or why she had regained consciousness when she did in that strange little medical clinic, only that something had jerked her senses into action.

It was a sensation so vivid, yet so opaque. She had tasted, heard and felt an internal alarm deep within herself. The best way she could describe it was like a child screaming, pulling, tearing at her insides, telling her to get out of bed and hide. A giddy sense of trepidation took over when she pulled out her IV. That part stayed vividly clear. The rest of her memories of it were hazy.

Almost in a trance, Myriam had ripped off cords and sensors before unplugging the machine that had been monitoring her. She then stuffed gauze and a pile of sheets from the laundry basket under the blanket in the vague shape of a person. The oxygen pump continued its cycle, making the compilation look almost lifelike if one didn't look too closely.

The next thing she remembered was scrunching herself inside a tiny room. She shut the door. She heard footsteps in the distance, and scattered voices, maybe in her head, maybe through the walls. Reality and her imagination disintegrated together.

Time passed. How much, she wasn't sure. People came in and out of the room. The Russian doctor entered and adjusted one of the machines attached to an intravenous drip. Its line fed under the blanket Myriam had arranged. Myriam remembered feeling very much awake while she watched through the gap in the folding door.

Then she nodded off again, waking when she heard a man enter. He seemed angry when he cleared the bedding, and he mumbled something about a control freak and someone doing everything herself.

Later on, she heard crashes and then footsteps further away. Her knee accidentally nudged the door open. She closed it once more, cringing as the metal clasp clicked shut despite her trying to slide it quietly.

That final commotion thankfully turned out to be Celia and Ana smashing through the clinic's entrance door.

***

Shafts of sunlight reflected off a massive cruise ship pulling into Valletta's waterfront for the evening. From the apartment, Gerardo had seen at least two other ships come and go over the afternoon. He turned back to where his group and their recently freed colleagues had congregated between the dining room, living room and kitchen. The open-concept layout allowed everyone to shift and move around comfortably.

Peter turned out to be in surprisingly good shape. Gerardo ran the same tests as they had for Carlos but Peter's bloodwork came back clean. Except for mild dehydration and hunger, he was relatively healthy despite the foul conditions he'd had to endure.

Saul, Celia and Ana were still humming from adrenalin after their rescue missions. Cristabel linked into the group from home, expressing how she wished she was there in person.

Gerardo savoured the buzz of success; his team had safely brought back all three of the missing folks. For once, he looked forward to making the call to his superiors.

Now he could concentrate on the remaining task of bringing down the rogue conspirators. He gathered them in the dining room, with Cristabel on video. "Okay team, we have less than forty-eight hours until the Big Reveal is due to begin on Saturday. Unfortunately, no one got a look at their captors. So we don't know for certain who we're after. But the intelligence gained so far points to two potential leaders among our Tartu Five."

Saul was already seated at the dining table. "So, after all my slogging in the city's trenches this afternoon, are you saying I can't even have a beer to celebrate yet?"

"That's why we're the elite team. I have the utmost confidence you can push on before we relax and celebrate. But go wild, grab yourself an alcohol-free beer from the fridge. I bought your favourite brand." Gerardo smiled and kept talking as Saul got up and grabbed a soft drink instead.

"Mr. Ast, or Man A, has the money and owns the yacht where the men have been meeting. Mr. Stokmane, Man B, holds a grudge and a criminal background and, I am willing to bet, is the mastermind behind the plan."

Peter crossed his arms from where he stood at the far end of the room. "That fits. Whoever put together the concept behind the repetitive messages playing in my cell would have to have been well-educated and had the time to scheme something this complex."

Gerardo nodded at Peter, relieved to have his buy-in. "Moving on. Saul put an end to Man E—the mysterious Mongolian classmate, or Tüvs. His full name was Tüvshinbayar Gurragchaa and he must have supplied both funds and muscle to the operation. Man D, or Davit Baboumian, on the other hand, has a record of smuggling Iranian artifacts and has ties to the trucking business. I expect we'll find a cache of relics with his signature. Cristabel found a list and they'll likely be stored in the tunnels beneath one of the historical buildings purchased by the group."

He took a breath and finished his overview. "I'm

willing to bet Aram Chikadze, the Georgian bricklayer, our Man C, made all of the alterations to the underground tunnels and archeological sites. We don't know much more about his involvement. But we have contracts and a pile of files from their server. Cristabel, have I missed anything of importance from your search?"

"No, you've covered the main points about who we're dealing with. As for the group's plan, I was able to access their secure files via the event's website. Most people don't realize that a server connected to a public-facing website leaves a trail. I located twenty files of interest. Of those, thirteen held routine backup data and didn't add anything new. That left seven files that *are* relevant. I've uploaded them to your machines now." Cristabel replied.

"Please tell me you have already summarized them!" Ana started to reach for her glasses case.

"Don't worry, Ana, you won't have to read them all." Cristabel continued as if uninterrupted. "As Carlos previously pointed out, data measurements from three of Malta's newest archeological sites were altered. In addition to the three sites Peter and Carlos found, there are two more. I only found the last one an hour ago, when I took a second look at the files of interest."

Peter and Carlos blurted out nearly the same question at the same time. "Where are the other two sites?" "What other two locations?"

Cristabel responded, as if expecting the question.

"This is where it gets interesting. One site is in Russia, Arkaim. It's an ancient settlement discovered in the 1980s up in the Ural steppe region. Archeologists uncovered cellars and underground water wells there. Some refer to the site as Russia's Stonehenge. The second location is in the Indus River Valley and spans parts of present-day Afghanistan, Pakistan and India. These Harappan communities existed much earlier than the sites on Malta, but soon after Malta's temples advanced, so too did one of their main cities, Harappa. Many consider this community to be the first to use wheeled transport and construct advanced drainage and sewer systems. From what I can see in the files, the Tartu Five wanted to flip that story around and claim the idea came from ancient Malta!"

Saul put his backpack on his lap and tore a strip of duct tape from a roll he had found in the apartment. "So, that explains why they didn't want anyone credible refuting their evidence. At least, not until well after the Big Reveal event scheduled for this weekend."

Cristabel started to speak quicker, showing her excitement. "Exactly! This means the upcoming event will try to convince the world that five ancient civilizations have direct lineage to Malta. From what I have read, whoever is behind this scheme intends to claim that the ancient Maltese people are the ancestors of everyone living today. Culturally, spiritually and genetically. Beyond the cultural and religious shock waves, their choice to use the number five is, in itself, significant."

"Besides the reality that five working days per week actually means seven—what is so important about the number five?" Saul stopped pressing the strip of duct tape on the tear in his pack to ask the question.

"Until this afternoon, I didn't see the links either. But get this, Saul ... and everyone listening—" Cristabel paused and the team could hear her tapping on her laptop for a couple of seconds. "Five pillars form the basis of the Islamic faith: the declaration of faith, five daily prayers, almsgiving, fasting and pilgrimage, or the hajj. Islamic law has five categories based on five prophets. Likewise, Persia's religion of Zoroastrianism holds the number five in high regard since the prophet Zoroaster's teachings, the Gathas, are grouped into five sections. These five groups make up the bulk of their most sacred text, the Avesta. Likewise, their sacred fire should be fed five times a day.

"In Christianity, the five-pointed star is associated with the birth of Christ. Although Judaism uses the six-pointed Star of David as a focal symbol, they recognize five in another way. They divide the ten commandments into two sets of five; the first relates to the person's relationship with God and the second pertains to their relationships with each other. Continuing on with this theme, Hindus and many Buddhist traditions believe the world is comprised of five elements: earth, water, fire, air and sky or space. And for those of different faiths, or those who don't have a specific faith, they like every human being rely on five senses to experience life."

Gerardo hoped Cristabel had not pushed herself too much. She must have been pulling data nonstop all day.

Cristabel moved on to the historical connections. "Human fingers and toes are naturally grouped into fives. For the Maya, these twenty digits represented the number of days in each Maya month. Five extra days were added to balance the annual calendar and complete their three-hundred-and-sixty-five-day year.

"Ancient Egyptians believed the five-pointed star represented the universe where the gods lived for all eternity. Pharaohs joined the gods in this universe when they died. Furthermore, the Egyptians believed the human spirit was made up of five parts."

The blare of a ship's horn silenced any immediate response from the group. After it weakened, Celia spoke up. "So, how are we going to stop this farce?"

50

AMATEUR HOUR

All eyes turned to Gerardo. Although she'd met him only hours ago, Myriam was impressed with his leadership. She could see that even Peter and Carlos, who did not directly report to him, had learned to respect Gerardo's advice.

"I need to make some calls," he said. "Ana, see if you can track down the owner of the phone number Saul found in Tüvs' shoe. Cristabel, compile all your data into a case file that can be passed along as evidence. Saul, can you go over the situation with Peter and Carlos to see if we have overlooked anything from their research? Myriam and Celia, keep digging. I can't explain it, but I feel like there is another aspect we're missing here."

Gerardo stepped away from the group into a small den. It offered quiet privacy for his calls.

Carlos looked over at Ana. "Do you have photos of the Tartu Five?"

Ana pulled up what she had. "The grainy shot on the top left is Lennart Ast. Over here, Juris Stokmane is shown standing beside his newest Audi. We think the third photo is Man C, Aram Chikadze, the owner of Excogitatoris Consulting. This next image captures Davit Baboumian from one of his busts when he crossed the Iran–Armenian border with stolen goods. Our fifth man, Tüvshinbayar Gurragchaa, who Saul can vouch for, passed through the airport last March and was caught on the security cameras."

"I recognize Juris. He came to see me about safeguarding a bunch of old maps and artifacts after one of my cybersecurity talks. At the time, I hoped he would give the university some funding, but he said something about another investment tying up his money. Overall, I remember it being an odd conversation. The man certainly came across as a quirky character." Carlos had confided in Myriam earlier how he had been trying to pinpoint what exactly had bothered him about the man that night.

Peter joined in. "I've seen him too. He attended one of my talks about a year ago and asked a question right at the end of the Q&A session. It stood out because my talk was focussed on maintaining data integrity over client files, like bank customers or supplier payment details. This man asked about something entirely different. He wondered what integrity measures existed to ensure scientific research could not be tampered with. At the time, news stations around the world were reporting the rise of fake news stories and vaccine conspiracies. I figured current events must have triggered his question.

"Then, the day before I was kidnapped, the same man stopped by to see me at the university. He offered one hundred thousand euros to authenticate a pile of data he had been given. He handed me a USB stick with a sample of the files to convince me he was serious. I admit, the challenge piqued my interest. After taking a preliminary look, I told him it was the work of an amateur and not to waste his money."

Carlos leaned in. "Was that why you called me that night? You said you found some worrying connections."

Peter raised his eyebrows. "Well, that was what started it. I recognized elements of the data from my earlier searches into Malta's recent excavation data. Except the files he gave me showed far fewer markers to indicate that the findings had been manipulated. Compared to the earlier data we pulled from the archeological registry, these results were far more refined. I'm not even sure I would have seen the shifted trajectories of the ancient ruts left in the rock if I hadn't recognized the data. The work wasn't amateur at all.

"And he wasn't there with a job offer. That man dropped by my doorstep to send a message—a warning. He knew where I worked and had seen me poking around his research files. Frankly, it made me nervous. That night, before I drove home, I got down on my hands and knees to check under my car to be sure nothing had been planted!"

The chain of events was evidently starting to fall into place for Saul. "I suggest we check to see which version of the files match those sent to the Superintendence of Cultural Heritage. We don't know if they are the original readings, the altered files Peter was given or those Cristabel downloaded from the event's administrative site. Or maybe they received another version altogether."

While he was comparing the sequencing, Ana discovered another connection. "You won't believe this! That number you found in Tüv's shoe is a local mobile number registered about a week ago to a man named Jim Tracker."

She looked over at Carlos and Myriam. "I have a feeling this is your friend James, a.k.a. Yakov. The SIM logged two phone calls, one to a known member of Russian state security. The other number, unbelievably, belonged to Lennart Ast, Tartu Five's banker with the yacht."

"So James—or Yakov—is either in serious danger or is part of this whole conspiracy." Myriam wasn't sure which option she preferred. At this point, she was not even sure which seemed more plausible.

The news seemed to fire up Carlos. "That explains why he travelled to Malta so quickly after I was taken. And explains how he was able to find me. His little team of sharks wanted to lure information out of me. James acted as their decoy."

He replayed for the team what he had told James, trying to remember exactly what he might have disclosed. His mind had been hazy during those days in the fisherman's hut.

Despite the overall situation, Myriam felt unusually calm. Celia had already helped her remove her implanted tracker. They had tossed it out the window on their drive away from the industrial complex. She rubbed her wrist where it used to be, anticipating the scar that would surely result. She glanced towards Carlos. Instinctively, she reached up to pick out a piece of fishnet still stuck in the fibres of his barretina. "Did you wash this yourself?"

He squeezed her hand, sending a boost of much-needed resilience through them both.

Gerardo walked into the room. His expression was grim. "My Russian contact was found dead in Moscow last night." He had more news to share. "The seniors in Havana have achieved their goal. Carlos, Myriam and Peter are back on secure ground. Scientific misconduct and the intent to spread false and misleading information falls under the jurisdiction of Malta's authorities. They can deal with it under the Maltese legal system. So, team, it is our turn to blend into the shadows. We did our job and the public face of security will take over from here."

Gerardo explained how he had relayed all the evidence the group had gathered to his superiors in Havana. They would liaise with the local police as well as their Russian counterparts. Sometime tomorrow morning, he would hand over the key and access card Saul had found in Tüvs' shoe. His team was to stay incognito and out of the final takedown.

51

THE FOOL, THE MEATHEAD
AND THE PUPPETEER

———————

T *hat fool.* Juris fumed as he tried to regain control over his master plan. He had locked himself inside his office after Tüvs lost contact from the tunnels. The small room was located at the back of the church—*his* church. When he first bought the historical building, this room only contained a dim light bulb hanging above an unadorned oak desk. Now, a Swarovski crystal chandelier cast golden orbs of light onto grey walls. A plush Turkish handwoven rug covered the knotty pine plank flooring.

Normally, the room's metre-thick rock walls offered solace and comfort, but this morning they made him feel boxed in. Imprisoned. It was a feeling he had sworn never to succumb to again.

This was not the first time James had strayed from their tight clutch of ships, navigating under his own sail. Juris did not like it. He did not like it at all.

When they'd first met, it was James' temper that had fascinated Juris. Never before had he met someone with such passion. James had a mind of his own and wouldn't be jerked around by expectations or social norms. The two men had met at an investor trade show. An exhibition kiosk promising to increase crop yields and lower unit costs caught Juris' attention. His father had been a farmer and from one year to the next he complained of too little rain, waves of mite infestations, pesky rodents or some combination thereof. Hope never came into the equation. Juris left home depressed and uninspired. His views started to change after five minutes of talking with James.

James' explosions of discontent grew on Juris. They were so different from his own ongoing dismay with life in general. Although he never invested in James' tech company, he admired James' ambition to devise entirely new solutions—alternative pathways, away from the obvious, well-trodden ways of the masses. Both of the men eventually learned to control their impulses, but their rage never dissipated. Perhaps that explained why they had kept in touch over the years.

As for Tüvs, his reliability was also starting to wane. Until Juris recently reconnected with him, Tüvs had been trying to expand his family's property business. No matter how hard he worked, he left half-constructed buildings in his wake. Despite Juris' attempts to give him a second chance, Tüvs' potential remained in question. Juris had recruited him to his Big Reveal project partly to tap into Tüvs' savings, but mainly for his brute strength. The guy was a quintessential gym meathead.

Just this morning, the screen into Peter's cell had turned fuzzy. Juris and Tüvs had assumed the wire on the camera had jiggled loose again. Juris sent Tüvs down to the dungeon to sort it out. Minutes later, Tüvs radioed back that an explosion had decimated the entry door and he saw no trace of Peter. The man was physically strong, but his ability to handle problems on the fly stunk.

Juris impatiently instructed Tüvs to chase down James, who he assumed was behind the incident and would have Peter with him. No one else knew of their little hideaway.

Tense lines crossed Juris' forehead. Twenty-five minutes had passed since Tüvs' last communiqué saying he'd taken care of it. He should be back by now.

Juris grabbed his handgun and tucked it in his waistband. He knew never to underestimate James.

When he reached the lowest level of the basement,

Juris pressed his shoulder against a panel fitted beside a private, secondary door used to access the tunnels. He had asked Aram to install it months ago when they designed their "storage" space. The panel's sensor released a pocket door, which rolled soundlessly into the wall and out of sight. Juris tapped a button on his remote control, quickly closing the barrier behind him. A layer of dirty-looking stucco applied to its exterior made the door look as if the contraption was part of the underground tunnel system itself.

Tüvs was nowhere in sight. Juris barked into the walkie-talkie once more, "Get your ass back here Tüvs. Now."

Just to be safe, he pulled out his handgun and slowly stepped into the darkened tunnel. The dungeon's light bulb still emitted a feeble bit of light. He could make out the outline of where the cell door used to be. It looked worse than he expected. Not knowing which direction Tüvs had gone, Juris followed his gut. His fingers trailed the wall, guiding him forward. After about thirty steps, he heard the trickle of liquid. Not droplets, but the slow echo of fluid soaking into porous rock. *Damn damp tunnels.* As if on cue, his foot hit something. He kicked ahead, trying to gauge what he had run into. A sort of fabric clung to his shoe. Juris let go of the wall and knelt down, still pointing the gun straight ahead as he slowly lowered himself.

He used the tip of the gun to prod whatever lay in front of him. It didn't move. But it was big, blocking the entire walkway. Juris pulled out his phone and shone its light around him.

"Shit. Tüvs, you let James get to you. How'd you do that? Shit, man." It was not water he had heard earlier, but a pool of blood soaking into the porous bedrock.

Juris stuffed his phone back into his pocket. He needed to move Tüvs' body and he would have to do it alone. It was best if no one on the team knew about this change of events, not just yet. He cursed James for the fourth time that morning.

Juris grabbed Tüvs under his arms and started to drag. "Damn, you're heavy."

Juris realized he was relieved to have this lug off his team. Tüvs' usefulness was fading anyways, and it would make the final rollout simpler. By the time he'd heaved Tüvs' body inside Peter's former chamber, sweat was trickling down his sides. He hadn't exerted himself this much in months. Juris left the body stretched across the dungeon floor to deal with later.

Posters surrounded Tüvs' bare grave with distorted ancient sites and twisted tales of long-gone civilizations. Much like the half-completed developments Tüvs left behind, this final debacle with Peter and James would add to the stains on Tüvs' legacy.

Once back upstairs, Juris fell onto the couch in his

small office. He texted Aram to get over here ASAP and replace the safety door in the dungeon.

Juris' trusted team was crumbling around him.

First James had promised to keep Carlos contained and find out what he and Peter suspected. That should have been simple. Extract information, destroy any evidence Carlos and Peter had found and then eliminate Carlos. He was a barrier who eventually needed to be removed *permanently*.

Peter, on the other hand, came across as more malleable. He, too, appeared to hold a grudge against the tentacles of government. Juris had been sure he could not only dull Peter's curiosity, but also get him on-board to believe in the "new" storyline. The professor could become an ally—or at least a passive observer.

It should have worked so smoothly. Then James screwed it all up. He got too impatient. He interrupted Peter's lessons and then lost Carlos.

James hadn't responded to any messages over the past day. A week ago, Juris had driven out to the hideaway where James was holding Carlos. He saw that whenever James left his post, anyone could break in to the exposed shack. That caused the first crack in Juris' trust.

Then he heard about the episode with Lennart at the bank. James was supposed to visit Peter, but not until closer to the main event. The visit was intended to test Peter's resolve and see if he truly believed the alternative story Juris had spun. Instead, Juris had had to increase the intensity of his persuasion tactics to bring Peter back into his altered reality.

Everything else with Peter had fallen nicely into place. Until now. The expedited mail system registered the university's receipt of the letter Juris wrote on Peter's behalf. He briefly tendered Peter's resignation, effective immediately. Considering Peter taught no classes and hadn't developed any research projects of recognition in more than three years, the university would have gladly accepted his notice. Juris had seen similar situations in many companies over the years. In every case, cash flow trounced employer loyalty. Because Peter's pay would switch over to his pension fund's responsibility, the university would be off the hook.

Just this morning Juris had felt so close. Too close for things to fail. Heat rose through his chest. It couldn't crumble this fast. He could still pull it off. He must.

Juris dialled the phone number of a trusted contact. The extension changed every six months to ensure their discussions stayed out of official records. Juris despised the guy, but recognized his usefulness. The confidant had ties to Russia's intelligence community and would be sure to relay the story Juris was about to tell about James' ulterior activities.

After passing along the location of the fisherman's hut, Juris hung up and sat at his desk. With a few clicks on his laptop, he sent a follow-up encrypted package with evidence he had collected over the years: copies of text messages, requests for funding and offers of anti-Russian side endeavours most investors were not aware of. James would drown quickly, likely painfully. Peter, sadly, would go down with him. A potential ally now lost.

Moving on, Juris tried to focus on his speech for his presentation in two days' time. He left the confines of his office and entered the nave of the church. From there, he turned on the stereo, already set to a jazz music station. The swell of a saxophone resonated against the stone walls and bounced off the vacant pews. Starting as a low rumble, a double bass clipped into the tempo. Its pulse grew alongside the sax. Juris breathed in the sounds, drawing more strength than any narcotic could ever provide. He pushed aside thoughts of Tüvs and focussed on his plan. It must move forward. He could not imagine a future without this destiny.

Over a decade had passed since he began formulating the plan. If there was one benefit to getting stuck in jail, it was having time to think. He'd realized his life was unfolding based on other people's expectations. Once he realized this truth, he found purpose. Its beacon carried him from the lowest depths into a life filled with ambition.

His dear mother had been the first to spell out a dire prediction for Juris proclaiming his inevitable path every morning at the breakfast table. She only ever saw failure and disappointment in his future. In an attempt to scare him towards some undisclosed path to righteousness, she would rail incessantly about his poor grades, impure friends and unjust mind. Whatever better future she wanted for him never came into the conversation. In her eyes, he was doomed to disappoint and fail.

His father took a different approach, although it did nothing to change Juris' fate. Juris could still picture his dad hunched over the table, dipping his chipped spoon into a bowl of cold millet porridge and grimacing as he took a swig of stale coffee. They could only afford half a cup of coffee beans per fortnight. The grounds were reused over and over until the drink looked more like the drainage from their hogs' watering hole than anything worth consuming. His father said little. He chose to communicate instead through the branch of a spruce tree, preferably loaded with sharp cones. Emotions took hold inside young Juris. Pain. Detachment.

So when Juris left school and the local bishop asked him to help keep track of the church's accounts, he thought he had landed a chance at redemption. Later, Juris moved up to manage the books at the main cathedral in Latvia's capital city. Old expectations trickled back. He started to siphon bits of the weekly donations for himself. No one noticed. He skimmed a little more. Initially, the bishop remained oblivious. But

Juris grew careless. He did not notice the watchful eyes. And in time, he landed in jail.

Years rolled past. Three dismal meals a day and manual labour filled the hours. He helped build roads, dig ditches and pour cement. He had time to think. Patterns fell into place. The world followed what they had always known. People followed a rhythm, copying one day to the next, agreeing with their bosses and passively acquiescing to politicians' wills. Complaining ended with good intentions lost and distorted in a web of bureaucracy. Apathy grew, dulling the general populace's sentiment. Blind expectations set in. A few leaders got what they wanted while the masses suffered.

Juris decided that when he left the iron bars behind, he was going to reset the stage. The blind mice would no longer run in circles around an archaic maze propped up by those with power. Not in Juris' reality. No, he planned to tip the scales of power. He would change the world.

52

FAMILY TIES

———

Cristabel switched off her computer. She should have felt satisfaction at the end of the job, but it felt half finished. Too many questions still flew around her head. She would love to see the men's faces when the authorities crashed down on their scheme. She craved a more tangible sense of closure than merely Gerardo's thanks to the team and request to lay low.

But that could wait. For now, she stretched out in her bed and savoured the cool puffiness of her pillow before letting her mind drift elsewhere.

Then, suddenly, something crashed. Pots clattered and a kettle hissed, disrupting her daydream. Their noise pulled her back to the present day, a reality she would rather avoid. Exams approached and papers sat unwritten.

It took a few moments to register, but today was a weekday. Her mother should have left for the bakery hours ago. She didn't remember any public holidays. Sometimes her mom closed the shop to take a day for herself. A possibility, but she had not done that for years.

Cristabel's shoulders tensed. Ever since the incident in the cellar vault, her mother had been acting erratic. Cristabel pulled a long-sleeved T-shirt over her pyjamas and headed downstairs.

An unrecognizable husky voice carried up the stairwell.

Plates clinked against the table. The scent of brewed coffee filtered through the air. *What is going on?* It sounded like a weekend morning of slow coffees and fresh pastries.

Her mother's laugh sailed through the kitchen doorway.

"Mom?" Cristabel looked from her mom to a tall man with dark wavy hair standing close by. Too close. "Why aren't you at the bakery?"

"Oh, Cristabel, dear, you're awake." Her mother looked uncomfortable for a split second, as if she had been caught kissing Santa Claus in front of her three-year-old. "I'm opening late today. Have a seat. There's something you need to hear."

The man took a step forward. He reached out towards Cristabel and then withdrew his hand uneasily. "Cristabel, I wish I didn't have to explain this to you this way or at this time. Honestly, I wanted to tell you a long time ago. Unfortunately, as you have found out recently, life doesn't always play by the rules you would like it to."

Cristabel hesitated. She had been through her share of uncomfortable situations, but having a strange man standing in her kitchen talking of lost opportunities as if he knew her was a new one.

Sasha handed Cristabel a coffee. "You're going to need this, honey. Sit down."

The man sat down as well, looking straight across the table at Cristabel when he spoke. "I know you have always been told that your father had to leave when you were very young. These semi-truths are how adults explain complex situations to children so they can understand."

Cristabel felt awkward looking directly into a face she did not recognize and who continued to talk so tenderly to her. *Have I fallen into some other world? This can't be happening.* Her mom simply stood to the side, allowing this stranger to take over their kitchen.

The man clasped his fingers in front of him, seemingly

considering each word with excessive diligence. "But in all honesty, it also helps us distance ourselves from our own realities. Years ago, your mother and I thought it would be easier for you if you did not know much about your father. I never wanted to leave you. Or your mother." He looked over and put his hand on Sasha's shoulder.

She reached up and clenched it with both of her hands. Her cheeks glowed.

Cristabel looked back and forth between her mother and the man. *Mom is really comfortable with him being here. Is he really my father?*

The man continued. "In those days, I worked with some nasty people. People with powerful connections. The situation was delicate. I was young and naive. I thought I could change the world and ended up ticking off the wrong person. Your mother paid for it with her business. We didn't think you remembered that awful day when the three of us hid in the cellar while gangsters ransacked the shop upstairs. But your mother tells me that is not the case. Well, I had become a target and had to divert attention away from my family." Tears glistened in his eyes. "Your safety was all that mattered to me. And so, I disappeared. You must know, I have always kept track of you."

The room seemed to darken and spin. Cristabel gripped the edge of the table. She shut her eyes, willing herself to grasp what she was hearing. Slowly, she opened her eyes. Black pupils stared back. Distant yet familiar dark eyes rimmed with laugh lines pulled her in. Cristabel absorbed the truth. Her father had disappeared—but he had not died.

"I am so proud of you. Your friend Gerardo keeps me apprised. He reports up a different line than to me, but we made an agreement long ago." He nodded to Sasha.

Cristabel sat frozen, unable to move or speak. *What is happening?* Anger, sadness, mistrust and relief all fought for attention inside her chest, leaving Cristabel feeling confused and vulnerable.

Sasha grabbed her purse. "Well, I'm going to leave you two to catch up. I have a bakery to get ready for the lunch crowd."

Cristabel stared at her mother in disbelief. Her once-certain world had shattered and all her mother could do was smile and walk away, leaving her to try to find the truth alone with this stranger who claimed to be her father?

Cristabel's father also watched the door close behind Sasha. He turned back, blinking away a look of sadness. "She still doesn't know all the details. When we married, her father did not accept me. Only a Maltese man was good enough for his daughter. It was hard on her, but it made my disappearance easier for her family to accept. They were just waiting for me to screw up." He wavered for a second and then seemed to remember something that gave him strength and focus. With his hand resting on the counter, he looked back to Cristabel. "Anyway, that's in the past. You've ended up earning yourself quite the reputation in the organization on your own. Admittedly, I've been a pain in the arse for Gerardo as an absentee father using him to watch over my little girl."

Cristabel's mind swam—against the current and immersed under a heavy fog. *Her father was part of the Cuban military? He had been involved all this time?*

"So, why are you back here now?" Her voice wavered. She wasn't sure what emotion was boiling up, but whatever it was, Cristabel was not ready for it.

Her father came around the table and took her into his arms. They were both crying, knowing and at the same time not knowing the person they held.

And her mother. Lies. Deceit. Cristabel could not process what this all meant. Protection. Realities crashing together. She wanted to go to the bakery to question her mother, but at the same time she realized she had been told omissions rather than falsehoods. Her mind had filled in the gaps, creating a narrative of its own.

After a long pause, Cristabel broke the silence. "Do you know Professor Ignacio and about this big scam claiming most major civilizations came from Malta?"

These were facts she was comfortable with, a truth she could rely on.

"That's precisely why I'm here. Carlos—or as you know him, Professor Ignacio—was sent to Malta as an undercover agent. His mission was to develop new technologies that could help protect our military's operations. Peter came on a separate mission to identify falsified science and potential insurgents. Neither of them knew that the other was an agent. Together they filled in so many pieces of intel that our puzzle rearranged itself into an entirely different portrait of the subversive plots being set around the world."

Cristabel stared at her father. Her coffee had turned cold. "This is a lot to digest. What does it mean for me?"

She had wanted to finish her degree and continue working for Gerardo in the military, at least on the side. For the first time, she questioned that plan. How could he keep such a secret from her?

Her father smiled. "In your case, I made sure it would be your choice. You can finish your degree and get a normal job. Or you can carry on with the military, working with Gerardo for now. I would like to see you finish your degree. Your mother has agreed to stay here while you do that. After that, we are trying to get her approved to move to Cuba. Maybe someday you'll want to relocate to Havana and climb the ranks at home."

53

SAFETY NETS

———

Aram laid down his tools. The door looked exactly like the previous one, except not blown to bits. He leaned back in the cramped cell and stared at the posters on the walls all around him. Who knew getting a degree on a foreign student's scholarship would lead him down this path? The friends he made during those four years had stayed solid. Almost more solid than anything else in his life. Almost.

He looked over at the black bag lying against the far wall. He had been surprised when Juris told him about

Tüvs, but he was relieved he hadn't been asked to dispose of the body—not yet, anyway.

Earlier in Aram's career, he had taught local boys how to maintain and repair the aging towers of Svaneti, Georgia, the region where he grew up. These fabricated pinnacles earned their protective image based on more than their straight lines and high vantage points. They were resolute. The towers endured for centuries, casting their narrow rectangular shadows across the valleys regardless of war, poverty or peace.

Perhaps the years spent resetting the same rock blocks with fresh grout and handfuls of gravel had shown him the secret to lasting strength. Each scar on his hands—and there were many—told its own tale. Every rock played a crucial role. Continual maintenance was critical. No exceptions, from the bottom row to the top rim. Beyond a few heavy blocks inserted to support artillery, the structure was strong because it was lean. A top-heavy tower would topple. It took standards and dedication.

The world today was not so straightforward. People believed what they saw and saw an interpretation of what they believed. Unlike Svaneti's towers, humanity's reality could be poked and shaped. Focus readjusted. Change manufactured. Like a fly's eye with thousands of lenses, each seeing a slightly different angle of the bigger picture, but as a whole it still couldn't find its way outside through an open window. Direction. Misdirection.

Aram understood this concept. Inspired to do more than simply maintain, he wanted to make waves. He imagined knocking out a few stone pieces near the peak and watching as the sanctimonious superpowers crashed down. Let a set of fresh-eyed leaders start anew, without the baggage of past relationships. This was the gift he longed to leave for his grandchildren. By now, his own life had turned stale. He could land in prison or die in the process. He didn't care. Such incidental damage would only add to his battle scars. No longer would he sit on the sidelines, moulded into the safe by-product of inaction too common among his generation. No more.

He breathed in the dusty air of the dungeon and savoured a moment of calm. It reminded him of dawn, that brief lull before the sun shattered the silence with its clarity. Normally, he loved the silence. Today, he anticipated the clarity, a new vision their team was about to show to the world.

The team held their positions. Juris had been clear in his instructions. *Leave nothing unchecked.*

***

While Aram covered the underground situation, Davit was driving on the far side of the island. He pressed his foot hard on the accelerator and his pickup's engine revved, gaining speed along the empty roads. Today marked the pinnacle of a plan he had been working towards with a group of his most trusted friends for the past two years. Today, he would seal his legacy.

Davit walked around the final archeological site. He wanted to check—one last time—to be sure the incisions and cut marks he and Aram had so carefully made looked natural. He would not allow any error. After retrieving a fallen drill from the dust, he tightened a tarp that had blown loose.

He gave silent thanks to his sailing buddies who had agreed to bring a number of heavy suitcases to Malta for him. While they thought the bags contained simply personal goods for his second home, Davit was actually smuggling artifacts in the folds of sweaters and hidden between book covers. Thankfully, his friends were frequent visitors and given a less-than-thorough inspection upon entering Maltese waters.

Once satisfied with the site, Davit returned to his truck and scrolled through his messages looking for any last-minute requests from Juris. *Nothing. Perfect.*

Then he typed the three-letter message to his broker to solidify his future. Years earlier, he had gifted almost all of his savings to his grandchildren. The funds were held in a trust. The kids did not know it existed. Only one other person did, a dear friend who managed the trust.

They had agreed on the details of the transaction months ago. Today, he only needed to confirm it. *BUY*.

Within minutes, his three grandchildren would unwittingly be shareholders in two weaponry companies. The companies were not listed on any stock exchange. Between the two entities, they held contracts with China, Russia, the United States and the United Kingdom for some of the most advanced drone devices and precision artillery ever developed. Davit felt certain their value would skyrocket alongside security fears after his team's little ruse.

His trust manager planned to cash in after six months, presumably at a hefty gain. His grandchildren would never know how they'd made the money. Their innocence would remain pure. After all, Davit's father had taught him long ago to always have a safety net.

He then thought about Lennart. That man had more to lose than Davit. He was the executive of a growing bank, owned multiple houses and a yacht. Lennart's father had passed on a different nugget of wisdom: fight for what you believe in with everything you've got. Lennart would never forgive the Soviets for taking his parents' lives, and time had only cemented that belief.

When their old university friend, Juris, came up with this grand plan to throw a cloud over religious dogma and shake up global leaderships, Lennart had jumped in with both feet. One evening Lennart confided in Davit.

Over the years, he had gathered damaging intel on a handful of very senior people involved in Baltic politics.

Davit understood these individuals were connected to the old Soviet regime, explaining Lennart's personal vendetta. They were trying to hide corrupt money using Lennart's bank. He did not approve their accounts, citing some mundane policy breach so as not to alarm those involved. But he held on to the evidence. Evidence that he planned to feed to their political base when the time was right.

Davit assumed that time was quickly approaching.

He looked down at his phone one last time to check for any messages from Juris. Nothing.

54

TAKEDOWN

A notification blinked on Cristabel's laptop. Gerardo had sent a secure email to the entire team, including Carlos, Myriam, Peter and Cristabel's father: *Called in a favour. Thought you all might want the inside view.* An encrypted link followed.

Cristabel moved the laptop over to the coffee table so both she and her father could watch from the couch. She clicked on the link. The single screen broke apart into four quadrants. Shaky video recordings started to play in each of the four views. Orange digits blinked the time and date on the bottom corner of each recording. They were livestreaming. She turned up the brightness to maximum, yet the pictures remained dim. Then she realized what they were watching.

She and her father both leaned in closer.

Cristabel pointed to the top left corner of the screen. "Here, they're in the tunnels under the church. That's where Peter was held. I bet each view is from a different police officer's bodycam."

The first feed in the upper left showed the tunnels. The second video, in the upper right corner of the screen, captured a row of chiselled stone pillars leading to the marbled foyer of one of the fastest growing banks in Malta. In the lower left corner, the third screen, showed low ditches dug around a myriad of grooves etched into rocky land. The corner of a blue tarp occasionally blew into frame. The fourth video captured massive rounded wooden doors carved with saints, crosses and kneeling devotees.

The team may have had to stand down, but their exclusive vantage gave them a clear view of the multi-location police raid about to go down. The officers must be waiting for instructions to move as there was not much going on. Minutes after Cristabel connected, all four videos rushed ahead. The raids had started. Her eyes darted from one screen to the next, trying to take it all in.

A blitz of explosions lit up the first screen.

Straightaway, a rush of shoulders crashed into the tunnel door, breaking through. A single light bulb lit up a small room plastered in posters and maps filled the view. The posters were covered in red circles, connected by arrows that ran all over the walls. A dark object filled the far end of the cell. This was the chamber Peter had described.

Cristabel's father groaned out loud.

An officer was photographing the scene. The officer wearing the camera turned away to investigate the outer tunnel. He bent down. Wire cutters clipped a thin wire just outside the entrance. The officer had clearly been briefed in advance.

Cristabel held her breath without realizing it until she gasped out loud.

A fury of movement jerked the camera as a dark bulk lunged at the officer. A hand swung past. Bodies collided. Moments later, a man lay face down with his hands pinned behind his back. The camera picked up the attacker's profile. His hooked nose and the scar on his left cheek matched the photos Ana had found of Man C, Aram Chikadze—caught in the very dungeon he had constructed.

"Did you see that?" Cristabel shook her finger furiously at the video feed.

Her father nodded his head rapidly, shifting his eyes from one corner of the screen around to the next.

In the second video, higher up, people turned and

stared in shock as police officers rushed into the main lobby of the bank. Two teams spread out, covering both the stairs and the elevators. The officer with the bodycam ran up four flights of stairs. Cristabel was sure if the stream had audio, they would have heard a breathless voice as the officer approached the executive secretary. The woman's face remained stoic, but her eyes were wide with alarm.

Lennart Ast was speaking on the phone when the officers entered. He quickly hung up and slammed his palms flat on the desk. Although his words were lost, Cristabel was certain he levied some hard-hitting assaults and warned the policemen that his lawyer would handle the situation.

"I can't believe Gerardo was able to loop us in on this." Her father leaned closer as if hoping he would be able to hear what was being said on the videos.

The officers closed in on him. One grabbed his arm, spun him around and slapped on a pair of cuffs. They led him out of the office.

The third video showed a team of police cordoning off the entire dig site.

"I think I can see an array of stone ruts fanning out from the centre. Look there!" Cristabel motioned to a dim part of the screen.

"Yeah, you could be right." Her father nodded slowly, still staring at the video.

The bodycam officer approached a truck parked off to the side. The man in the driver's seat looked up from his phone as the officer yanked open his door. One hand tensed on the gear shift, as if the phone call was a warning to leave. Unfortunately for him, it arrived too late.

The officer dragged him out of the vehicle. The man sprawled on the ground and the officer bent to cuff him. As he stood up, the camera showed another officer rummaging through the truck bed. Before he fell out of view, Cristabel saw him hold up what looked like an ancient Persian statue and piece of Maya pottery. The driver must be the infamous Davit Baboumian.

In the fourth video, the tactical team stormed the cathedral doors. A solitary man stood at the pulpit while a slideshow played overhead on massive screens. The Big Reveal heading was plastered across the current slide, so the man was presumably practicing his speech for the next night's scheduled event.

The pews sat empty. The nave looked ominous, half-lit by candlelight and the glow from the presentation's screen. Cristabel recognized some of the slides from the files she had seen on the website's administrative portal. So this was the mastermind, Juris Stokmane.

The video feed vibrated as the police officer ran inside. The left shoulder of another agent blocked a section of the screen.

"Move over Shoulder Officer!" Cristabel yelled at the screen.

It seemed to take Juris ages to react. The tactical team must have been quiet, or the man was so engrossed he tuned everything else out. Just then, the officer in front on their camera view rushed towards Juris. A third agent came into view from across the room, running towards the pulpit.

Juris darted to the back of the room, apparently aiming for a set of stairs that led up and out of the main hall. The agents must have been screaming at him to stop because as Juris reached the top of the stairwell he paused. From the way his elbow bent, Cristabel knew he was reaching for something inside his jacket or a pocket.

The officers recognized the move as well. Before Juris could pull his arm back out, his chest arched at an odd angle. Then his arms jerked up as if trying to fly away with only one beat before his shoulder blades buckled backwards. Seconds later, he lay on the ground. Two officers ran up the stairs and surrounded his corpse.

Before falling asleep the night before, Cristabel had become engrossed in the character profile Ana had compiled on the man. She almost felt sad to see him fall when he thought he was so close to achieving greatness. Almost, but not quite.

Cristabel's phone vibrated. It was a message from Gerardo: *Turn on TVM2 at noon.*

An hour later, Cristabel turned on the TV. Malta's national news station would start its midday report in three minutes. As they waited, Cristabel tried to access the Big Reveal's website. A *404 Page Not Found* error message landed on her screen instead. Clearly, the authorities were on top of that as well.

She turned her attention back to the television as the news anchor began passively reading the top story. "We have breaking news. Earlier this morning, Malta's police force took down a well-known executive for criminal activity and attempts to spread false and misleading information. Three other men have also been taken into custody, and one man was found dead. All are believed to be linked to the case. More details will be shared once we receive them. For today's weather, expect a cloudy afternoon and rain showers by this evening."

Cristabel slouched back on the couch, unable to control the flood of emotions rushing to the surface. So much had come to a head after so many long hours of work. On top of that, her father, who she thought was gone, was sitting beside her. It all seemed too hard to believe.

One question, though, remained unanswered. "I wonder what ever happened with James—or Yakov?"

Her father turned to face her, "Well, I can add some colour to that one. We passed along his details to the

Russian authorities. They prefer to handle their problems in-house."

"What do you mean?" asked Cristabel.

"He was involved in some side dealings of his own. That business in Canada was a front to give tactical intel to a group of defected KGB agents. Yakov knew these men from his childhood. Over the years, they had all grown disillusioned with the traditionally slow and top-heavy style of Russia's intelligence service. From what I hear, a special Russian team found Yakov on a little fishing boat not far offshore a secluded inlet. They'll take him back to Moscow and deal with him there. I don't suspect he will be returning to Canada any time soon."

About an hour later, Cristabel's father's phone buzzed. His eyes widened as he read the message. "Unbelievable."

He looked at his daughter, glancing at his phone again before relaying the latest message to Cristabel. "So Juris' plot thickens. The police found an email on his computer scheduled to be sent tomorrow at midnight. That would have put it just a few hours after the Big Reveal event was meant to take place. The message included a number of attachments—documents from James' Canadian company. It seems James' surveillance technology wasn't monitoring just insects, but military pests as well. Somehow, he tracked covert Russian operatives near the disputed Arctic border between Canada and Russia."

"Wow. You mean he had the option to double-cross

Russia or Canada, and he chose Russia?! They don't handle personal grudges politely." Cristabel raised her eyebrows and slowly shook her head, disbelieving his judgement.

"And listen to this, Cristabel, there's more. The email was addressed to a group of investigative journalists in Canada—who would certainly follow up and share the information with the military as well as the public. If Juris wanted to ignite another fire in global tensions, this move would do it. He must have intended a secondary uprising, one that taunted sovereignty and aimed its arrow at the strategic heart of two government treasures: shipping rights and oil reserves. A dangerous dance, especially if NATO got pulled in."

Cristabel's mind whirled. She realized Juris was a grand manipulator, but this latest news exposed the extent of his reach. It also explained why James seemed so cagey. James obviously knew how cunning Juris could be, so he'd played both sides, leaping from Russian insider to Russian infiltrator and then back again. James probably thought he was protecting himself. In reality, it was these supposed safeguards that ultimately pulled him down.

While she gained some comfort knowing the authorities would pass any valid information on to the Canadian military to handle, she knew its fallout would take a long time to fully clean up.

55

HOMEWARD BOUND

———————

"I would have liked working on a live mission with you—if I had known about it." Carlos put his arm across Peter's shoulders.

"Still," Carlos said, "these past few years at the university, thinking you were simply an innocent, yet brilliant, professor have been some of the best years of my life. We should start an archeology group back in Havana. You never know what we might dig up!" Carlos beamed from the back seat of the minivan where he sat between Peter and Myriam. His old barretina hat sagged on his head, a little more ragged and a little more slouched, but he couldn't help feeling it perfectly suited his traditional yet tenacious ways.

Myriam grinned. "You two are on your own. History can stay in the past. I prefer to look forward. Biotechnology and medicine are evolving before our eyes. I want to be part of it—real science advancement without these conspiracies or subplots that you two seem to find."

Carlos felt a sense of relief knowing he was finally going home. He looked through the tinted glass as the vehicle drove past the main entrance to the airport. They were headed for a lesser-known runway. Parallel to the international airport but beyond the industrial canopies and cargo facilities sat another landing strip. It was reserved for private jets and military attachés.

After they cleared security, their van pulled alongside a similar navy shuttle. Its rear window rolled down. Carlos recognized Cristabel's curly hair even before her face came into view.

"I've come to say goodbye to all of you ..." Cristabel paused and turned inside the vehicle to look at a man sitting next to her. She turned back to Myriam, Carlos and Peter. "... and to my father. Maybe next time, we'll meet on Cuban soil."

About the Author

Nancy O'Hare is a Canadian author who has travelled to over ninety countries and lived on five continents. Before writing *The Man in the Barretina Hat*, she published two travel books: *Dust in My Pack* and *Searching for Unique*. Influenced by her former career in finance where she lived and worked in Australia, Oman, Switzerland, Nigeria and Canada, she writes about diverse cultures and destinations less touched by mass tourism.

www.bynancyohare.com

CPSIA information can be obtained
at www.ICGtesting.com
Printed in the USA
BVHW082312040123
655621BV00014B/97